Life at the Top

by John Braine

Life at the Top

The Riverside Press Cambridge

HOUGHTON MIFFLIN COMPANY BOSTON

1 9 6 2

For Maurice Temple Smith

Life at the Top

one

SHE WOKE me up by lifting my eyelids; then she slipped under the bedclothes beside me and lay there smiling, her arms around my neck. She had no business to be there, and she'd have to go before Susan awoke; but I could never regret her presence, no matter what Spock said. She was so small, so vulnerable, and at this moment so beautiful, her face pink and her fair hair tousled, that something dreadful was bound to happen to her; this is no world for children.

I kissed her to get rid of the picture of her body broken by accident or illness, and held her tightly to me; here at least she was safe — as safe as houses, for what *that* was worth these days.

She looked at me with large, brown eyes — Susan's eyes — and stroked my chin. "You haven't shaved, Daddy."

"Never mind that," I said. "You shouldn't be here, Barbara." I said this to her every Sunday morning.

"You're lovely warm, Daddy. You're a giant warm."

She put her words in the wrong order sometimes — which

was forgivable at the age of four — but the right message always got through. I was security to her, whatever I might be to myself. The sun caught the silver backs of my hairbrushes on the dressing table; suddenly I felt enormously happy.

I lay back and closed my eyes. There wasn't any need to go anywhere and I was more tired than I had thought. Susan was still asleep; I could hear her even breathing beside me. I smiled to myself; after nine years of marriage, last night I had not known her. I had kept my eyes open so that I could find out who this naked stranger was, but it hadn't helped. And perhaps it wasn't necessary, or even wise, for me to attempt to find out; warm giants accept things as they are.

Barbara lifted my eyelids again. "Wake up, Daddy," she said.

"Let Daddy sleep, Barbara."

"Why do you want to sleep?"

I yawned. "Daddy works hard all week earning pennies. He needs to rest on Sundays."

"Why do you earn pennies?"

"Because Mummy and Daddy and Harry and Barbara need a house. And things to eat and drink —"

"Harry lives at school. He has a house there, he has. And things to eat and drink."

"But Daddy has to earn pennies to keep Harry at school. And pennies for pyjies and frocks and dollies and bicycles and all sorts of things."

And the light gray fitted carpet and the gray and primrose yellow wallpaper and the built-in wardrobe and dressing table and the candy-striped sheets and the divan bed with the Continental headboard; we were always buying something new, the house itself was only three years old. The building of a Council estate nearby had been the excuse for leaving Linnett Road; the neighborhood — we had to face it — was going down. And the birth of Harry had been the excuse for leaving Pudney Lane, on the road to Gilden; the house was too old, too big, too much for Susan to look after; and too cut off. I'd liked it myself, and still missed it; it was my choice, it had belonged to me. At least, I'd paid the deposit myself and could keep up the mortgage repayments. I remembered the visit to our solicitor to go over the deeds of our present house and the expression which had flickered across his face when he'd realized where the money — or most of the money — was coming from. There was nothing I could put my finger on; but there was no mistake about either his contempt when he looked at me or his envious lubricity when he looked at Susan. The expression wasn't too obvious, of course; and perhaps no one but me would have noticed it. But when you marry a rich man's daughter you become expert about these matters.

Barbara tugged my hair. "You're still not up, Daddy," she said.

"All right," I said. "I tell you what, we'll make some tea-pot tea for Mummy."

"And juice for me. Nice cold cold juice. With ice in."

My dressing gown was on the floor; I reached down, but Barbara ran out of the room with it. She threw it over the stairs, then began to cry. I looked at her in bewilderment. "What is it, silly-billy?"

"I won't like it," she said. "I won't like it, I never. I want the fuzzy one."

"Put your dressing gown on first, then. And your slippers."

I went back into the bedroom to fetch my own slippers and the fuzzy dressing gown. It was of camel-colored wool, and I'd bought it when we lived in Pudney Lane; it was now mangy rather than fuzzy, and always had been too large for me. Its thickness had been welcome enough in the drafty corridors and icy bathroom of the house in Pudney Lane; it wasn't really necessary now. The oil-fired central heating, in fact, kept the house so warm that we hardly needed clothes at all; I didn't object to this, but there were times when, perversely no doubt, I missed the comfort the old dressing gown had given me on winter mornings, just as I missed the open fire in the big kitchen. But I didn't mind; more and more frequently these days I didn't mind. Barbara reappeared in her pink dressing gown, the hood pulled up over her head. "Be my horse," she said. "Be my furry horse."

I knelt down and she sat astride my shoulders. She wouldn't go upstairs or downstairs any other way; I walked downstairs very slowly, keeping to the wall. She talked all the time, running her words together, as she always did when excited; as far as I could gather a story had begun and in some way I — both as myself and a furry horse — and the castle on Squirrel Gorge were part of it. There was a danger in the shape of a giant — but not, I think, a warm giant — and Barbara was both rescuer and rescued.

When we reached the hall I knelt by the window and put Barbara down on it. I pulled back the venetian blinds; southward, on the far side of Squirrel Gorge, I could see Sindram Grange. Tom Sindram had been dead now these twelve years; I remembered Bob Storr pointing him out to me at the Thespians one evening. He was a small, wizened old man who wore what was obviously a dickey; Bob, with a certain awe in his voice, had said that he was the meanest old bastard in the West Riding, which meant the whole world, and that he could cash a check for a hundred thousand and still have left as much again. But when he died — not long after I first came to Warley — he owed the Inland Revenue almost exactly a hundred thousand; and they never got a penny of it. Nor did they ever find out what he spent the money on; and for this reason he was remembered in Warley with something like affection.

And now he was dead and Sindram Grange had been taken over by the County as a Further Education Center. A weekend course on the theatre — or was it Aspects of the Contemporary Theatre? — was being held there at this moment; I'd spent most of yesterday afternoon showing a party round the Thespians. I hadn't accepted the invitation to attend the course; now, looking at the turrets and battlements of Sindram Grange, hazy through the morning mist, I wished that I had if only to tell Barbara that I'd been there. For Sindram Grange was her castle; this look at it through the hall window had been an early morning ritual for fifty days now. The ritual didn't change, nor did the story; she always looked at the Grange in silence for a while and then, jerkily — she always seemed to find it necessary to hold her breath when concentrating — tell me that Barbara went home then.

But there were variations according to season; in February Barbara went home and there was snow. And cheese pie. This morning as we went into the kitchen there was flowers.

Flowers — she repeated it over and over again — all kinds of flowers. Then she put the story aside as she watched me fill the kettle at the sink.

"My juice," she said and began to hop up and down. "My juice. Give me my juice."

I switched on the hotplate. Her face puckered. "Daddy, don't stop getting my juice! Why have you stopped getting my juice?"

"Don't be so impatient, cheeky-face," I said.

"*I'm* not cheeky-face. *You're* a cheeky-face."

"You mustn't think that the world's just made for you, darling." I didn't believe it even as I said it; as far as I was concerned she was entitled to the whole world.

I'd never felt like this about Harry; even when he was Barbara's age he'd been curiously withdrawn and self-sufficient, so much so as to make me feel unreasonably guilty at times. And now, after a year at prep school, he seemed to need me even less; I suddenly realized that I didn't even know where he was at the moment. The morning seemed less bright, the Formica-topped wall table with the four stools against it seemed to belong to a café rather than to a private home, and the pink wallpaper — depicting a fiesta scene in, presumably, Mexico — was rather too garish to be comfortable. The cupboards were built-in, and Larry Silvington, who did most of the Thespian sets, had decorated them with some of his special murals as a Christmas present to Susan. They showed Susan in each of her four big parts — *performances, darling, we'll always remember with wonder and gratitude* — and they were very lively and very gay and very witty and Larry really knew how to handle line, how to suggest movement and detail with a few strokes of the brush. It had been the very best Christmas present Susan had ever had, and she really had to kiss him; Larry was a real friend, and it was so good of him to give so much of his time and his talent; he had imagination, which was more than some people had . . . But I still missed the old kitchen cabinet which had now been relegated to the garage; I missed it because it was mine, a wedding gift from Aunt Emily, I missed it because no one else but me would miss it. It wasn't likely that Aunt Emily would notice its disappearance, for it wasn't likely that Aunt Emily would visit us. She had to be invited first, hadn't she?

I took a tin of orange juice from the refrigerator, shook it, and poured it into a jug. I took the tray from the freezing compartment and ran hot water over it; when the cubes loosened, I put four into Barbara's pink plastic mug and gave her three straws. There had been a time when I derived a great pleasure from the mere fact of having cold orange juice available when I wanted it; now the refrigerator was, as far as I was concerned, only there for Barbara.

I lit a cigarette; she coughed a little, and looked at me reproachfully. This was an expression for which her face was well suited; it was of the type which I call Victorian, oval with a short upper lip and high forehead and a nose which one day might well be Grecian. "It's naughty to smoke before breakfast," she said.

"I know. But I could do worse."

"What worse, Daddy?"

"I could drink before breakfast."

"*I* drink before breakfast," she said. "You're silly, Daddy."

"So I am." And so I was, I thought; why mention these

things to a four-year-old child at all? And why had I? The truth was that I actually wanted a drink now, I wanted something to blur things slightly, to put a haze between me and the pink wallpaper and the pink cupboards and the white refrigerator and the electric oven and the mixing machine and the pink wall table and the pink-covered stools; it was too bright and shiny and hygienic at eight o'clock on a March morning with Harling Crescent quiet under the weight of Sunday, it reminded me rather too coldly that I was thirty-five and father of two children and at least ten pounds overweight.

I sat down and pulled Barbara onto my knee. I wasn't shielding her any more; she was shielding me. I didn't know what she was shielding me from; I only knew that as long as we could be so close together nothing really bad could happen to me. She sucked up the last of her orange juice noisily, put the mug down on the wall table, and said: "I love you, Daddy."

"I love you, too," I said.

She kissed me and said, without alteration in her tone: "Harry's had his breakfast, he has. He's gone birdwatching."

"Good luck to him," I said. I looked around the kitchen; there was no dirty crockery, not even a crumb to show that he'd eaten a meal there. He was unnaturally tidy for a boy of nine; at his age every room I passed through looked as if a hurricane had hit it. Thinking of him eating his breakfast alone in the kitchen here, I felt obscurely that somehow I had failed him; I should have been with him. My own father had taken me for a walk every Sunday morning of his life; but my home had been with my parents, not with strangers. But

Harry had to go through the middle-class sausage machine; which was in this case the St. Clair sausage machine; his prep school had been chosen by his grandmother, just as his public school would be.

The kettle was boiling; I put Barbara down gently and made the tea. Warm the teapot, bring the teapot to the kettle, one spoonful to each person and one to the pot; but now there were refinements, one experimented with different blends, the latest being two of Hornimans' Directors' to one of Twining's Earl Grey. And Susan drank hers with lemon and without sugar. This would be one of the topics of conversation today either at my in-laws' or Mark's; it was all part of the campaign to make me lose weight. When the tea had stood for three minutes I poured myself a cup, put in five spoonfuls of sugar and filled up the teapot with hot water. I drank it quickly and rinsed out the cup; it was a small triumph, almost as stimulating as a double whisky would have been.

When I took the tea into the bedroom Susan was still sleeping. I gently shook her and then lifted up her eyelid. She smiled. "What a good Joekins you are." I gave her a kiss; she pulled me down on top of her, her arms so tight around my neck that I had to disengage myself in order to breathe.

Barbara had put the hood of her dressing gown over her head again. "He *is* a good Daddy Joe, he is," she said. "He gave *me* juice and ice and straws."

Susan leaned over and kissed her. Barbara accepted the kiss with no show of enthusiasm.

"I can see through your nightie, Mummy," she said. "You can't see through my pyjies."

Susan laughed. "Well, there isn't much to see yet, is there, dear? Now run along to your own bed."

"I'm not sleepy any more," Barbara said.

"You don't want a spanking, do you? Mummy only says things once, Barbara."

Barbara went out, her shoulders drooping.

Susan poured out the tea. "You spoil that child," she said.

"She has a nice nature. You can't really spoil Barbara. Of course what she really needs is someone of her own age — or nearer her own age . . ."

"We've been into that before." She reached down for the bedjacket, which as usual lay on the carpet beside the bed.

"Not really," I said. "Not really." I sipped my tea. We, Joe and Susan Lampton, had never really gone into the question of having other children; but after Barbara had been born, my father-in-law and mother-in-law had.

I saw Susan's mouth assume the pout which was always, these days, the precursor of a quarrel. Once it had been the precursor of kisses; but once she'd wanted five children all like me.

"If you'd been through what I went through when Barbara was born —"

"All right, all right. Let it ride."

"You're absolutely selfish. I suppose you'd like me to die. Then you could go off with that little tart Jean Velfrey whom you're so fond of. Don't think I didn't notice you the other night. Or that no one else did."

"She's nothing to me. Look, I said let it ride. I won't mention it again."

Susan took a cigarette from the pocket of her bedjacket.

Like most women, she made a great business of smoking, inhaling and exhaling with great noisiness. "I'd rather you didn't," she said.

Let it ride again. I'd given way. I let things ride for the sake of peace; but they weren't riding away from me. They were riding over me, on me, trampling me into submission, and sometimes I felt that everyone knew it. I felt something very near hatred for Susan; she'd won again, the pout had been replaced by a faint smile. And one of these days *I'd rather you didn't* would become *You'd better not;* and then I'd be forced to start thinking. Thinking constructively, to use my father-in-law's favorite adjective. And clearly and boldly, to use a couple more. And big; I mustn't forget Thinking Big.

Susan hadn't bothered to button her bedjacket; I couldn't help looking at her breasts. I wasn't pleased with myself for it, nor pleased with her when she put her hands over them and said in a voice which was almost a whine: "They're nice, aren't they?" I nodded; things were riding over me again. We hadn't gone to sleep until four in the morning, we'd just come near a quarrel, and in any case Barbara was next door and fully awake. But if Susan made the signal, I knew what would happen. I got out of bed and pulled on my dressing gown.

"I'm going to have a shower."

"A cold one?"

I turned at the doorway. "I'll come back to bed if you're not careful."

She giggled. "The child," she said. "Remember Spock, Joety." She took off her bedjacket.

"There'll be tonight," I said, slamming the door. Her giggle seemed to follow me down the passage.

After breakfast I went out into the garden. Spring had come late that year, making nonsense of last year's grandiose plans; I was two Sundays of hard digging behind schedule. Harling Crescent was part of a new housing estate off St. Clair Park, or off Earl Road, depending on which way you wanted to look at it. (The estate agents generally called it the Park Development, the word Park having more cachet than Road.)

With the exception of a few big houses on Earl Road itself, there'd been no building in the district until after the war. We were the first occupants of Number Seven Harling Crescent, and the garden had been a wilderness when we moved in. Now, after three years during which I seemed to have done little else but weed and dig and add cartloads of lime and manure, it was beginning to look credible that in about ten years time it might be remotely like the garden in Hunlitt and Lesper's brochure. It wouldn't, I knew, boast quite as many roses and cherry trees or have such a smoothly green lawn or such agreeably fantastic topiary work, nor could I ever hope for a limousine of anything near the dimensions (the hood, according to my calculations, being some fifteen feet long) to stand in the drive. I had few illusions left about my value to my father-in-law's business. But it would be definitely a garden, and we'd have tea there in the summer and eat our own strawberries and there'd be a Wendy house for Barbara and, as she herself would put it, flowers. Barbara would come home and there would be flowers. Above all, the garden would be something I'd made, something which belonged to me. The poet who wrote about God walking in his garden in the cool of evening had got it all wrong; I valued my garden because it was about the only place in the world in which I, Joe Lampton, could walk as Joe Lampton.

And, since I'd been thinking of being two Sundays behind schedule, it was the only place where I didn't live to schedule; in a garden one did things by season and weather, not clock and calendar.

The St. Clair mansion stood north of Harling Crescent with the St. Clair Folly on the crest of the hill above it. It was still a pleasure to look at, its propositions of balance and order and simplicity were still acceptable to me; and there had been a time when the fact of my mother-in-law being a St. Clair had given me a feeling of part ownership of the place; because the St. Clairs were my children's ancestors they were mine too. If anything I did the family credit; among the more notable St. Clairs were at least two known murderers, three convicted traitors, and one particularly ambitious gentleman who was rumored both to have procured his fifteen-year-old son for Edward II and to have helped to arrange Edward's murder at Pontefract. Heiress-hunting and robbery of one kind or another they all seemed to have taken for granted; Peregrine, who built the Folly in 1810, went through two wives' fortunes and then made another as colonel of a regiment. He even was supposed to have taken a rake-off on the teeth which the denture makers of the time extracted from the dead on the field of battle; I came across this tidbit in an anonymous Chartist pamphlet which Reggie Scurrah showed me — surreptitiously as a Port Said photograph — at the Library.

Reggie had expected me to be shocked; instead I was mildly

titillated. That had been some seven years ago; now the St. Clairs had lost their glamour as far as I was concerned. True, when away from Warley I always managed to bring my wife's ancestors into the conversation; I had never disliked an association with a name which — all the more so for the family being extinct — was a symbol of doomed aristocracy, pennons against the sunset, trumpets at Roncesvalles and all the rest of it. But now I used this social gambit only when I remembered to.

My heart wasn't in it. I couldn't remember exactly when I discovered that they were really dead; all I knew was that I no longer looked northward as often I did. The three turrets of the Folly, swart against the skyline, deliberately and successfully spectacular, the way in which the great bulk of the mansion seemed to be suspended from the sky instead of pressing down into the earth — this still gave me pleasure, but not pleasure of an important kind.

I looked southward to Squirrel Gorge now, but not towards the town, not towards Snow Park, on the riverbank, not even towards Warley Forest on the far side of Snow Park. I had seen all these before; but until Barbara had discovered it I hadn't seen Sindram Grange. I tried to look at it through her eyes, inhabit a world of giants and rescues and enchantments. It didn't come off; I kept thinking about old Sindram. Still, it was a fair enough replica of a castle, right down to the now dried-up moat and the big courtyard and the arrow slits in the turrets; looking at it I began to nourish fantasies of my own, wilder in their way than Barbara's.

One thing was certain, I reflected: my own house would never nourish any child's fantasies. It was, when I came to think of it, just the sort of house which a sensible child, given enough roof tiling, reconstituted stone blocks, and cedar boarding would have built for himself. A child would have seen the necessity of varying the gray stone blocks with a selection of red cedar boarding, and of having the garage jut out from the side of the house to break up the roof line. And I suppose that a child would have seen the advantages of oil-fired central heating, a double garage and all the rest of it. It was a good house, and worth every penny of the four thousand five hundred which had been paid for it; and it was a capital asset which, my father-in-law never lost the opportunity of informing me, was increasing its value almost daily. But it still wasn't a really grown-up house; no child living in Sparrow Gorge would look across at it this morning and see princesses and dragons and warm giants. And somehow — and not entirely because it was in Susan's name — living in it had diminished my stature as a man. I'd lost something by coming to live there; and perhaps Barbara had, too.

I looked round the garden to release myself from the gloom that had come over me, indisputably and for no good reason on a fine spring morning. There was plenty to do this afternoon and God knows I needed the exercise. My spirits lightened; I'd have a spring bonfire. And then, unbidden, anarchistic, the thought came to me: there was more than garden rubbish that I wanted to burn. I felt weighed down by things, all the material possessions which had accumulated during ten years of marriage, some two thousand seven hundred pounds worth, not counting my Zephyr and Susan's Morris 1000. To make the inventory afresh every year instead of merely adding on the value of our new possessions had, up till now, been a ritual which gave me a sober but keen satisfaction. Up till now, up till now; and now I wanted some kind of fresh start.

Barbara came running out of the house towards me, "Daddy, it's nearly time for church!" As always, she spoke as if there were some dire emergency threatening us all; I picked her up and held her in my arms for a moment, speaking gently. "There's lots of time, my darling, oceans of time." But she wriggled out of my arms and tried to drag me by the hand to the garage. "We'll be late, Daddy, we'll be terrible late —" She started to weep.

Harry came to the door. His hair was ruffled and there was a black smudge on his forehead. He watched us with a faint smile on his face. That smile had been the more or less permanent tenant of his face since he'd gone to prep school last year; stretching a point, it might have been called inscrutable, but I had my own definition of it. I called it Carruthers; behind it a sahib was watching the natives at work and play — rum customers, these wogs, almost human in their way . . . That's what Carruthers seemed to be saying, not directly to me, but to some invisible companion, some chap of his own totem.

I wiped Barbara's eyes. "You'll cry your lashes away," I said. "Look at Harry. He never cries."

Her tears began to flow again. "Harry's a boy! Harry's a boy!"

I knew what she meant. She was entitled to weep; and to long eyelashes also. In actual fact, Harry's eyelashes were longer than hers; her grandmother had only last Sunday pointed this out to her, and it still rankled.

Harry's smile broadened. Now it was identifiably an impudent little boy's.

"*You* can wipe that grin off your face," I said. "You haven't as much time as all that. You're absolutely black. Go on, get to the bathroom."

I gave him a little push; he winced away as I touched him, but he still made no move.

"What are you waiting for?" I heard the irritation in my voice; there wasn't any need for it, but Harry almost always rubbed me up the wrong way.

"I can't go to the bathroom," he said.

"Why can't you?"

"Because Mummy's there. So I'll just have to resign myself to wait." He yawned, and then Carruthers came back to his face.

"You know what I mean. Wash your face and hands and put your Sunday clothes on."

"I haven't any Sunday clothes," he said.

"I take your point," I said. "One has heard your grandmother on this subject. But stop arguing the toss and go and do what I tell you."

Barbara, who had been listening intently, had at last stopped crying.

"You're naughty, Harry," she said. "You always talk back to Daddy."

Harry shrugged his shoulders. It was a strangely adult gesture, and typical of him; he meant, without actually saying so, that whatever I said or did wasn't of the least importance.

"Don't panic," he said. "I'll go and wash and put on my

Sunday clothes." He strolled into the house leaving me feeling rather mean but still aware, however confusedly, that I was in the right.

Once actually inside the church I began to feel better. We'd been going to St. Alfred's for some ten years now; I suppose that I'd begun to go originally to please my mother-in-law but now I went to please myself. (I had long ago, in any case, abandoned the attempt to please Mrs. Brown.)

I don't know why I liked to go there so much; it was damp and musty, and the benches could more properly be termed ledges than seats. And, being the St. Clair family church, it seemed sometimes to be more like a private museum than the House of God; the place was full of memorials extolling their virtues as warriors, statesmen, employers, parents, and patrons of the Arts. But mostly as warriors; there was even on display a tattered banner said to have been taken at Ramillies. But it still remained the only place, outside of the bathroom, in which I couldn't be got at, didn't have to make any decisions, didn't have to hear my father-in-law recommending me to Think Big or my mother-in-law explaining to my son that well-dressed people don't have best clothes, because this implies that there are times when they wear inferior clothes; even if what I was hearing now didn't make any sense at least it sounded as if it should make sense. *Whatsoever is born of God overcometh the world, and this is the victory that overcometh the world, even our faith. Who is he that overcometh the world, but he that believeth that Jesus is the Son of God?*

I looked at Harry's face: almost imperceptibly, Carruthers was there. One of these days he'd let it show to the wrong person and that thin straight nose — his grandmother's rather than mine or Susan's — would have its shape altered for the worse and those dark blue eyes — mine, everyone said, but had mine ever been so cold? — would be ringed by bruised flesh. And I couldn't save him from being hurt, because I couldn't communicate with him any longer.

And how much longer would I be able to communicate with Barbara? But that wasn't any problem, unless I was to make some catastrophic mistake with her we'd always be on a direct line one to the other. She was fidgeting on her seat now, obviously bored; all Barbara's feelings were obvious, her face was a human face, not a mask or a pudding. Unaware that I was watching her, she put out her hand to tug the pigtail of the little girl in front of her. I frowned at her; she subsided into her seat. She smiled at me, as if to say that she bore me no ill-will for the frown; I smiled back. She'd always be the same; the only mistake I could make would be not to love her enough.

You spoil that child, Susan had said, and no doubt would say again. It was a risk I'd have to take. Once Alice, talking about her childhood in Harrogate, told me that I must never be frightened of loving children too much. Her words came back to me: "It's not being loved enough that spoils children. When you have children, love them all the time. Don't forget; love them all the time." I hadn't forgotten; she'd said too that in the world today for people to discuss the ill-effects of loving children too much was exactly like giving lectures on the dangers of obesity during a famine. There was a comfort in remembering her words; they were my authorization to love Barbara.

The church was, as usual, full. It had always been the rich
man's church — Mark called it the Big Needle — and Canon
Tintman could always be relied upon to give his congregation
just what they wanted. And what they wanted, to judge
from his sermons, was to be assured that they could indeed
have their cake and eat it too; he was at his best when casti-
gating the crass materialism of the working classes and the
machinations of international Communism. But I liked him
and I liked St. Alfred's: his voice, beautifully modulated and a
little husky, always soothed me no matter whether or not I
agreed with him. And the church, despite its dampness and
mustiness, was obviously prosperous; there was always a positive conservatory-ful of flowers on the altar, the floor was
spotless and the metalwork always gleaming. And the sunshine this morning had brought out the women's summer
dresses; I seemed to smell, from the younger ones at least, an
exciting collective aroma like new morocco. Thinking of all
those clean and lightly clothed bodies I began to play my
own variety of Patience. Jean Velfrey, sitting on the right
across the aisle, was obviously an ace, if not all four aces; the
tiny circle of black straw and net which she was wearing did
nothing to hide her hair. In fact, it accentuated the gleaming
and gloriously false fairness; Jean was not merely a blonde,
she was *the* blonde, the archetypal popsy, in whose proximity
every man not actually moribund straightened his tie and
threw his shoulders back. I took my eyes away from her with
an effort and looked at Eva Storr. Eva was putting on a
little too much weight. Once her black hair and general
sleekness had put me in mind of a bird, a starling or a robin,
say; now there was a certain stiffness about her contours, and

the bird she reminded me of was something larger and more domesticated. Still, a queen at least.

Barbara turned round in her seat. "Stop it, you naughty!" she yelled, her voice rising above the second Collect. "Give me it back, you naughty!" The small boy behind her had snatched her tam-o'-shanter; he was clutching it firmly to him.

His mother pursed her lips and frowned at the little boy; he gave the tam-o'-shanter back to Barbara and began to cry noisily. I turned back; the game was over. It was harmless enough, even if rather immature, to arrange undressed women in a circle and deal them out like cards; but the girl next to the little boy's mother wasn't someone who could be dealt out . . . I didn't know her, I'd never seen her before in my life, but I knew that much already from one glimpse I'd had of her face, calm and smiling. *Defend us in the same with thy mighty power; and grant that this day we fall into no sin, neither run into any kind of danger; but that all our doings may be ordered by thy governance, to do always that is righteous in thy sight . . .*

Calm and faintly smiling; I went over the synonyms for calm. Tranquil, serene, quiet, undisturbed, at rest, at peace; and tranquil was the right one, being positive. I didn't dare to turn round again; I could sense that not only Susan but the Browns were looking at me.

I glanced over to the left; they were sitting near the front. There weren't any pews at St. Alfred's any longer; but my mother-in-law didn't seem to recognize the fact. There was a pew around them and their guest, Ralph Hethersett, even though to all appearances they were sharing the same kind of bench as the rest of the congregation. There was a barrier, there was an order of precedence; I felt a spasm of hatred and of fear when I looked at his thick red neck and her sharp profile. And what was Hethersett doing here, so far away from home? This was his third weekend visit this year; and I knew that my father-in-law never as much as bought anyone a drink without a purpose.

The congregation rose for the hymn; I was a few seconds behind everyone else, which I knew would be another item in the score against me. Reproof wouldn't follow immediately, of course. But at some future date my mother-in-law would refer to the sort of people who were so stupid or impious — really one didn't know which — that they couldn't even follow the order of the service. And I would know who she meant and from the tone of her voice and the direction of her glance, so would everyone else.

My mother-in-law was adept at making herself unpleasantly clear without ever actually being explicit and since Hethersett had started becoming a regular visitor to her home she was excelling even her past performances. There had recently been conversations about the general undesirability of fortune hunters, the proclivity of low people for low pothouses (this was after I'd helped one of the laborers at the works to wet his baby's head) and the importance of Harry's speaking properly. He had to go to boarding school; it was too easy to pick up the wrong accent at home — I mean, in Warley . . . But I'd known that the slip wasn't Freudian, I knew who had the wrong accent. Her son-in-law had. Hethersett hadn't; he'd been to Harrow and there had acquired a genuine public school face; it was as if the bones had been taken out of it and replaced by some harder and smoother but far more malleable substance, something that could be set overnight into any shape desired. Presumably there he had also acquired gentlemanly tastes: he actually went shooting and fishing and would have loved to hunt, but couldn't spare the time, old boy. Most important of all, his father was the managing director of the Hethersett Steel Corporation, a huge concern in the Midlands with which we'd done business from time to time. I wondered again what exactly was the purpose of Hethersett's visit and then ceased to care. It suddenly seemed more important to re-create the face of the girl behind me. Gray eyes, close-curling brown hair, rather large teeth, a rosy complexion. She'd be in her middle twenties. This was the inventory of the items which made up her face: it didn't explain it, didn't explain that expression of tranquillity.

When the service had ended and I had at last the opportunity to look at her again, I turned expecting disappointment. It was the spring, I said to myself, it was the sunshine and stained glass windows, it was the words of the Book of Common Prayer; it was perhaps only my own need of tranquillity. Her face would be as dead or as disturbed as the rest. But it was exactly as I'd remembered it. I started to think constructively from sheer force of habit. Warley being a small town, and she being a newcomer, I would meet her sooner or later. I would make it sooner. On surface appearances alone she seemed the kind of person with whom we might credibly be friendly; her clothes were good but unobtrusive and she had the appearance of someone who had a bath and changed her underwear every day.

Above all, there was the fact of her being in church. Once

it would have been almost obligatory for one to attend church, so there was no particular social cachet attached to church-going in itself. Then it became unfashionable; and now, in Warley at least, it had become fashionable again. No one would lose the good opinion of the community because they didn't go to church; but they wouldn't lose it if they did go.

Or so Mark had said the other night; and rather to my surprise I found myself resenting the fact that I was using someone else's opinions, even this. He was undoubtedly right, I thought as I went out of the church; but I should have preferred him to be wrong.

But whether he was right or wrong, there was no point in thinking constructively about the girl. It was better that she should remain a face and no more than a face, a kind of superior pin-up to carry in my wallet. I had to be realistic about the situation; realistic enough in fact to acknowledge that no situation could exist between me and the girl. But this acknowledging it wasn't the same thing as liking it; watching her disappear round the corner into Market Street I suddenly felt tired, middle-aged, and in need of a drink.

two

Brown scowled at the letter as if to browbeat it into submission. "The awkward old bastard!" he said.

I smiled to indicate how right he was but didn't bother to answer him; I knew my father-in-law's Monday moods all too well.

"He's trying it on, that's what he's doing. He knows bloody well he's got us by the short hairs —" He crumpled the letter into a ball and threw it across the room. "I'd like to break his sodding neck!"

I stifled a yawn. There seemed to have been a great many of these scenes lately; before making even the simplest decision he seemed to find it necessary to lash himself into a blind rage.

I rose and went to the window. I looked eastward towards Warley. On a clear day I could distinguish the spire of Hawcombe Parish Church. Hawcombe, a drab little village on the outskirts of Warley, had no great interest for me; but I preferred it to the straggle of brick boxes which constituted

Brown and Co. This afternoon there was no escape; the hills were hidden by the rain.

Behind me I heard his fingers drumming on the desk; I knew the act by heart now. I stared out of the window into the scrapyard, the place from where, as Brown had explained to Harry time and time again, it all started. And the place where Grandad had started, and I'm not ashamed to admit it, sonny. Yes, I shoveled scrap in a yard just like this. Mind, I was younger then. My mother cried the first day I came home. You're covered with rust — that's funny, isn't it, sonny? You don't seem able to scrub it away; and everything you eat tastes of rust. And you're always thirsty. The scrap? From airplanes and cutlery and motorcars — look, that's a fork stamping, nothing's wasted, you see.

And then Grandad took charge of one of the arc furnaces. And he worked hard and he went to night school and he got to be a foreman and he went on learning all the time. And, whatever they say, sonny, people were glad to help him. Everyone respects a man who's come up the hard way.

I could see Harry's face now. Carruthers hadn't been anywhere near it, despite the fact that the story of Grandfather's Early Struggles must by now have become tiresomely familiar. There was respect on his face. Respect; that word had been chosen for him but it was the only one that fitted. Respect; and unfeigned love.

Perhaps my big mistake had been made ten years ago: perhaps I should have bought myself a pair of overalls and started work in the scrapyard, perhaps if I had done so then that look of respect and love on my son's face might have been directed to the proper person. But it was too late now;

I should have to continue as the despised administrator, the nasty unsympathetic accountant who kept his eye on office materials and methods and who, every now and again, firmly checked any attempts at empire-building. (Or at least attempted to check it; I had a shrewd suspicion that my immediate senior, Donald Middridge, despite all that I'd said to Brown on the subject, was going to acquire an assistant in the very near future.)

I heard a match strike and smelled cigar smoke. Tantrum over; decision coming up. I turned and glanced at him expectantly. That was, as they say, the drill. There was nothing personal in it, I told myself, repressing the thought that he would have behaved far differently had I been a director.

In my early days with the firm I'd tried to discuss matters with him before he made the decisions; but I wasn't so naïve these days. And I didn't relish being called a jumped-up nowt and a sapless bookkeeper, which were two of his mildest epithets when he realized I was actually putting forward opinions of my own. I had taken his abuse then; now I knew that I couldn't. So I waited for him to speak.

"You'll have to go down to see him," he said.

"Are you sure I'm the right person?" This was as near as I dared approach to questioning the necessity of anyone's going to see Tiffield; it seemed to me that a polite but firm letter would easily settle the matter.

"*I'm* not sure you're the right person. *I'm* not sure at all."

He must have seen from the look on my face that he'd gone a little too far. "Nothing against you, Joe, nothing against you. It's just not your job, you're not really concerned with the sales side."

"You'd better send someone else then."

"He wants you for some reason. You must have made a deep impression on him. Dammit, he's only met you once. What the hell did you talk about?"

"He likes my stories," I said.

"Nay, you're not the only one that knows a lot of mucky stories." He laughed. "He's not just a big customer, is old Tiffield. He's a funny customer. You'll have to keep your back to the wall, won't you, lad?" He laughed again; this time there was a note about the laugh which I didn't like.

"When do you want me to go?" I asked.

"You've worked here for ten years and you ask that? Well, I'm surprised at you. The answer is, you go as soon as possible. Which is this very moment." He blew out a cloud of cigar smoke.

"All right," I said. "You phone Susan. She won't be pleased, though." I went to the door.

"I'm only joking," he said. "Can't I have a bit of a joke?" His tone was that of a starving man who has a crust of bread snatched from him. "You're all so serious-minded, you young ones. Catch the first train tomorrow. Get your secretary to book a room at the Savoy."

I raised my eyebrows. He didn't look at me but mumbled something about our biggest customer and being able to afford it.

When I was at the door he called me back. "Joe, have you thought about what we discussed yesterday?"

I sat down again, this time on the sofa to his right instead of the office chair in front of his desk. The sofa was part of the new executive suite designed for him by his wife; I found it too low for comfort, but deliberately sat there because it was presumably intended for guests, for private people and not employees.

"I've thought about it," I said, and saw to my delight that he looked ill at ease. Or was it the new executive suite, the handsome walnut desk that wouldn't have looked out of place in a drawing room, the matching cocktail cabinet and coffee table, the lilac-covered sofa and chairs, the cream fitted carpet and lilac and cream curtains? It needed a young American style executive — crew cut, Old Spice, Italian silk suit — behind that handsome desk: Brown didn't belong there.

He rose abruptly and began to pace up and down the room.

"You've got the wrong idea, Joe. You don't *have* to do this. It's a private matter between you and me."

"I know," I said. "But I don't spend very much time at home as it is."

"Neither do I, neither do I. I'm not asking you to do anything I wouldn't do myself, lad."

"I grant you that," I said automatically. But it didn't really apply; he hadn't a young wife, two children and a hundred interests he wanted to do something active about before it was too late; and what was more, he enjoyed being a councilor.

"Well, what do you say?" He pushed across the box of cigars. I hesitated, then took one.

"I called in at the Club last night," he said. "They're very keen. We need young blood, that's a fact. Last year was a sad year for us all. Men like Harry Runcett don't grow on trees."

I looked at him coldly. He meant that he wouldn't easily replace so useful a yes-man as Harry Runcett.

"They were agreed you'd be the ideal candidate. I was a

bit surprised —" He held up his hand to silence me. "Now, hear me out and don't fidget as if you'd got piles. I was a bit surprised because it's not often that lot all are agreed. George Aisgill —"

I stiffened. "What about George Aisgill?"

"He was most enthusiastic. That's all I was going to say. Now, you're not going to go on about something that's dead and buried long since, are you?"

"Dead and buried," I said. "You're right. Dead and buried." My father-in-law didn't only want a new yes-man; he wanted to tidy up the past. This could be a good way of doing it: instead of the triangle of lover, wronged husband and dead mistress there'd be those two respectable citizens Councilor Lampton and Councilor Aisgill. Members of the same great party, that great party to which we have the honor to belong. Councilor Lampton and Councilor Aisgill are great friends. Councilor Aisgill is a widower . . . It all fitted.

"You'd have to come up to the Club a bit more often," Brown said.

"Yes," I said. "I'd have to do that." It wasn't any use fighting against him and it wasn't any use avoiding George Aisgill. It was dead and buried; everything had changed, and what had happened ten years ago was as ludicrous to contemplate as an old film. Councilor Lampton would drink with Councilor Aisgill at the Conservative Club. Councilor Lampton and Councilor Aisgill would sit on the Council together; seeing them together, who would believe the old story?

"You'll let your name go forward?" Brown asked.

I nodded. "It should be interesting."

He clapped me on the shoulders. "I knew you would, Joe. Believe me, you'll not be sorry. Lots of people jeer but the councilor's the backbone of England. By God, what'd they do without us?" He grinned maliciously. "Beside you're just the chap to make things hum. It's not many of us that's worked at the Town Hall. That'll make that bloody clerk think twice!"

I grinned back at him. "Reformed poachers make the best gamekeepers."

He unlocked the cocktail cabinet. "This isn't going to be a regular thing, mind. I'm off spirits, anyway. But let's have a drink on it." He poured out two measures of Black and White. His own scarcely moistened the bottom of the glass.

"I may not get in," I said.

"Never mind. We'll have a drink on it just the same." He looked at me with something like affection. "We'll celebrate you doing what I want for once."

I lifted my glass to him; suddenly for no reason I felt sorry for him. It was a long time since I'd seen him so pleased about anything unconnected with his grandson; I began to wonder what the catch was. He couldn't possibly care about whether I was nominated for the Council or not, he couldn't possibly take it seriously. Then I saw from the smile on his face that he did. I'd only seen that smile twice: once when Harry was born and once when, after the birth of Barbara, I'd told him that Susan was out of danger.

It was a smile that made his red, heavy-jowled face surprisingly young; the harsh lines of power were still there, but they were warm without arrogance. For a moment I found myself almost liking him, I was almost able to persuade myself that I might find the flatulent mummery of local government as fascinating as he did.

But driving home that night, the double whiskies at four o'clock already transforming themselves into a faint but persistent headache, I was already beginning to regret having given way to him. And there was the trip to London, too; Susan wouldn't be pleased about that. I generally enjoyed my drive home; the quarter of Leddersford where the works were situated was so unmitigatedly, blackly hideous, the contrast with Warley so extreme, that every day I renewed my enjoyment of Warley. It was something I could rely upon; my reactions were always exactly the same. There was mild relief driving out of the works along Rawdon Road into Birmingham Road; but that was a feeling shared by everyone in the crowds I threaded my way through. It was shared, so it lost its value; the real elation began when I turned off Birmingham Road into the Leddersford Ring Road, a short stretch of dual carriageway running through an open-cast mining area now restored to farming land. This evening the fields looked more than usually desolate under the drizzling rain, their dreadful unvarying flatness an even worse insult to the eye. On another day I should have been glad of this, just as one's glad of a dry throat before a drink. For soon I'd turn left into the Leeds Road, then right into Warley Road and then there'd be a straight run into Hawcombe. And once at Hawcombe I was home. I never needed the Warley sign to tell me that; at Hawcombe the air began to smell different.

The real elation, the authentic joy, began at Hawcombe; but this evening, it was only a village like any other. The air couldn't smell any different; Hawcombe was at the bottom of Warley Road and Warley Road climbed to a thousand feet. The fact was, I realized, that I didn't want to go home. It wasn't only that Susan would be angry about both my trip to London and my going on the Council; it was something much worse. For ten years now this drive home had been an escape; every inch nearer to Warley had been a further distance between me and my father-in-law and my father-in-law's world. I naturally saw him frequently now, but only in the capacity of grandfather, only as a private person.

I could accept that, even find him almost human at times. But now he was going to be a fellow councilor. Or rather, was going to continue being my boss. There wasn't going to be any escape, there wasn't going to be any time when I could pretend to be a free and independent person. And there was nothing to be done about it once the Selection Committee had made their decision; as Harry Runcett had once said in his cups, the Park Ward was so safe a seat for the Tories that they'd elect a fucking cat if the party chose to run one. I've got a Siamese tom at home, he'd said, and if the party nominates that cat they'll all vote for it . . .

It came back to me now; I'd heard it at second hand through Eva Storr, who still was the clearing house for all Warley scandal. There'd been a mild stink about it; in a watered-down version and naming no names it had even reached the local press. Brown had cleared it up of course; I suppose the editor was gently reminded of the political affiliations of the Clarion group's principal stockholders. At the time I hadn't been anything but mildly amused by Harry Runcett's outburst, if you could call it an outburst. Now, driving along

Hawcombe Main Street in the rain I knew what the cat was. And it wasn't a tom. It was a neuter, a big fat neuter, that always did just whatever its father-in-law told it to do.

I put my foot down and the Zephyr gathered speed up the slope. The sooner I was home, the sooner it was over with; the speedometer crept up to sixty. Then I was over the crest of the hill and I could see Warley; despite myself I began to feel more cheerful. The day was behind me and Leddersford hidden behind Hawcombe Hill; before me was Forest Road and the river. I slowed down and opened the window to let in the rain and the smell of the forest. And as always, even now when I didn't dare hope for it, there came the quietness, the palpable dark green quietness. There was no reason for it; the road was a short one running through the narrowest part of the forest, with the town in full view over Forest Bridge. There was no reason for it, but it was there, there so strongly this evening that for a moment I was tempted to stop the car and for the duration of a cigarette sit quietly with the quietness.

I changed into second, then back again; what I wanted to do was innocent and harmless and utterly impossible. I could hear the voices now as I crossed the bridge and turned into Market Street; he's drunk, of course, they said. Why else, my dear? Why should he stop so near home? Trying to sober up, frightened to go home . . . Or meeting someone . . . that's more likely.

That was exactly how they'd chatter on; I'd heard those voices before. The three sets of lights in Market Street were each against me; at the third set, before St. Clair Road, the car in front of me stalled and I missed the green. The voices went on to other subjects; as I waited there I wondered if there ever had been a time when they hadn't ruled my life.

I didn't tell Susan about my trip to London until after dinner. I didn't admire myself very much for putting it off; but that day I seemed to have used up my small stock of courage. It was rather like being in the RAF again; every day one was forced to do something one didn't want to do, every day one was tested, the men were separated from the boys. I was sick to death of it, I'd proved myself often enough, I only wanted to sit back in my armchair and sip my coffee and let my meal digest, I only wanted to live in the present.

In the drawing room I was always happy to be in the present. Like that last stretch of Forest Road it was a pocket of quietness; it was the one room in the house where I felt at ease. And it was the solid testimony of how far I'd come in ten years; the parquet floor and the Maples suite alone had carried me through many bad moments.

It was the sort of room I'd dreamed of when I was living in that little house in Dufton; and now I possessed it, now I was living in the dream, and the flowered linen loose covers matched the curtains and the cream and gold wallpaper set off the dark walnut of the writing desk and coffee table and sideboard and the Grundig radio-phonograph. The great blank eye of the television was the only discordant note; but if my bonus this year came up to expectations, I'd change it for the new model with the cabinet door. And there was the chandelier which I'd picked up cheap in a Birmingham Road junk shop just before Christmas; it belonged with the parquet floor, it provided the finishing touch.

And the pictures, early nineteenth century prints, had mostly come from the same source as the chandelier. It was Alice who'd given me that tip. Originals, she'd said, were too dear, and you could easily go wrong; and everyone had reproductions. But you could pick up old prints cheap and everyone admired your taste, particularly if the subject was architectural or zoological. And old maps too were always safe; the great point was that your guests didn't have to know anything about art to admire them.

I went over to the cabinet for a drink. I didn't want to think about Alice tonight. Sometimes I had the notion that this was her room, that she, not I, had made it the kind of room that it was. Her taste had never been her husband's; he was all for pale, bleached woods, chromium and plastics, and not only knew what he liked but insisted upon having what he liked. His house, except for the books on the shelves, had entirely reflected his tastes, not Alice's; this room, about which I'd had my own way despite some opposition, was the only room which could accurately be said to belong to her. And she'd never know it. And no one else would ever know it. There was no one I could tell it to, no one who would understand. The whisky I was pouring into my glass would help a little; but if I tried to make it help more than a little then tomorrow morning I'd become aware of the existence of my liver, an organ which now was more and more frequently registering its protest against alcohol generally and spirits specifically.

"You might give me a drink," Susan said.

I spilled a little of the whisky; I'd forgotten she was there.

"A little brandy, darling." She looked at my glass. "I wouldn't have *your* head tomorrow," she said.

I didn't answer, but poured her out her usual medicinal dose of brandy. "Just enough to wet the bottom of the glass," I said, as I always did. Sometimes I made jokes about using an eye dropper next time; but just now I wasn't in a joking mood.

"You might as well tell me," she said.

I brought the drinks over to the coffee table. "I was thinking how pretty you look in that new dress."

That was true enough; the dress was bright red with a button-through front; the kind that only a pretty young woman with black hair and a good figure could get away with. She crossed her legs; she had good knees, neither too thin nor too fat. It isn't many pretty young women whose knees live up to the rest of them; without thinking, I leaned down and kissed each in turn.

"Wicked!" she said.

I pulled up her skirt a little; she pushed me away gently. "Mark's coming in for a drink, soon," she said.

My hand returned to her skirt. "He can watch us. Do him a world of good."

"Don't be horrid," she said.

I laughed. "It's Sybil it'd do a world of good to, actually. Mark doesn't talk much about it, but from what he's let slip, your dear cousin's no bargain in bed."

"They've three young children."

"Ah, come off it. He probably raped her. Or put something in her tea."

"You really are revolting," she said. But her cheeks were flushed a little and she wasn't bothering to push her skirt back; looking at her it was obvious she wasn't like Sybil, and I felt, along with desire, an uprush of tenderness. She wasn't the Browns' daughter; she was my wife. And unlike other men's wives she desired me physically. I looked in the direction of the sofa. That had been one of the great pleasures of married life; to make love at other times than night, at other places than in bed. In the bath, in the car, on country walks, wherever in fact we had as much as a quarter of an hour alone together; we'd pretend that we weren't married, pretend to be star-crossed lovers. And I, though I'd never told her, had sometimes pretended that she was married to someone else, to one of the men whom she might have married, one of the Jaguar and Porsche set like Jack Wales. Or like Ralph Hethersett. Thinking of him made me think of Brown; I swallowed my whisky at one gulp and went over to the sideboard again.

"*I'm* not revolting," I said. "Sybil finds sex revolting, that's all. No wonder Mark strays —"

"They say she didn't use to find sex revolting," Susan said. "She was quite gay once." She giggled. "*Awfully* gay with all and sundry. Can you imagine it?"

"People change," I said.

"There was a big scandal," Susan said. "They had a party when her parents were away and it got out of hand. Mummy told me a bit about it . . ."

Mummy, it transpired, had told her more than a bit about it; I found myself seeing Sybil, fat, harassed shrewish Sybil, with the spectacles always steamed up, in quite a new light.

When Susan had finished, I whistled. "Gay is the word," I said. "Gay is the word." Then I had a mental picture of the Sybil of twenty years ago, of the drunken faces hanging over her, of her inevitable posture, of the inevitable actions; gay wasn't the word.

"It's disgraceful really," Susan said. "I mean, we shouldn't drag up these things. It's all over and done with now, anyway."

"Dead and buried," I said. "Dead and buried." I lit a cigarette. "By the way —" I stopped.

"Go on," she said. "I know something unpleasant's coming up."

"I'm going to London tomorrow."

"You might have told me before," she said angrily. "You know perfectly well we're having Bob and Eva to dinner on Thursday."

"I'll probably be back by then."

"Probably is good. You're well aware you won't be. You'll be having too nice a time in London. You're absolutely selfish, Joe."

"Goddam it, it isn't my fault. Complain to your father, not me."

"I've a good mind to," she said. "He doesn't push anyone else around like that. I'm always being left alone with just Gerda for company and this week I haven't even got Gerda. You're mean and horrid and I hate you!" She began to cry. I knelt down beside her and put my arm round her shoulders. "Don't be upset, love. Joe doesn't want to go, but Joe has to earn pennies. Joe'll bring you something booty back, you'll see. Don't cry, precious, don't cry, there's a good girl . . ."

I put my hand on her knee; suddenly the tears stopped.

"Bolt the door," she said, suddenly.

"Mark —"

"They won't come for half an hour yet. Bolt the door, Joe, bolt the door." Her hands were at my body then at her own, feverishly. Bolting the door and switching off the main light, I heard something rustle to the floor; I walked over slowly to the sofa.

"Hurry," she said. "Hurry. You do, too, you know you do, you know you love it —" Gay, I thought, gay is not the word; then I cried out in pain as she bit my hand. "The big pretend," she said as I shook her by the shoulders. "The big pretend, the hurting pretend — I can't stop you, you must, you must —" and I emerged after what seemed a long time later to hear the front-door bell.

"Damn them," she said. "Help me up, darling." I pulled her up by her hands, noticing that it wasn't as easy as it used to be. The bell rang again.

"You'd better let them in," she said. "I'll tidy myself." Her smile broadened. "You're all undone. And your hair —"

I made myself decent hurriedly on the way to the door; but under Mark's and Sybil's eyes I felt a curious embarrassment. It was a night too when I could have done without callers, particularly Sybil whose voice that night seemed to be at its shrillest; they had, she breathlessly explained, just been to a *disastrous* management meeting, and she'd had the *hell* of a day, the children had been fiends —

I put my arm round her shoulder and kissed her on the cheek. Her skin tasted of powder and fatigue and her up-swept hair straggled at the nape; she was only three years older than Mark but at the moment she looked far more than that; she was one of those fair, delicate-featured women whose good looks fade almost overnight, who go to bed young women and wake up matrons.

"I've got the cure for you, love," I said. "Don't worry your pretty little head, I've got the cure."

"For me, too, I hope," Mark said as they followed me into the drawing room. "I've been coping with the little fiends, too."

"For both of you," I said.

"They've been playing Night Clubs," Sybil said. "Lisa's simply frantic. I'm afraid we won't keep her much longer." She sighed. "Oh God, these bloody foreign girls! Where've all the good servants got to?"

"They never existed," said Mark. "It's a legend, a beautiful bourgeois legend."

He looked at the sideboard. "Ah, my cure's coming along splendidly. Nothing with it, Joe, thank you."

He looked more than usually spruce this evening — though it was still raining there was no trace of it on his person. But there was mud on Sybil's shoes and the neck of her purple dress was dark with moisture. She was unlucky in that way, unlucky in the minor things, an attractor of small annoyances; Mark was one of the lucky ones, one of those who walked through the rain without getting wet, who ate and drank just what he liked without putting on weight, whose dark good looks would be unchanged twenty years from now. He'd always been able to attract women all his life. Or rather, stupid young girls, I reminded myself sourly. Then I caught sight of myself in the mirror across the room, and felt a spasm of envy; my spare tire was becoming too pronounced to be funny and my face was beginning to be blurred by fat.

Susan came into the room, her hair brushed and her dress buttoned up and her seams straight, completely the respectable and tidy hostess, but on her face the unmistakable satisfaction of a woman who had recently made love. She might as well have said as much; I noticed that Sybil, after the first glance, turned her eyes away from her. But Mark's face betrayed his envy; for a moment he looked all of his forty years. I leaned back in my chair smiling and poured myself another whisky.

three

TIFFIELD was in high good humor. So he should have been; I'd given him a lunch which would have fed a family of ten, I'd taken him to a strip club afterwards, and now here we were in the American Bar at the Savoy knocking back double martinis and devouring olives and potato crisps, as he would have devoured anything that was free; I was content to watch him, rather queasily.

"The black ones are best," he said, putting the last of a saucerful in his mouth. "The oil renews the stomach lining." He looked at me sorrowfully, as if making some weighty pronouncement about sin or nuclear warfare.

"I'll try to get you some," I said, and beckoned a waiter.

The furrows on Tiffield's face assembled themselves into an expression of regret. "No, thank you very much. It would spoil my dinner. But another one of these —" He nodded towards his empty glass.

I ordered another martini, his third in twenty minutes, and as he'd specified, each had been well and truly dry. It was going on top of four double Scotches, half a bottle of Burgundy, and three brandies. I looked at him with a certain envy. Already I felt rumpled and liverish and was beginning to talk overcarefully; Tiffield, thirty years older, looked and sounded as grave and precise and sober as when I'd collected him from his office that morning.

He hunted in his pockets for something, then looked expectantly at me. I passed him my cigarette case; he snatched one greedily, as if afraid that I might change my mind.

"Dear me, I must remember to get some," he said.

"Leave it to me," I said. "Benson and Hedges?"

He smiled, showing a set of ill-fitting false teeth of the same yellowish tinge as his linen.

"That's very nice of you, my boy. How did you know?"

"I remembered from the last time we dined together." It was a lie; I remembered because I'd bought a tin of Benson and Hedges for him at lunchtime; it would now be reposing unopened in his pocket. Probably he'd keep them for Christmas boxes, if he ever gave Christmas boxes.

A tall blond girl entered; close on her heels and giving the impression of sniffing at her hindquarters, were two short fat men. The men were ridiculously alike, each wearing the same kind of lightweight blue suit, American from the cut, and white shirt and narrow tie — the capitalist's dungarees. When they sat down they began to talk to each other rather than to the girl; she didn't seem to mind, or to want any kind of attention, but looked straight in front of her, her face blank. It was a face I'd seen before somewhere in two dimensions; and in two dimensions and in two colors it had looked more real. Her eyes focused upon me for a second; I fancied I saw a faint smile. One of the men spoke to her sharply; her glance jerked away from me.

Suddenly it was as if everyone were speaking very loudly; wave after wave of sound was sweeping over me. At home now Barbara would be having her bath, two hundred miles away she'd be splashing and singing, singing her own gibberish songs which to me often made as much sense as anything I'd heard during the day. And sometimes after she'd been put to bed I'd hear her singing to herself for a few minutes, softly and happily as if recapitulating every good thing which had happened to her since morning. But I was in the American Bar and unless I was lucky I would be there again or in some place very much like it tomorrow night and the following night; and Tiffield had finished his third martini and very soon was going to tell me dirty stories.

I would have to laugh. I thought as he began the sad little classic of the vicar and the prostitute, I would have to laugh aloud. A smile wouldn't be enough. Keep him happy, Brown had said, give the old bastard everything he wants. Antagonize him and you antagonize me . . . No, he hadn't said that. But it was true. Tiffield was Brown and Brown was Tiffield. Tiffield weighed about one hundred and fifty-five pounds and hadn't bought a new suit since 1930, Brown weighed around two hundred and ten and made regular visits to Savile Row and Bond Street; but these were only surface differences. They were the same person; an old man with power over me, an old man whom I had to keep happy at all costs.

The voices mounted, matches struck, cigarette lighters clicked, ice tinkled, money passed; I was two hundred miles away from home, listening to a rich old man in a prewar fifty-shilling suit tell a story I'd first heard at Dufton Grammar School. Word for word, almost; though Tiffield didn't tell it so well as Charles.

" 'I've tried it that way,' she said, 'and it always gives me the hiccups.' " Tiffield exploded into laughter — it was a desiccated laughter, old dry tissues forcing themselves into a kind of dance. I echoed the laughter as best I could, and to cover its falseness told him the one about the elephant and the nun. He laughed so hard that he began to cough. The cough wouldn't stop; it seemed to have picked up his skinny body by the scruff of the neck in a determined effort to shake the life out of him. His face turned a dull red; I became seriously worried. He hadn't signed the contract yet and his was the only signature which counted. If the old swine had to die now, it wouldn't help me at all. I was wondering whether to loosen his collar when suddenly the cough let him go. He pulled out a big red dotted handkerchief, of the kind that workmen used to wrap up their dinners in.

"My boy, you'll be the death of me," he said. "Where did you hear that one?"

"From an actress friend," I said. Jean had told me it at the Rinkmanns' party on Saturday; she'd also told me her London telephone number. And she'd be in London now. And I was in London. And surely Tiffield would want to go home straight after dinner. The voices were as loud as ever, and I was still in the American Bar and two hundred miles away from home; but the voices didn't matter any more. And Barbara had stopped singing.

"From an actress friend," Tiffield repeated. "If only I

were young . . ." He cackled. "I think I'd do with another of these martinis. In fact, I deserve one. You young men have actress friends and we have a drop of gin, that's the way it is . . ."

"Are you sure —"

"Yes. And then we'll think about dinner. Does she live in London, your actress friend?"

"Kensington," I said.

He looked at the blonde. "I've seen her on TV," he said. He named her. I hadn't been able to identify the fashionably kittenish face, but I remembered the name. It had been in all the papers some six months ago; too much drink, a wife on the way up, and a husband on the way down.

Tiffield's eyes were bright. "Strange lives these people lead," he said happily.

"Some of them," I said. Jean hadn't been cited twice as a co-respondent, nor had she virtually driven a husband to his death, but Jean hadn't climbed very high yet. And Jean, when she'd rested for too long, could always return to Warley and home cooking; there was always a safety net, there was never any need to be frightened.

I looked at the blonde again; she was leaning forward to listen to what one of her companions was saying. Her black dress was so low-cut that it didn't seem possible for the nipples not to be revealed; but I turned my eyes away. I felt ashamed to lust after her; I knew what had made that face blank, I knew what it was like up there on the tightrope.

"Delectable," said Tiffield. "If I were younger, I'd ask you if your friend had a friend." He pulled out a watch. "Five shillings," he said. "Five shillings in 1930. And it's never cost me a penny in repairs. It'll be going long after that pretty little toy you're wearing has ceased to function . . ." He peered at the watch. "They stir you up, they really do. But time is running on. Yes, time is running on. We really must think about dinner . . ."

He thought about dinner to some purpose, beginning with *foie gras*. This was the only moment at which he showed any indecision; he wasn't sure whether or not he preferred caviar. He went on to trout, chicken *en cocotte* and *crêpes suzette;* he didn't talk much, but ate with enormous concentration, his napkin tucked into his collar. Between courses he smoked my cigarettes and drank the lion's share of the wines — hock, *vin rosé*, and Madeira. The wines were his choice, not mine, and as each bottle was brought out he treated me to a short homily on the reasons for his choice.

We had a good view of the dance floor; that evening there appeared to be a great many young people there. They were mixing, they all seemed to know each other, there was an air of celebration. They would be private persons spending their own money; this would be a big night, they'd be enjoying themselves, an evening at the Savoy would be something worth remembering. Eleven years ago, I'd gone regularly to the Dufton Locarno; there too I'd sat upstairs, and ate and drank and watched the dancers. I'd eaten sausage rolls and drunk tea or coffee and my suit had cost nearer ten guineas than thirty-five; but I had been a private person, spending my own money. And I had been free to join the dancers.

I pushed aside my *crêpes suzette*. Tiffield looked up from his emptied plate. "You haven't touched them," he said, rather reproachfully. "Off your food, my boy?"

"I'm not very hungry," I said. I looked at the dancers; the girls' skirts were flying up in a rumba. Off your food; a horse is off its feed, an employee is off its feed, a son-in-law is off its feed.

"You should eat it," he said. "It's really delicious." His fork was still in his hand.

"I'm sure it is," I said. "But I can't eat any more."

"You've not eaten anything," he said. "Orange juice and an omelette — that's not a dinner." He looked longingly at my plate. "It'll only be wasted," he said.

"The waiter will eat it."

"You don't mind if I have it?"

I pushed my plate over to him; for the first time I began to like him. There was something endearingly childish about his gluttony; after all, what else did he have? He'd never married, and never had any interests outside his business; and the business now ran itself. He had got into light industry on the ground floor in 1919, and now wherever you threw a stone in East London you were pretty well bound to hit a Tiffield Products factory.

The particular kind of steel which he wanted was necessary for a brand-new process; it was in fact a brand-new kind of steel. We'd spent a great deal of time and effort in giving him just what he wanted; but he wasn't prepared to order enough of the stuff. Enough, for him, was roughly half the amount we needed to sell in order to break even; and we couldn't sell it to anyone else because there wasn't anyone else who needed it. But we knew this when we began research, we had set a sprat to catch a mackerel. My father-in-law had been wrong to describe Tiffield as a big customer; he really meant that he hoped he would be a big customer. To me it appeared as if he were going to swim off with the plump juicy sprat XA 81 triumphantly between his yellow teeth. And if he did I knew who would get the blame.

Tomorrow I had an appointment with his production manager and he'd ask me questions about XA 81 as if he couldn't read or as if he didn't believe what we'd written: yes, I would say it really does resist that temperature, yes it really does resist corrosion by this that and the other chemical; and blood and benzine and pineapple and chutney, and why the hell are you wasting my time? No, I wouldn't say that; but I'd want to say it.

Tiffield had finished his second helping; I handed him my packet of cigarettes. If he wasn't approachable now, he never would be; I wasn't going to let him evade the subject again.

"We're rather worried about your order, Mr. Tiffield."

He finished his glass of Madeira. "You needn't be, my boy. Of course I'm not an expert, but I know you've done a fine job. Mottram — and he knows about steel if any man does — was talking to me about it only the other day. He's delighted, my boy. Quite frankly, he thought that you couldn't possibly meet all our requirements. What you've done with Z — no —" he snapped his fingers — "XA 81 is to solve a series of technical paradoxes. And you couldn't," he said, "be guided very much by previous experience."

I cut him short. "It isn't XA 81 we're worried about."

"I'm glad to hear it," he said. The waiter appeared with

the cheeseboard; he looked at it as greedily as if it were the first food he'd seen that day.

He selected a piece of Gorgonzola, then, as the waiter was taking the board away, pointed out a *petit Suisse*. "Yes," he said absently, "I'm glad to hear you're not worried about the XA 81."

"There was an understanding about KY —"

"KL," he said, his mouth full. "KL 51."

"You wrote us last month. Apart from that, your Mr. Mottram himself expressed an interest, a very great interest, not so long ago."

"But of course. That's just as it should be. That's Mr. Mottram's job." He put sugar on the *petit Suisse*. "Mr. Mottram's very interested. Mr. Mottram's on top of his job. He's on top of his job because he knows my guiding principle: I appoint a man to a job, then leave him to it. *My* dogs, you might say, do their own barking. If he's as interested as you think he is, then you'll hear from him."

They were taking their partners for a waltz now, a slow waltz, an old waltz from the days of Carroll Gibbons and the Orpheans. He'd been in a cigarette card series; and Henry Hall and Ambrose and Billy Cotton and Harry Roy who married a princess; I knew all about the dance band leaders in those days. They were music from glamorous places, they sent messages from a world one couldn't really hope to inhabit.

Wish you were here, the music said, assuring one of the existence of that world, the gayer, richer world of the Café Royal, the Café de Paris, the Savoy, and now I was dining at the Savoy. Carroll Gibbons wasn't here; but even if he had been, I wasn't free to join the dancers. I went on arguing with Tiffield; there seemed to be no point in beating about the bush now. But my head had begun to ache and I had a frighteningly sharp pain just beneath my breastbone; I didn't just then, care whether or not he gave me the order for KL 51 and he seemed to know it. He had defeated me; I couldn't think of any way to get through to him. I didn't feel any hatred for him; he was too old, he was enjoying his free dinner too much.

Sipping his brandy, he said in a surprisingly disconsolate voice, "I suppose you'll want to go now."

"There's no hurry," I said.

"I'll send a car round here tomorrow."

"There's not much point in doing that, sir." I accented the *sir*; I was tired of the pretense of our being companions.

"Why isn't there any point in it? Have you forgotten your appointment?"

"Send him my apologies."

He shook his head slowly.

"Now, we have a mystery. Your father-in-law sends you all the way from Yorkshire to do a job for him. You're halfway through the job and doing it to everyone's satisfaction — and then you throw the job up. Why?"

"Because I might as well get the row over with," I said. "You're not going to give me the order, and my seeing your production manager won't alter that."

I beckoned the waiter. "The bill, please."

"You're jumping to conclusions," Tiffield said. "You've not been in business very long, have you, Joe?" It was the first time he'd used my Christian name.

"Ten years," I said.

"I've been in business fifty years. Man and boy, as they say. I started at the same time as your father-in-law. I was in business in the same part of the world."

"I didn't know that."

"Not many people do. I wasn't very successful at first. In fact, I came a cropper. I knew it all. Yes, a real purler. I was young and I thought I knew it all. We were after the same young woman. I expect you know who she was."

I kept my face expressionless. I didn't want to discourage his confidences; but if he told me too much he might be sorry the next day.

"It's the old story," I said.

"Yes, the old story." He folded his napkin and rose abruptly. "I'll see you tomorrow," he said.

My cigar was lying unlit by my brandy glass; I handed it to him. "They're wasted on me," I said.

He smiled and put it in his cigar case.

"You understand me, Joe."

He patted me on the shoulder.

"Your father-in-law must think a lot about you," he said. "He'll think even more of you after tomorrow. There's nothing for you to worry about."

"There's quite a lot," I said. "But it doesn't matter now."

"Well, we'll go into all that tomorrow, when we look at the draft contract. A most forbidding document, I may add." He held out his hand. "Thank you again for a really admirable dinner. And now I'll go home to bed and a nice mug of Ovaltine and an hour with Sherlock Holmes. . . . The pleasures of an old man . . ."

I hardly heard him. "What draft contract, sir?"

He put his hand to his mouth; the gesture was almost roguish. "I mustn't tell you," he said. "It's Mr. Mottram's decision. But it'll be the contract that you're *really* interested in, take my word for it."

I looked at him dumbly.

After I'd put him in a taxi I went up to my room. I kicked off my shoes and loosened my collar and lay on the bed; it was the first moment that I'd had the chance to relax. The pain in my chest began to diminish; I was in, I was home and dry. I'd got the order. He'd played cat-and-mouse with me for a bit, because that was his nature; but I'd succeeded where other men had failed.

I ran my hand over my chin; it was six o'clock in the morning since I'd shaved last. A shower, a shave, a clean shirt, and a large Scotch on the rocks; and Jean was having a party. I hadn't expected to go to that party when she'd told me about it on Saturday; but neither had I expected to all but clinch the deal with Tiffield. I threw off my clothes and went into the bathroom; as the cold shower jerked my body back into well-being it suddenly occurred to me that there was nothing more I could reasonably wish for.

I dried myself on one of the huge white towels and put on clean socks and underwear; I hesitated for a moment over the choice of a shirt, then picked the brand-new one I'd bought that morning in the Burlington Arcade. It was plain cream silk and with it I could wear the rather loud Charvet tie I'd bought myself in Paris last year. Susan always made a minor scene when I wore it; so I didn't wear it in Warley. But I wasn't in Warley now and I didn't want to think of Susan; and the tie had cost me nearly two thousand francs. And I was going to a party at an actress's flat.

I didn't feel married, I didn't feel an employee; in that warm room with the wall-to-wall beige carpet and heavy curtains I threw off my Warley identity. There were no responsibilities in this room, no worries, no sound except my own breathing. The day's work was over and I was free in London. In other hotels at this hour I'd always found myself thinking of Warley, overcome by nostalgia, but now there was no nostalgia. I'd pulled the deal off — there was no arguing with my instincts — and Warley had ceased to exist.

One of these days I'd have a suite here, one of these days I'd be so big that old bastards like Tiffield wouldn't dare keep me on the hook.

I went over to my dressing table and rubbed my face with pre-electric shave lotion. It seemed to smell different here; I didn't feel self-conscious about using it, as I did in Warley. I unpacked my electric razor; while I was shaving I'd order a drink. And I'd phone Jean. I smiled at myself in the mirror. I'm just confirming your invitation, darling. I didn't want to burst in on you all unexpected-like . . . Yes, I'm phoning from London , surprise, surprise. The Savoy. Not really, I'm in the peasants' quarter, just one little room . . .

Then my smile stopped. I wasn't taking part in a drawing-room comedy and I knew, alone with the beige carpet and heavy curtains and smell of Old Spice, just what I intended to do with Jean.

four

Night was falling as I left the Savoy. The rain had stopped, leaving the air moist and heavy, brassy on the tongue; it seemed to hold sounds — footsteps, voices, the swish of car tires — long after it should have let them go. But it was fresh air of a kind, it had once moved over trees and running water; I was outside, I was walking, I was alone, I'd just had a shower and I was clean from top to toe. One bath a week it had been once, on Saturday, the big night; and no one had brought me a large Scotch-on-the-rocks either. I stopped to look at the Savoy Taylors window; suddenly I realized that I had all the clothes I wanted.

I walked on in the direction of Charing Cross Road, feeling better with every step. I turned up St. Martin's Lane and went past the New Theatre and then stopped at the British and Colonial showrooms to look at a pink Thunderbird. And then there was something else you couldn't afford — so you worked still harder . . .

I turned away from the Thunderbird and hailed a taxi.

It wasn't as simple as all that; in the first place, I didn't want the Thunderbird. I wouldn't have refused one, just as I wouldn't have refused a vicuña overcoat; but I had stopped wanting things. I wanted power, power to put through my own ideas; I wanted to be taken seriously, I wanted to be something more than the boss's son-in-law.

I leaned back for safety and comfort as the notice told me: taxis remained a great pleasure, I didn't want to undervalue the things which came along with four thousand a year and an expense account. The power would come; Brown couldn't live forever. Or with luck he might have a stroke; he was exactly the right build and age and temperament. And I was the father of the Crown Prince. I would have to get to know him better, we'd have to become chums, real chums. Because if we didn't, one of these days Daddy might be pushed out in the cold. It had happened before in family businesses; my position wasn't unique.

The pain under my breastbone returned; this time it was so sharp that I bit my hand to stop myself from crying out. The sweat was running into my eyes, but I didn't dare to wipe it away: the pain held me rigid, my hand in my mouth like a baby. It had gone by the time we reached Kensington High Street; but I still sat stiffly, my right hand to my mouth, my left arm pressed against my side as if to hold back its return. It didn't return; instead I kept thinking about Harry's model railway layout. He'd finished it — as much as one ever finished a model railway — last year, just before he'd gone away to boarding school; it lived on two trestle tables in the loft. It was a mixed sort of railway, mostly Tri-ang Transcontinental stock, running from Warley to Zurich. It was open country all the way from Warley to Zurich; there were three windmills and two churches in the middle of the fields, but that was the only sign of human life. And on the road which ran parallel to the main line there was a steam lorry, a traction engine, and a steamroller. There were cattle browsing beside the bright blue river; and, in the shadow of what I took to be Zurich Cathedral, a shepherd and a flock of sheep. But beside them he'd put an elephant and a leopard.

That was on the first night of the Easter holidays when we'd gone to the loft and switched the lights off; as the big silver diesel came out of the tunnel its headlight had illumined the cathedral and the sheep only. The elephant and the leopard were vague shapes in the background. He dropped the mail at Zurich, a tiny Zurich full of British soldiers, and there the headlight picked up the elephant and the leopard.

He'd drawn in his breath sharply and then slowed down the train. "The people in the train can't believe their eyes," he whispered. "But they're not frightened." He speeded up the train. "They're safe, they're on their way to Warley."

"What about the shepherd and the sheep?" I'd asked.

"The soldiers will look after them," he said. "That's what soldiers are for."

The train speeded up; then at the last moment before the bend he stopped it dead. "The people on the train are frightened now. They think there's a breakdown. And the elephant will break down the doors and then the leopard will get in . . ." He'd started the train again. "They're all right now, though. They're glad they're not where the shepherd is. They're all laughing —" The train had gathered speed into the next bend; but he didn't slow it down and it went off the rails.

"They thought they were safe," he'd said. "They weren't, you see. Now they'll never see Warley again."

I'd switched the light on. "Time for bed," I said.

I could still see his smile. "Sorry about the crash, Daddy."

"You're not, but it doesn't matter."

He'd not played with the railway again. And what I'd said was true enough; it didn't matter. But that night we'd lost something. I took my hand from my mouth. The pain had gone. But I could still see the big silver diesel crashing at the bend, still see Harry's smile.

Kensington High Street seemed deserted; I wondered gloomily where everyone went to at night. When I was younger there always seemed to be a lot of people about; now there were only cars. When you came close to them you saw there was always someone in the driving seat; but it wouldn't always be so. One day they'd drive themselves, without passengers, to whatever destination cars choose for themselves and we'd all hide indoors waiting for them to pass. But they'd never stop passing; it was like watching Chinese march by.

The taxi turned off to the left past Olympia into a district of greengrocers and laundries and dry-cleaners and florists, then sharply right into a long street of three-story terrace houses, then sharply left into the mews where Jean lived.

"Know where your number is, sir?" the taxi driver asked.

"I'll soon find it," I said, and paid him off.

I didn't: the numbers ran in no regular order, and I walked round the whole square, or rather oblong, before I found 14a tucked away in a little alley next to 23. The alley was cobbled and lit by a Victorian gas lamp on the wall.

There was an electric bulb inside the lamp, but the wattage was low enough for it not to appear too glaring. The door had been newly painted pale yellow and the brass knob had been newly polished; I smelled money. I pressed the bell.

The young man who answered the door was more than a little drunk.

"There's nobody at home," he said thickly, pushing long black hair out of his eyes.

"This is Jean Velfrey's, isn't it?"

He swayed and recovered himself by putting a hand out against the wall. Looking at him more closely I saw that he wasn't quite as young as I'd first supposed; nearer forty than thirty, in fact.

He scowled at me. "You'll know me again, won't you, mate?"

There was an oak chest beside me with a pile of coats on it; I added mine to the pile. I didn't need to ask him again whether Jean lived here; I recognized the framed playbills.

"Through that door?" I asked him.

"That's the bog," he said, sitting down heavily on the oak chest. "The opposite one, that's what you require, my friend. But there's nobody home. These objects on the walls represent all the shows in which Jackie and Jean have taken part. Jean on the left, Jackie on the right. Nothing has come amiss, you see. *The Beggar's Opera, Cymbaroon, She Strips to Conquer*, Anouilh, Coward, Novello, the lot. But they're not home tonight." He stood up and took my lapel between his fingers and thumb. "That's a nice piece of cloth," he said. "I have seen it, or you somewhere before."

"I don't think we've met." I said, feeling my antagonism towards him sharpening violently.

"I didn't say we had. But I've seen you in Warley. I come from Warley."

"How exciting," I said. "I'm sure we shall be great chums."

I turned my back on him; at that moment the door opened and Jean came out. She flung her arms around my neck. "I thought you'd got lost," she said. "Has Jeff been tiresome?"

I shrugged.

"He's tight, you see. He's in between jobs and it's a great strain for him."

"You're breaking my heart," I said. I put my arm round her and nuzzled her neck. "Diorissimo," I said.

She kissed me again. "How clever you are. And my dress? You like my dress?" Superfluously, she smoothed it over her hips.

"Hardy Amies," I said. "But mostly Jean."

"She's done that with everyone tonight," Jeff said. "It isn't Hardy Amies. Madame Winterbottom, High Street, Warley, that's where she got it. Cut price; no decent woman would wear it."

Jean kissed me. "It's lovely to see you," she said. "Now I don't feel homesick any more."

"The big act," Jeff said. Suddenly he seemed less drunk. "Christ, you only came back on Monday night." He pushed his hair out of his eyes again; he had a high broad unlined forehead which didn't match the rest of his face, which was pretty rather than handsome with a dimpled chin and full but well-cut lips. If it hadn't been for the forehead and tufts of black hair on the cheekbones he'd have made a very pretty girl. I wondered why he was in such a bad temper, and why Jean had put up with him. He'd have to be slapped down somehow; I tightened my arm around Jean's waist.

I felt young again. It was all so easy. He was jealous. He wanted what I wanted. He was jealous even of Warley. And ahead of me lay pleasure. Not just the pleasure of having Jean but the pleasure of taking her from someone else, whom I had disliked at first sight. I'd spent the whole day pleasing a gluttonous sadistic old man for the sake of my bread-and-butter, for the sake of my wife and children. I'd spent the whole day from catching the London train at six in the morning, looking at notes and specifications and letters with aching eyes, as an employee, as something less than a man. And now I was free, now I was a man again, now I would join the dancers.

There were thirty of the dancers. They weren't dancing; some of them weren't even drinking. It didn't seem to me as if there was going to be an orgy; everyone there seemed to be very young. Or maybe, I thought, I'd come ten years too late. "I'll get you a drink," said Jean. "Name it, sweetie."

"I will name it, and I'll name him," Jeff said. "I've just remembered. It's Lampton and he wants a large Scotch; that's what the successful businessman drinks in Warley." He flattened the first vowel of Warley into a bleat, looking at me to observe the effect. I felt a spurt of anger; automatically I measured him up. He was two inches taller than I but he was painfully thin. It wasn't an athletic thinness, it was a disjointed, underfed thinness; he seemed somehow brittle. Or as if his bones hadn't hardened yet; there was more than a touch of childishness about him.

"You've guessed right," I said. "You seem to know Warley quite well." I offered him a cigarette. It suddenly seemed important to please him, not because I cared about pleasing him but as an exercise in handling people.

"I lived there once. And I have worked for your father-in-law," he said. "During the war. We never saw eye to eye."

"Who does?"

"It's different for you," he said. "I was just a clerk."

"We all are," I said. "Every last one of us at Brown and Co." At the far end of the room, half hidden behind a studio couch, was a big tape recorder; its profusion of knobs and switches put me in mind of the Flamville computer which, against my advice, Brown had just acquired. Firmly I put the recollection out of my mind.

"He's the big boss," Jeff said. "No togetherness for Abe Brown. He's a throwback, a nineteenth century throwback."

Jean came back with the drinks; he took his from her absently and drank half of it at one gulp. She looked at him anxiously. "Are you all right, Jeff?"

"I'm fine," he said. "Just talking about old times with Mr. Lampton." He giggled. "I know him, you see. He drives around Warley in a big white car. He doesn't know me, though. I see him but he doesn't see me. He lives at the top —"

"A friend of yours has just arrived," Jean said, rather coldly.

"Mr. Lampton's my friend. Everyone knows Mr. Lampton. He reminds me of dear old Warley. I visit Warley now and again, you know. Dear little Warley, dear residential Warley. My mum lives on Tebbutt Street. At the bottom —"

A plump hand fastened on his shoulder. He turned round. "Judy, my love! I've been missing you all evening!" He took her by the waist and held her out at arm's length. "God, you look wonderful. I'm going to monopolize you, absolutely monopolize you." He took her to the long table near the tape recorder. "You look wonderful," I heard him say again; then he whispered something to her and she laughed happily. For a second she looked the younger of the two; then her face became middle-aged and greedy again.

"He's in advertising," Jean said.

I grimaced.

"Don't be bitchy," she said. "It's not your thing, darling, it really isn't."

"It isn't me who's been bitchy," I said. "Who is he anyway? He knows me but I'm damned if I know him."

"You mean you don't know him?" She seemed incredulous.

"If he comes from Warley I might have seen him about the place."

"His name's Kelstedge."

"I've heard it somewhere before. A long time ago."

"Hasn't Susan ever talked about him?" There was a sly smile on her face.

"Come off it," I said. "Tell me the truth. They say the husband's the last one to know —"

She laughed. "Jeff? He hardly ever goes to Warley. No, he's an old flame. Extinct, in fact."

The memory was coming to the surface now. The clerk who'd been run out of town by my father-in-law. He looked as if he'd run away.

"I suppose he's told you all about it," I said.

"He never discusses it."

"Susan doesn't either," I said. "It wasn't anything — just calf love." But she hadn't seen it like that; those were my father-in-law's words, spoken a long time ago, before I was married. And when my status hadn't been very much different from Jeff Kelstedge's. How had she seen it? When had she talked about it to me? If you live ten years with a woman not much is left unsaid. I could remember now the night when she'd screamed that Jack Wales was twice the man I was and she wished to God she'd married him. I could remember — it was as if the dragnet was bringing up old boots and rusty tins — the party at which she'd met Adam Loring, Warley's own stage celebrity, fresh from an American tour, and had wondered, rather too loudly and vehemently, what it would have been like to have been married to him. But I couldn't remember her mentioning Jeff Kelstedge. It seemed essential that I should; I stared at him scowling with concentration.

"Never mind him, darling," Jean said. "He's Jackie's pal anyway, not mine. She's the lame-dog collector in this establishment." She moved closer to me. "You haven't told me how you like our flat."

"It's cozy," I said.

"This room is the studio," she said. "It's the wrong shape and size, but if you call a room a studio you needn't have much furniture. The studio couch and the suite are rather grand, but Mummy and Daddy gave me those. And Jackie and I did the distempering." She looked at my empty glass. "Do you need another, Joe?"

"Presently," I said. I had a feeling of being let down. Here I was at a party in a mews flat in London; and I didn't feel any different. I was in a rather bare room with streakily distempered pink walls and an odd assortment of furniture, talking to a pretty girl who happened to be an actress; there was no more to it than that.

Jeff and Judy had moved into the far corner of the room; he was still whispering to her. Now he was stroking her bare shoulder; her face was stupid with pleasure. I felt a queer kind of regret on his behalf. It was as if he were being exploited, not she. But why should I care, and what did it matter?

"You really do need another drink," Jean said. "Come on, honey. And then we'll circulate."

Three hours later I was still circulating. I had stopped counting the dancers now or trying to remember their names.

And now they had rolled back the big Indian carpet and were actually dancing; I was waltzing with a tall thin girl who said she was a model. The walls had ceased to look streaky, their color was a soft rose. At some point in the evening, the tape recorder had been switched on and we stopped dancing to listen to the playback. Everyone's face was excited, flushed, half ashamed; as always the machine seemed only to regurgitate malice. *False, of course*, it said, *sponge spheroids. Ask Tony, he knows.* And then there'd be a confusion of voices and an assortment of minor noises — glasses clinking, matches being struck, the central heating rumbling and a girl's voice would say very clearly: *The latest? Jesus, he's ancient. Full of whisky — no darling, no we couldn't I've told you;* and a different voice, the voice of the red-haired girl from RADA whom now I dimly remember talking to earlier. *I'm just a working girl,* and my own voice, thicker and more Yorkshire than I'd imagined it — *You give me great delight . . .*

The model had left me and was chattering to Jackie, Jean's friend. Jackie was small and dark and plump and reminded me of Eva Storr; I went over to the table to pour myself a drink, reflecting as I did so that I'd already had quite enough. I started to worry about the Tiffield order again; Mottram was bound to talk about delivery dates tomorrow. The red-haired girl from RADA was sitting on a young man's knee; to judge from the expression on his face she was giving him great delight too. I filled up my glass again and moved over to the fireplace. There was a firescreen in front of it impossibly big red and white satin roses covered by glass. There were logs in the fireplace festooned with red and blue crepe paper; the logs looked as if they'd been dusted and polished. The red-haired girl from RADA pushed the young man's hand away from her leg; he said something to her and she blushed. She lifted an arm to put a curl back into place; I saw the tuft of hair in her armpit. Suddenly I wished her dead; I wasn't with them, I hadn't joined the dancers, it was ten years too late. I looked at the invitation cards on the mantelpiece; there were too many for them all to be visible but somehow all those from celebrities were at the front.

Jean came into the room. She smiled at me and I went over to her. She looked over at the tape recorder. "How long has that been on?"

"Long enough," I said. I put my glass down.

"It's Jackie's bright idea. Sheer sadism I call it." Her lipstick was a little smudged and a shoulder strap had slipped.

"I'm making some coffee," she said. "Would you like some? Honestly?"

"Honestly."

She put the strap back. "Do I look very dissipated?"

"Fresh as the morning."

"It *is* morning. But they'll go on for hours yet."

Jeff's voice was whispering over the tape recorder. It carried farther than a shout would have done. Jean's eyes dilated.

"He's terrible," she said. "She's forty if she's a day."

"They don't seem to be here any more."

"She whisked him away an hour ago. She's got a huge American car with fins and a built-in cocktail bar and seats that let down into a double bed — you know the kind of thing."

"I can guess," I said. "I can guess. I began to stroke her arm. She drew in her breath sharply. "No," she said. "Not here."

The kitchen was very small and smelled of new paint and garlic. Above the electric oven was a tea towel with a recipe for *Ratatouille Niçoise* printed on it. There was a crate of empty beer bottles by the sink.

On an impulse I knelt down and kissed the hem of her skirt. The silk smelled faintly musty. The floor was stone: I felt its cold hardness through the carpeting. I put my arms round her waist and my head against her belly and stayed like that for a moment. She pressed my head closer to her. I shut my eyes.

There had been no impulse; this was Stage Two. If I kept my eyes shut, she could be someone else; but I had to look at her during the next stage. And the floor seemed to be growing harder and colder. I rose a little stiffly and kissed her on the mouth.

"You're beautiful," I said. "And kind. And good. And — tranquil. Did you see me looking at you in church last Sunday?"

I loosened her shoulder straps; the dress stayed where it was.

She giggled. "They don't hold anything up, silly." I kissed her again, my hand stroking her neck. "You got in between me and my prayers," I said. "I couldn't think how to describe your face." My hand left her neck. No, her face wasn't kind. Or good. Or tranquil.

There had been a face in church last Sunday that had been all that, but this wasn't the face. This was a lively face, a pretty face; it was full of good nature, it was healthy, it was normal, it would be agreeable to have it on the pillow beside one at waking; but it wasn't the face I really had in mind.

"I saw you," she said. "It was naughty of you. Susan —" I kissed her again to silence her; this was a no man's land, Susan had ceased to exist.

"I'm only here because of you," I said. "I wangled this job specially. I shouldn't be in London at all really." My hand worked its way inside her dress; she sighed and relaxed in my arms. "I couldn't manage without seeing you again. I thought of you all the way, every minute of the journey — "

She jerked herself away from me. "There's somebody coming," she said. "Give me a cigarette, darling. And fill that kettle."

It was Jackie. She looked at us, with a rather prurient smile. She was somehow welcoming us into a circle, a secret and tight and cozy circle.

"I only wanted some ice," she said. "And some more whisky."

"We're having coffee," Jean said.

"Of course you are, dear. Joe must have a clear head tomorrow." She took out the ice-cube tray.

"I'll do that," I said. I ran hot water over the tray and tipped the cubes out into the bowl which she'd brought in.

"You're nice," she said. "I think you'll be very good for Jean. She needs someone solid." She picked up the bowl. "Enjoy your coffee, children."

When she'd gone we both burst out laughing.

"She talks as if I were a kind of medicine," I said. "Shall I really be *good* for you, darling?"

"She thinks affairs are good for everyone." Jean took down a tin of Nescafé.

"I think they'd be very good for you. Just one, that is."

"A real one?" she said. "A real actressy one with presents of mink and dinner at Prunier's?"

"I wouldn't get in the way of your career," I said. "I'd understand, like in the French films. Tell me what you'd like for a present." I put her hand on my leg for a second. "A falling in love present," I said.

She took her hand away from me. "There'll be someone else in at any moment," she said. She bit her lip. "You choose it," she said.

I put my arm round her. "It'll be the finest present you ever had."

We stood there silently, holding each other very lightly. The smell of garlic and new paint seemed to grow stronger; but I didn't mind, it was part and parcel of no man's land, the territory where I was free.

The kettle boiled and she made the coffee; we drank it and returned to the studio hand in hand. No one commented or even bothered to look at us; the tape recorder had been switched off and so had all the lights except one table lamp. Jackie went over to the hi-fi and put on a record; I recognized Pearl Bailey's voice.

There was a space on the sofa; I sat down and pulled Jean onto my knee. The record player was turned low, but the slow creamy voice seemed to fill the whole room, the words seemed to expand inside the head. *She had to go and lose it at the Astor, she had to go and lose her honest name* . . .

Jean kissed me: I had joined the dancers now. I was in no man's land, I was free. "Tomorrow," I whispered to her. "Tomorrow."

"Don't talk," she said. "Don't talk, darling."

five

"WE'LL MAKE a salesman out of you yet," my father-in-law's voice said. "By God, I never thought you'd bring it off."

His tone seemed half regretful; I took another sip of whisky and stuck my tongue out at the mirror on the wall.

"I didn't think so myself," I said. "I'm still a bit worried about the delivery date —"

"That's not your concern, lad."

"Just as you say."

I stretched luxuriously. Until now I hadn't noticed how comfortable the bed was; it had been three in the morning when I'd returned to the hotel. Jackie's boyfriend had given me a lift; he'd seemed impressed by the fact of my staying at the Savoy. Jean had wanted me to stay; why hadn't I?

"You don't have to see Tiffield again?" my father-in-law asked.

"He's been called away to Paris."

My father-in-law cackled. "Dirty old devil, you've got everything sewn up, then?"

"Sewn up well and truly. There's only the delivery date —"

"Sod that. What the hell do you think I pay Middridge for? You've not promised them to deliver sooner, have you?"

"Of course I haven't."

"You had me frightened." Frightened; Jean had used the word last night. We'd gone back to the kitchen again; this time we'd gone a stage further, the last stop before the terminus; it was bliss, she'd said, sheer bliss, but she was frightened.

"You needn't have been," I said. "By the way, I think they're interested in HJX too."

"We'll look into it. I'm well content as it is. When are you coming home?"

"I'll catch the four o'clock."

"Sure you've no one else to see? This meeting tonight can be put off. It'll be awkward; George is going away tomorrow. But you don't have to go if you don't want to."

Not much I don't, I thought. I have to go because I have to be inspected before they adopt me and most of all I have to go because George wants to make sure how he feels about it.

"It's all turned out very nicely," he said. "I thought you wouldn't be back today. I'll see you at the club, then. Nine-ish."

"I'd better come straight from the train."

"You can't do any other. Never mind, lad. The next time you go down to London I'll let you have a night on the razzle. Or you can take Susan along and have a little holiday. You've earned it. See you tonight then. Be good."

"I'll try," I answered automatically; and hung up.

All the first class compartments seemed to be full; finally I got a seat in a non-smoker and nodded off into an uneasy sleep. When I awoke everyone else in the compartment was reading typewritten reports or the evening paper; one man was actually making notes in red ink. There was a bulging briefcase above him in the luggage rack; a thick calfbound book protruded from it. A lawyer, probably, on his way to get some poor bastard hanged. The bearded man next to me took a tin of peppermints from his pocket, opened it, and inspected the contents.

He put one in his mouth and returned to the news-paper. He read as if he thoroughly disapproved of its con-tents. I closed my eyes, surprised at the intensity of my ha-tred. I opened them when the ticket collector tapped my shoulder; I couldn't find my ticket immediately and as I hunted through my wallet I seemed to detect a half-ashamed enjoyment of my discomfiture on the faces of my compan-ions. I knew what was in their minds; either I hadn't got a first class ticket or I hadn't a ticket at all. That would make their day for them, that would give them something to talk about at the club.

The lawyer wasn't making notes any longer; he was glanc-ing first at me and then at his neighbor, a bald man with gold-rimmed glasses. The words were on his lips: *Extraordinary how one can tell, let's admit it . . . There's a lot of that sort of thing these days . . .*

I found the ticket. The anticipation on the lawyer's face vanished. It was a pink, plump face with heavy lidded eyes; I began to be frightened. There was no good reason to be frightened; I was a respectable and responsible citizen, father of two children, candidate for the St. Clair Ward, returning from a successful business trip. I had as much right to be here as anyone else; why did I feel out of place? Outside the fields were flat under a pale sun; there was no one about. It was reasonable enough for no one to be about in the city; but surely someone should be working in the fields? Perhaps the deficiency might be noticed soon and someone might take some assorted farm workers out of a box. Or a leopard. Or an elephant. Or a platoon of soldiers. I looked at my watch; half an hour until dinner.

I thought of Jean. She'd seemed disappointed when I'd told her I was going home, but far from heartbroken. There'd be other men to share the big sofa with, there'd be other men who'd share the trip to the last stop before the terminus. Or to the terminus itself. I didn't care; I had been far enough, I had fed my curiosity, I had fed my pride. They had both been on short commons for long enough; now they wouldn't bother me again. And no harm had been done, no lawyer would ever earn a fat fee out of it. I wasn't out of place in the First Class, I was where I belonged, with the sensible ones. I rose and took down my briefcase and pulled out the Tiffield file. I started to make notes but the train was going too fast, seeming actually to roll from side to side. But I kept my pen in my hand like a staff of office.

There wasn't a taxi in sight at Leddersford Victoria; I waited for a moment then walked across to the Central Station. The wind struck cold through my thin suit and my briefcase seemed very heavy. I was the commercial traveler coming home, the tired bagman; it struck me as typical of my father-in-law that he hadn't sent anyone to meet me.

I took the short cut through Ingerton Close. Ingerton Close began as a narrow alleyway, broadened out into a little square and then narrowed again; it was, now that I came to think of it, a dingy parody of the mews where Jean lived. Once it had been a residential quarter, Leddersford's answer to the Albany; now it was mainly populated by West Indians and Pakistanis. And they wouldn't be there much longer; soon it was all coming down. There wasn't really anything else to be done with Leddersford; everything had gone too far for repair, everything was too black, too dirty, too old, too badly planned; there had to be a new city, but who would live in it when they'd built it?

There was a knot of youths by the lamppost at the far end of the Close; I slowed down for a second, wondering whether to turn back. But they were looking towards the jazz club in the basement at Number Seven; someone was trying to cut loose on the trumpet but still was in Leddersford blowing his lungs out on a piece of brass; he hadn't cut loose into pure sound, he hadn't made music, and the grass still grew between the cobblestones and the Close still smelled of cabbage and rancid cooking oil. And the expression of expectancy on the faces of the youths didn't alter. It was as uniform as their style of dress. Bootlace tie, Slim Jim tie, blue suede shoes with crepe soles, black leather shoes with brass curb chains, tapered slacks, tight jeans, jackets halfway between raincoat and shirt, jackets with tinsel woven into the fabric — none of them wore the same outfit, but the effect was as if they did. Disquietingly, they all wore crew cuts.

They were a gang, they were expecting to enjoy something together. I came closer to them, I hoped they wouldn't smell the fear on me. I walked on past them; they stopped talking for a second and stared at me. I forced myself not to look back or run; after the alley came Webb Street and the only way out of Webb Street was Humber Stairs. One thing was certain; they'd be able to run faster than I.

But they weren't interested in me. They were laughing about something. "Right up," I heard one say. "Black bastard. I'll fucking well show him. And that sodding little whore —"

"You show him, Killer. You show him." It was like a Greek chorus.

"I'll shove that fucking trumpet right up —"

I saw a policeman in Webb Street. He gave me a quick cold glance, then went into Ingerton Close. Councilor Lampton would have put him in the picture about Killer and his friends; but I wasn't Councilor Lampton yet.

Humber Stairs were very steep and the steps were worn and uneven; I took them slowly, keeping close to the iron handrail. Though the day had been cold and dry the handrail was warm and greasy to the touch. I quickened my pace; soon I'd be home, and Leddersford and two hundred miles of traveling would be soaked away in a hot bath.

I got into a taxi and, my eyes half closed, gave myself up to the thought of a hot bath and sleep. It wasn't until I'd reached Market Street that I remembered my appointment with Brown. For a moment I was tempted to tell the taxi driver to turn left for St. Clair Road; Brown after all had said that I didn't have to go. And I didn't want to see George Aisgill.

We'd not spoken to each other for over ten years now, instinctively we'd avoided each other. There had been no agreement that it was better so, and no need for any agreement. Now we were going to break the silence. Now we were going to pretend that there never had been a silence, now we were going to be polite and friendly and sensible. I could manage that; I wasn't the person who had fallen madly in love with Alice Aisgill eleven years ago. Madly in love; that had been the truth. I rubbed my eyes; they were smarting from lack of sleep. I didn't want to meet him when I was tired, not fully in control of my wits or my temper; he would still have a sharp tongue, he would still have the ability to hurt me in some way or another. If we hadn't spoken for ten years another day wouldn't make any difference. I'd turn to the left up St. Clair Road, I'd turn into the road for home and for sleep.

And then as the taxi approached the traffic lights I knew it was futile, that there wasn't any dodging the meeting; it wasn't of my choosing, yet I had chosen it.

"Straight on," I said. "Straight on and first to your right."

When I got out of the taxi I looked at my watch. It was three minutes to nine. I put down my briefcase and pulled out my cigarette case. I tapped the cigarette on the case, then took out my cigarette lighter. What Alice used to call my Phileas Fogg fetish had hold of me; I like to keep appointments exactly on the hour, to enter when the clock is striking. I moved away from the entrance to look at an old election poster, even when you spin it out it doesn't take much longer than fifteen seconds to take out a cigarette and light it. I looked at the poster for about thirty seconds then bent down as if to tie my shoe.

Brown's Bentley drew up beside me. He didn't look in my direction when he got out, but went round to open the passenger's door. I straightened up, then bent down again as if to tie the other shoe. A minute to nine now; if he didn't notice me I'd still be able to enter as St. Alfred's struck the hour. It would be a tiny victory over him; and tiny victories mounted up.

But he'd seen me. "Looking for cigarette ends, Joe?"

There was a whirring and the church clock struck the hour. He smiled.

"On the dot, you see. I'm always on the dot, aren't I, Joe?"

"Punctuality is the politeness of princes," I said. I looked at his passenger. Good legs. A white trench coat. A blue headscarf. Twenty-six, twenty-eight at the most. It was difficult to tell with the trench coat but she seemed to have firm and high breasts. She smelled pleasant; was it lily-of-the-valley? She was nearly as tall as I; but she wasn't ashamed of her tallness, she stood up straight. *The spine that bears all brightness;* the words came back to me and they were the right words; I had not forgotten them but merely put them aside to await their owner. Then, remembering the words, I remembered their owner: she was the girl I'd noticed last Sunday at St. Alfred's. Now that I could look at her properly, I could see that I had had no alternative but to notice her. At long last I'd met an adult woman again.

"This is Joe Lampton," Brown said. "Joe, Norah Hauxley. Mrs. Hauxley's from the *Leddersford News*," Brown interjected, as if excusing himself.

"How do you do?" I put out my hand.

She smiled. "Mr. Brown tells me you've come all the way from London today, Mr. Lampton."

I held her hand longer than I should have done; I wanted to be as near her as possible. Her smile didn't break her face up, but belonged to it; and now, I thought, I was finished. I let go her hand. I was finished because I wanted to give myself to her here and now on any terms, I wanted to be drawn into her tranquillity. I had known it was impossible when I first saw her on Sunday. Mrs. Hauxley; a young married woman, apparently childless, apparently not long married. It was impossible, no good would ever come of it.

"My father-in-law keeps me hard at it," I said.

"He'll be grateful to me one day," Brown said. He turned to Mrs. Hauxley. "We'll have to leave you now, Mrs. Hauxley. Council business."

He nodded towards the grimy stone façade of the Club. "More gets done there than at the Town Hall, you know. But don't quote me!"

"Thank you again," she said. "I'll send you the proofs. Goodbye, Mr. Brown. Goodbye, Mr. Lampton."

At the top of the steps we watched her walk away.

"Lovely girl, that," Brown said. "See how she carries herself." He pushed open the swing door. "Teeth a bit too big though."

"She seems a very pretty girl to me."

"She's determined. They're doing a series — a day in the life of — you know the sort of thing." He helped me off with my coat, an act of unusual consideration for him. "She's been trying to catch me all week. I wasn't interested, why the hell should I be? But I got tired of putting her off."

I'll send you the proofs, she'd told him. She was going to write an article about my father-in-law. She'd think about him, try to remember his appearance, the things he'd said, the things he did. I wouldn't be mentioned; but that wasn't to say that she wouldn't remember me. And I would see her name in print; that would be something I could hang on to.

"Publicity never does any harm," I said. "Did you show her round the works?"

"Ralph did."

"Ralph?"

"Ralph Hethersett."

"I didn't know he was on our staff."

"He's trying to do business with us. Or his father is."

"I don't see why he should show her round the works."

"He had an hour to kill. All steelworks are the same, you know. Matter of fact, it was bloody impossible to stop him." He chuckled. "He'd better watch his step. You know what widows are."

"Widows?" I said.

"Her husband died last year. Swimming accident. Don't you remember it?"

I'd been looking around the entrance hall like a prisoner on his first day in jail; suddenly the green and buff walls, the proliferation of notices, and the smell of pine disinfectant lost all power over me. I was standing on a rather dirty terrazzo floor in the entrance hall of the Warley Conservative Club and that was all.

"You're giving a boy man's work," I said. "I'll show the young widows round in the future."

"I'll bear it in mind," he said.

"I'll just show her steel processes, of course." I kept my tone light; it was best to take no chances. This was the way men talked about young widows; and we went on talking about her with the same heavy waggishness as we walked up the steps towards the bar.

Brown and I sat down at a corner table. I slumped down into my chair; though the color scheme of the bar was the same depressing green and buff as the entrance hall, the chairs were new and comfortable. I took a gulp of whisky and felt its warmth smooth away the rough edges.

"I needed that," I said.

"Have another." Without looking behind him, he raised his hand; the waiter appeared from the other side of the room. Brown was the kind of person whom waiters notice; so too, I thought with a twinge of envy, was Ralph Hethersett.

"I'll have a pint of bitter," I said.

"Whatever you like, lad." He gave the order. "You're entitled to it, if ever man was. I appreciate your coming here tonight, don't think that I don't."

"I don't mind," I said. "I might as well see him now."

"You're free to change your mind," he said. "I've been thinking about it. I'm not sure —"

"What aren't you sure about?"

He sighed. His sighs were generally deliberate and gusty but this was a sigh despite himself.

"Susan won't like it. Margaret won't, either."

"It isn't a question of what they like."

"No, it isn't. A man's got to do what he thinks best. But are you sure you want to go through with it? There's time for you to change your mind."

There were only four other people in the bar; they were all in Brown's age group. I knew them all, or knew what they did for a living: timber, flour, textiles, insurance. Timber and Flour were standing at the counter discussing the cost of labor; Textiles at a table on the opposite side of the room was complaining about his garage bills. Insurance was listening patiently, waiting his turn. From the room next door I heard the click of billiard balls and a confused shouting. There would be a thousand other evenings like this, a thousand other evenings listening to people like these. The prosperous middle-aged grumblers, the solid sensible citizens; I would sit in here or in the committee room listening to them; taking great care not to offend them, and, without my realizing it, I would become exactly like them. Waiting my turn to grumble, waiting my turn for thrombosis, waiting my turn for death. And Harry would continue to grow away from me and Barbara, even Barbara, would stop loving me. The world would laugh her out of it; and she'd marry some sleek type like Hethersett, she'd make up no more stories about warm giants, she'd see no more castles at Squirrel Gorge. And Susan would become Susan's mother. It was all settled; I had taken what I wanted, and now I was paying the first installment.

"I haven't changed my mind," I said. "Unless you have."

"No, no. One or two in the Club have been a bit — awkward. But no one who matters."

"I wonder who," I said.

"Look for those who drink ginger beer and orange squash and you won't be far out."

He meant the nonconformist element; in a place like Warley that gave me a pretty wide field from which to choose.

"I'm not really bothered about that lot," I said.

"You needn't be. Just keep your nose clean, that's all."

"I never do anything else," I said.

"You've settled down very well, Joe. But watch your step."

That ruled out Jean. It would even rule out going to parties in London without my wife. I wondered whether to tell Susan about the party. Not everything about the party naturally; but it would be wisest to get my story in first. Warley and London weren't exactly incommunicado. I remembered Jeff.

I hadn't been all that drunk; he'd been jealous of me. He'd transferred his attentions to Judy because Judy would be his bread and butter; but it had been Jean he'd really wanted. And Jeff's mother lived in Warley and Jeff visited Warley from time to time and Jeff would in any case be able to use a telephone. It was too late to worry about it now; but I'd have to remember these things in future; I was a citizen of the green and buff country of watch your step keep your nose clean you can't be too careful. I had to remember who I was, I couldn't afford the smallest indiscretion.

"You needn't tell me that," I said. "Warley's a small place."

"Too bloody small sometimes." He looked at his watch. "Where the hell's George?"

I gestured towards the door. "Speak of the devil," I said.

Brown remained sitting; I rose and shook George's hand. In that room and in that company it was almost like seeing a friend; he was ten years older than I, but he was of my generation. I had hated him once, he had been the barrier between me and Alice. Now I saw only a middle-aged man of middle height, spruce and hairline-mustached, with rather cold eyes. Cold, or withdrawn?

"It's nice to see you, George," I said. "What are you drinking?"

He sat down. "Brandy, Joe, please." He looked at Brown. "What's up with you, Abe?"

"You're late."

"I've just been seeing my young lady." He spoke the last two words with a mock affectation.

I ordered the drinks. There were advantages in being a citizen in the green and buff country; ten years ago I would not have greeted him so easily nor could I have afforded to lubricate the moment with brandy.

"You're looking very well, George," I said. "How's business?"

"Never better," he said. "Don't look so shocked, Joe. No point in telling lies about it."

"It's nice to hear one businessman who doesn't bellyache," my father-in-law said.

"I never have, Abe." He inspected his fingernails. They were gleaming from a recent manicure; he flicked off a smut from the little finger of his left hand. The impression wasn't one of effeminacy, but as if he were keeping a weapon in good order.

"No reason to now," my father-in-law said. "We've got rid of those Labor bastards."

"I did just as well under Labor," George said. "In fact, better."

"You're a card, George."

"I always have been," George said. He took his glass of

brandy from the waiter. "That's the secret of my success."

His voice was as light and cool as it had always been; nothing could touch him.

"Well, George, what do you think of our new candidate?"

"I've already told you. We need new blood. Maybe Joe'll wake us up a bit. I only want to be sure he'll be happy with us. If an old man's memory isn't playing him tricks, Joe used to be a rebel once. Didn't you, Joe?"

"You're not so old," I said. "But I was never exactly a revolutionary."

He smiled faintly. "Not exactly that. And you've been a member of the club for quite a while." He looked at the green and buff walls and grimaced. "Not that it proves anything. Half our members vote Labor. They come for the beer and the billiards. And to get away from their wives."

Brown stood up. "I'd better go back to mine. She'll be wondering if I live here. Have a good trip, George." He turned to go, then came back and, to my surprise, shook my hand. "I'll be seeing you, Joe."

We sat in silence as he strode out, self-assured, heavy-footed, the fixer who had fixed everything to his complete satisfaction.

"A red star on *your* composition," George said. He hadn't missed the handshake.

"The grass grows green over the battlefield," I said.

The room was filling up now. Everyone's eyes seemed to be in our direction; the general reaction was one of mild shock.

"It's because they don't see you very often," George said.

"I don't think so."

"You'll get used to it. Tell me, how's Tiffield these days."

"Keeping his strength up."

"You know he once was full of mad passionate love for your mother-in-law?"

"It's news to me." When someone gives you information always be grateful for it. And if you know it already, why deprive your informant of his pleasure? I assumed a look of interest.

"It's donkey's years ago of course. Before they were married. Brown bounded ahead of Tiffield — and there you are. I doubt if Tiffield's ever forgiven him for it."

"If Tiffield knew her as well as I do," I said, "he'd thank him on his bended knees."

George shook his head. "Forty years ago she'd look like Susan, not your mother-in-law."

And forty years from now, Susan would look like my mother-in-law. Time went quickly in the green and buff country.

"It's useful to know these things," George said. "You still don't think of businessmen as human, do you?"

"I try."

"Try harder," he said. "If I were you I wouldn't forget it. Your father-in-law thinks that Tiffield's changed. He hasn't. You're walking on a minefield."

"You mean my father-in-law is."

"You too. Because you're the one he'll blame."

"That's true enough."

"I'm telling you this for your own good." He called over the waiter. "It's odd, but I feel a kind of responsibility for you. You go blindly ahead, butting your head against stone walls . . ."

"Sometimes through them," I said.

"You can when you're younger. Not now, Joe, not now."
He passed me his cigarette case. The cigarettes were fatter
than usual and bore his initials. I reached for my cigarette
lighter then took out instead one of the books of matches I'd
taken away from the Savoy. He looked at the matches and
grinned. "Snap," he said. The grin made him look younger;
for the first time I was beginning to understand why Alice
had married him.

"I didn't want to come here this evening," I said.

"I can see that. We needn't go into the reasons, need we?
I didn't want to come myself, actually —" He bit his lip.
"We can't talk here."

We talked at his house on Pennack Lane. Pennack Lane
was a narrow unpaved road off Poplar Avenue; it was for
some reason a better address than even Poplar Avenue.
George's house wasn't the biggest but it was the newest; it
was a staunchly traditional chalet bungalow in local stone, an
entirely different proposition from the concrete box on Lin-
net Road in which he'd lived with Alice.

It was the kind of house which Alice would have liked;
but his tastes otherwise didn't seem to have changed. Only
the bourbon whisky ("I remember your weakness, Joe")
which I was helping myself to kept me from acute depression; the colors were too light, the furniture too stream-
lined, the abstracts altogether too abstract. And the house
was too neat, too tidy, the home of a neat and tidy man who
lived alone.

George did most of the talking, wandering restlessly
round the lounge. The bourbon seemed to be soaked up by

my tiredness, leaving my head clear and my tongue articulate; but George, now that he was on home ground, was letting himself go. He didn't redden or turn pale, but very quickly his face and his voice became disheveled.

"It was Maureen's idea," he said, abruptly leaving the subject of my father-in-law. He brought a framed photograph over from the mantelpiece. The girl in the photograph didn't look much older than thirty; she had dark hair and a firm mouth. She seemed amused at something, but not in an unkindly way. I handed back the photograph; he took it from me very carefully as if to drop it would be to injure her.

"She's beautiful," I said.

"We're going to be married."

"Congratulations."

"It's unofficial. But soon."

He sat down. The chair, silver-colored in the shape of half an eggshell, was of a kind which I thought only existed in *New Yorker* advertisements. George looked comfortable in it; George had twentieth century anatomy. I was the wrong shape, this was the wrong room, I'd be hurt here . . . I was too tired and I'd had too much to drink. I had only to say something pleasant to George and then go home.

"I'm delighted for your sake," I said. "It's miserable to live alone."

"I lived alone for a long time," he said. "All my life. Do you know —" he filled up his glass — "when Alice died —" He stopped and looked at me almost with tenderness. "When Alice died, I was glad. It's better to be lonely by yourself than lonely with someone else. If there'd been children it might have been different."

It was eleven o'clock; Susan would have gone to bed by now. I'd undress on the landing then creep in beside her very quietly. But first I'd go into Harry's room and there leave the roll of color film he'd asked me for. And then I'd go into Barbara's room to put in beside her the panda I'd bought from Hamley's. It wasn't Susan I was going home to, it was the children. Momentarily, I felt sorry for George.

"Do you ever think of her?" he asked.

"There'd be no sense in it."

"Have another drink," he said. His voice was thickening now.

"No thanks, George. I really must be going."

"I insist. It's ten years since we had a drink together. More than that. Come on, sup up."

I handed him my glass. "Not big enough," he said, and filled up a pony glass.

"Cheers," he said. "Whatever that means. But do you ever think of her, Joe?"

"Sometimes."

"You're stupid. She wouldn't have been any good for you. She'd have eaten you up alive."

To my surprise, tears prickled my eyes.

"Let her rest."

"Maureen says that. She's been saying that ever since we met. You're happy now, aren't you, Joe?"

"As happy as anyone is." I could say no more than that; because he had been Alice's husband I couldn't lie to him. He was well aware of it.

"Not gloriously happy. Just as happy as anyone is. And you have a daughter."

"And a son."

"But the son's his mother's son."

"And his grandfather's."

"The daughter's *yours*. It happens like that sometimes."

"It may happen to you," I said. I rose, with some difficulty; my chair, though not quite as twentieth century as George's, seemed to have forced me into a reclining position.

"You're flaked out," he said. "I'll run you home." His voice had suddenly lost its aggressiveness, and he seemed to have forgotten about my still untouched pony glass.

On the way home we didn't talk; but he seemed curiously pleased about something. I guessed what had made him happy, what now and again brought him to the verge of a chuckle; I felt myself warming to him. He got out of the car and went to the garden gate with me. I saw to my relief that the house was dark. I was home and knew that the aubrietia and the morning-glory had come out. I recognized them now only by their position. Tomorrow I should see them opened out, blue and pink and lavender and crimson.

"Come in for a drink," I said to George.

"It's too late," he said. "Thanks just the same."

"Bring Maureen here sometime," I said, as he was getting back in the car.

"I'd love to," he said. "Goodnight, Joe."

The car door slammed. It was a solid railway carriage slam; George had a Mercedes now. I watched him till he went out of sight then opened the front door. I didn't go in immediately; I turned and had a last look out. Everything had been settled now, I thought, there was no pain left. Warley had stayed the same, Warley had won in the end,

George would give his wife children and the dead would rest. I went indoors, closing the door softly, and opened my briefcase to look for the color film and the panda.

six

"Use the record player if you like, Gerda."

"Thank you, Mr. Lampton."

She bobbed her head as if to begin a curtsey. She looked very plump and blond and submissive; I wondered, not for the first time, how she would react if I made a really determined pass. How did one begin? *You've been a good girl, a very good girl;* then a pat on the rosy cheek. *I've a little present for you* — but I hadn't a little present for her, and I didn't mess about with the servants. Not that she was a servant; her father was a customer of ours and she'd come over to learn the language. So she was one of the family. There weren't any servants now; I'd been born too late.

"In Hamburg now we shall all be out of doors," Gerda said. "We shall dance out of doors also."

"We haven't the facilities here," I said. "But there's a flannel dance tonight."

She wrinkled her nose. "You dance in flannel?"

"You can wear summer clothes." I looked over her shoulder at the mural. The venetian blinds were half closed and the kitchen was full of shadows; there were lines on the drawings which I hadn't noticed before.

Susan's costume in the "Night and Day" number in the last revue had been abbreviated and skin-tight; but had it been as tight as all that? I twitched the cord of the venetian blinds and looked at the murals again. The sharp line between her legs had disappeared and the shapes of her breasts were merely hinted at.

"It is too cold for summer clothes," Gerda said.

"You don't have to wear them," I said. "But maybe it'll be warmer later on."

"I shall not be here," Gerda said. She sat down on one of the stools against the wall table and pulled out a packet of Peter Stuyvesant. I lit her cigarette for her.

"Thank you," she said. "You are very kind. When I go home I won't smoke at all. My father doesn't like it."

She wasn't wearing any stockings; the down on her legs glittered when she crossed them, as if they'd been dusted with spangles for a cabaret performance.

"I expect your father knows best," I said.

"You are very like my father, Mr. Lampton. He is a big man and very kind. I am very happy here."

"Then why do you want to leave?"

"My father is not well."

"I'm sorry," I said.

"So I must go very soon. I must go next week."

"We'll be very sorry to lose you. The child will miss you."

"No." She shook her head. "Little children only care for their father and mother. It must be so. And Barbara is Daddy's girl, isn't it?"

"It happens like that sometimes," I said.

"It's so with me, though I love my mother too." She swung her leg and the spangles weren't there any longer. Now that her legs weren't simply objects to look at, but objects to touch, to stroke very gently, feeling each separate hair, I took my eyes away with an effort; it was just as well she was leaving.

"Have you told Mrs. Lampton, Gerda?"

"I have only now decided. And you are the man, aren't you? It is you I must tell first."

I remembered Maria, whom I had had for a packet of cigarettes in Berlin. Those had been Woodbines; as if it mattered now. She had been like Gerda, though she was as dark as Gerda was fair and as thin as Gerda was plump. She had been submissive — *you are the man aren't you* — she had cared only about making the man happy. Susan's purpose all day seemed to have been the exact opposite; I'd never known her to be so bloody-minded. And she got a great deal more from me than twenty Woodbines; though the house was hers Brown didn't give her any allowance. We lived up to every penny of my income and sometimes hundreds of pounds beyond. There had been a bill from Maudsley's, Leddersford's most expensive department store, today which I'd put in my pocket unopened. It was I who should have been bloody-minded today, not Susan.

"You look serious," Gerda said.

"I was thinking that Mrs. Lampton won't be pleased with the news."

"It's only a little house," she said. "And Harry is away at school mostly."

I seemed to detect contempt in her voice.

"You're a great help though, Gerda. Mrs. Lampton will be very much housebound now."

Gerda shrugged. "All married women are housebound. That's why I don't get married for a long time." She giggled.

The kitchen was beginning to seem cozier; it was almost as if there were an open fire and hams hanging on the oak beams, as if it were a different kind of kitchen and a different kind of home.

"I'd better go and tell her," I said.

Gerda frowned. "Mr. Lampton, you are like my father."

"You told me that before," I said.

"Wait. It isn't *that* I want to tell you —" She was blushing.

"You needn't be frightened," I said.

"You are a good man. You are very kind and very warm. You are a very good father and very generous. And you work very hard and now you're a councilor because you want to give service, isn't it? And your children are beautiful. I like you, Mr. Lampton. Well —" She was silent for a moment. "I don't know how to put it," she whispered.

"You seem to be expressing yourself very well," I said.

"Thank you. What I must say is that, because I like you —" She was silent again.

"What is it, Gerda?"

She looked down at her skirt and pulled it over her knees. "Just that I am sorry I have gone before I said I should. And I have been happy here until — until my father was ill. You understand?"

"Don't worry," I said. I felt slightly embarrassed, but at

the same time happy. One day Barbara would be twenty; I'd have a daughter who'd cut short a stay abroad to look after her father. I would have kissed Gerda then if there were any possibility of a kiss not being misunderstood; I compromised by smiling at her and patting her hand, and went upstairs to Susan.

I looked in at Barbara. She was sleeping soundly, her arms round Mr. Mumpsy, the panda I'd bought her in London. She'd kicked her hot-water bottle out of bed, as I had guessed she would; she'd only insisted on it because it was in the shape of a piglet — a blue piglet with a stopper on its head — and the piglet sometimes went on voyages with her. She'd chosen the wallpaper herself — pink galleons sailing on a pale blue sea with dolphins and sea horses following. She'd wanted ships not fairies or Mickey Mouse or Little Noddy and on the ceiling she'd wanted sky and stars. So the ceiling was dark blue and dotted with silver stars for the galleons to steer by.

She stirred to the edge of the bed and murmured something I couldn't catch. But whatever it was that was in her mind, it wouldn't be hatred or fear or unhappiness. She was too full of love, there wasn't any way in for the darkness. And when she was born, she'd pushed the darkness away; five years ago there'd been a darkness over my marriage, a darkness which at the time I couldn't explain. But when Barbara was born the mystery was solved. Those fits of weeping, those harridan tempers, those scratching and biting attacks of passion, those long periods of sullen silence — I didn't need to be a psychiatrist to explain them. And now it was beginning again. The solution was in my hands, if hands weren't a euphemism.

I knocked at our bedroom door. There was no answer. I knocked again.

"You'll wake the child," Susan said. "Come in, for God's sake."

"Are you nearly ready, darling?"

I kissed her bare shoulder.

She moved away. "Don't do that!" she snapped.

"Sorry," I said. "Your husband humbly apologizes for kissing you."

She didn't seem to be listening. "Oh hell," she said. "I can't do anything with it." She flung her hairbrush down. "I've a good mind not to go."

There were dark smudges under her eyes and her hair, generally so glossily black that it was almost midnight blue, looked dull and lifeless. But she would still be the best-looking woman there; her appearance of ill health seemed to me to make her more attractive, to rid her face of its slight plumpness and harden its lines.

"It'd be a shame not to go now," I said. "We don't often get the chance to go out together."

"Have you just found that out?" She lit a cigarette. I noticed that the ashtray on her dressing table was full. She'd switched to Turkish cigarettes recently; the bedroom was full of their heavy odor.

"You're smoking too much," I said.

"Mind your own business."

"It *is* my business." A thought struck me. "I hope you don't smoke in bed when I'm away." She had always been used to servants picking things up after her, tidying up her messes, emptying ashtrays, switching off lights and gas taps.

And emptying ashtrays; I smelled the burning cotton bed-spread, I heard a child screaming, saw a small charred body. Suddenly I hated Susan. "You don't realize how easily it can happen," I said. "Barbara —"

She turned round to face me. "Shut up," she said. "Or I won't go."

"Please yourself," I said. "It was only for your sake."

"Only for my sake! Do you know how many evenings you've been in this week? Not one. You're out every damned night. Council meetings, party meetings, the Thespians — you come home, you shovel your food down, you say goodnight to Barbara, and then you're off. Why do you bother to come home at all?" She started to brush her hair again, so savagely that I would not have been surprised to see it lit up with electric sparks.

"Leave it," I said. "Let it ride. I must do these things. Don't let's argue."

"No, we mustn't argue. We must just do what you want. My father matters to you more than I do. Even George Aisgill matters more than I do. And more than the children do. Yes, George Aisgill matters more to you than even your daughter whom you claim to love so much. I haven't forgotten that."

"Oh God!" I said. "It's a month ago."

"You come back after two days in London. A trip which you said you made with the greatest reluctance. A *tiring* trip. A *strenuous* trip. A *boring* trip. You'd think that any normal man would want to come straight home to his wife and children. But not you. My father wants you to meet him at the Conservative Club. Off you go, tired though you are. But that's not enough. You still can't go home. It's too early. You go to George Aisgill's house and sit up boozing till midnight."

"Look, we can't go into that again. I've said I was sorry —"

"George Aisgill, of all people. You've managed not to talk to him for ten years. Couldn't you keep it up? What was it you had to talk about? It was Alice, wasn't it?"

I looked away from her. "She's dead. It's over and done with."

"I wonder," she said quietly.

"It was before we were married. It wouldn't have happened if George had treated Alice properly. And I was young and stupid and Alice was ten years older . . ." My voice trailed away.

"Yes, blame her. And blame her for killing herself when you threw her over. You might as well."

Suddenly I wanted to hit her. "Shut up! Shut your bloody mouth! What the hell are you trying to do, you crazy bitch?"

Part of my anger was with myself. I was blaming Alice, I was casting myself in the part of the innocent young man led away by the older woman. It would have been better if I hadn't tried to justify myself; I was betraying Alice in doing so.

Susan laughed. It wasn't a real laugh but a harsh and forced one, a gesture of contempt. "That gets you on the raw, doesn't it? You still don't like to think about it, do you, Joe?"

I sat down on the bed. If only Susan weren't here, I thought, I'd like to lie down and go to sleep. I'd look at the primrose and gray wallpaper and the gleaming white paintwork and think about nothing at all. I closed my eyes.

"Joe, do you hear me?"

"No," I said. "I'm not listening any more." I stood up. "I need a drink."

"You've gone away, haven't you?"

"I don't know what you're talking about."

"Suddenly you go away. You're not thinking of me, you're not thinking of anyone." She unstoppered a scent bottle. It was a kind she'd not used before, heavy and rather too sweet, a chrous girl's perfume. But briefly, perhaps because of its unfamiliarity, I saw her as an attractive young woman in a black slip, an undressed stranger.

"I get tired," I said. I picked up the scent bottle. "This is new."

She snatched the bottle from me. "I thought I'd try it."

"That's right," I said. "You only live once." I looked over her shoulder. "They really are pretty," I said. "Why can't you go to the dance like that?"

She put her hands over her breasts.

"Don't stare," she said. "Go and mix me a drink. A nice dry martini."

"I'll just say *vermouth* to the gin," I said.

"That's my Joe." She dabbed the perfume behind her ears. "I'm sorry for being so bad-tempered."

"Forget it," I said. "Life's too short."

"I'm a possessive, jealous bitch," she said.

She sniffed at the scent, then put back the stopper. "It really is rather tarty," she said.

I pulled out my wallet. "Five pounds for all night, miss?"

"Wicked!" she said.

I kissed her on the cheek; that schoolgirl expression, which she didn't seem to have used for a long time, provoked in me a queer avuncular tenderness.

"I'll begin to worry when you're *not* jealous and possessive," I said.

"That'll be the day." She gave me a little push. "Now go and mix my martini, slave."

I mixed an extra one for myself while I was waiting for her. The quarrel was over, over almost as quickly as it had begun; the air had been cleared. But there would be other storms. And one of these days I wouldn't be able to ride the storm. One of these days Susan was going to say something to which there would be no answer except to leave her.

Gerda was singing in the kitchen. The song was German; I could only catch something about a ship of death. The tune had a strange raucous poignancy; it wasn't music so much as sorrow, a hoarsely real sorrow; that ship of death, as far as I could tell from my scanty knowledge of the language, was going to come soon to take away a lot of people. They didn't expect the ship of death, but it was on its way.

I put down my empty glass and went over to the sofa. For a while, supine there with a cushion under my head, I had an illusion of happiness. I wasn't tired, I told myself; I had just laid aside my pack for a moment.

There was a bunch of honesty in the copper jug on the writing desk, the oval white flowers translucent in the evening sunlight. I'd helped Barbara to pick them in the afternoon; she called them paper flowers. I'd told her the prettier names — satin flower, money flower, moonwort — but to her they were paper flowers, too elegant and smooth for reality.

Suddenly the pack was on my shoulders again; there was no quietness in the room. I got up and looked through my pockets for cigarettes. There were none. I went to the silver box on the coffee table. Susan filled it when she remembered; I'd seemed to have seen her open it today. The left-hand compartment was full; that was always reserved for Turkish cigarettes. The right-hand compartment was empty.

It didn't matter, I told myself. It didn't matter. I'd buy some on the way to the Alexandra Hall. I didn't want one badly; if there hadn't been any cigarettes there at all, it wouldn't have bothered me. I slammed the box shut and went over to the cocktail cabinet.

seven

My father-in-law's Sunday morning sherry parties were something of an institution in Warley. He gave about ten a year, generally on the first Sunday of the month; the number of times one was invited was a pretty good index in Warley of how one stood socially, or of how one stood with the Browns, which amounted to the same thing. It was a convenient way of working off social obligations and at the same time was a sort of screening process; if you were invited to a Sunday morning sherry party it didn't necessarily mean that you'd be invited to dinner, but if you hadn't been invited to a Sunday morning sherry party then it meant that you didn't exist as far as the Browns were concerned.

Susan and I, being members of the family, had a standing invitation, which I knew better than to refuse. But that Sunday morning I should have much preferred a pint of bitter at the Clarendon. Incautiously I said as much to Susan as we were driving away from St. Alfred's.

"I'm sorry you feel like that," she said.

I changed gear for the sharp turn into St. Clair Road.

"Nothing for you to feel sorry about," I said. "It was just a stray thought."

"It was a peculiar stray thought," she said. "You're going to a sherry party with me but you'd rather go to a pub without me."

"I didn't say that."

"But you never like me to go to the Clarendon."

"You've never said you wanted to go."

"I don't want to go," she said. "But you do. Why don't you drop me at Daddy's and then go back into the town? All your irresistible pub friends. All your damned constituents. All your admirers. I'll tell Daddy why you couldn't come —"

"Tell him to stuff himself," I said.

"That's pretty," she said. "You always express yourself so nicely, don't you?"

"I'm sorry," I said. "Let's forget it."

She didn't answer; when I glanced at her I saw to my surprise that she was crying. I turned to the right and then stopped the car on Royden Lane, a narrow and rocky cart track south of Poplar Road.

"What's the matter, darling?"

"Nothing," she said.

I gave her my handkerchief. "There must be something. Don't you feel well?"

"I'm all right," she said.

I put my arm round her. "You mustn't cry in that pretty dress."

"I'm not a good wife," she said. "You'd be better off without me."

"Hush, baby," I said. I took the handkerchief from her and

gently wiped her eyes. "We'll stay here and smoke a cigarette and admire the view. There's no hurry."

"It's quiet here," she said.

I looked at the wide expanse of rock-strewn turf behind the drystone wall, sloping sharply upward to Warley Moors. Behind us and to the left the land was level and lush; it was as if the moors had reached out a great rough tongue. It was very warm inside the car; I cranked down the window.

I put my hand on Susan's knee. Last night we'd both drunk a little more than we usually did, and had fallen asleep as soon as our heads touched the pillow. And this morning I had at last told her that Gerda would be leaving us; it was then that the bickering had started, the dreary bickering of man and wife. But now I didn't feel married: now we were a man and a girl in a white Zephyr on a lonely road. "We could go for a walk," I said.

"Not in stiletto heels," Susan said.

I unfastened the top button of her dress. She slapped my hand and refastened the button.

"No. Not here." She said it without anger.

"It's your dress," I said.

"It's very prim and proper."

"It's virginal. High-necked and blinding white." I put my nose against her sleeve. "Starched, too. Most aphrodisiac. Like raping a nun."

"Don't be filthy," she said. She took out her cigarette case. "Give me a light, darling."

As she leaned towards me she knocked her open handbag to the floor. I was suddenly aware of a heavy cloying smell; a bottle of scent had been dropped. I picked it up and put the stopper back.

"Your new scent, darling," I said. "There's still some left." I sniffed. "The car'll smell like a brothel."

She looked at the scent bottle and began to cry again.

"It's nothing to cry about," I said. "I'll buy you another bottle."

"I don't like it," she said. "It's horrid. I don't want any more."

I lit my own cigarette. "Throw it away then."

"No, that'd be wasteful."

Still crying, she dabbed the scent behind her ears. I burst out laughing; she had never seemed so illogical or silly or feminine or — to roll all the words up in one on a fine June morning — so lovable. I kissed her. "Powder yourself and we'll be off," I said. "It's funny but sometimes it's as if you weren't my wife at all."

"What do you mean?"

To my surprise she seemed angry.

"It was only a compliment."

She opened her powder compact. "It's a funny compliment," she said. "You put things in a very odd way."

I squeezed her closer to me; she jerked herself away. "Someone might see us," she said.

"We're married, aren't we?"

"You didn't feel as if we were. You just said so."

"Let it ride," I said. "It doesn't matter."

She brushed off a fleck of dust from her dress.

"That's right," she said. "It doesn't matter."

She continued powdering her face. It was a social mask I was looking at now, a churchgoing and sherry party face; it was impossible to believe that there had ever been any tears in those large brown eyes.

When she'd finished powdering her face she picked up the scent bottle. She held it to the light; there was still a little left. She turned away from me, and holding the neck of her dress away from her, let the scent trickle down between her breasts. I looked at her without tenderness; for no reason she had gone away from me. Her body was still there beside me, just as the cloudless blue sky was still there outside. But I meant no more to her than I did to the sky; she had gone away from me.

She didn't speak until we were driving along Poplar Road. Looking away from me, she said: "Please circulate this time."

"What the devil do you mean?"

"Please don't talk shop to Daddy all the time. Or run after that Haxey woman."

"Hauxley," I said. "Not that I knew she was coming."

"If you had known, you'd have been a damned sight more eager about the party, wouldn't you?"

"Oh God, I met her once. Just once for two minutes."

"You wish it had been for longer, don't you? I've seen you staring at her in church, I've seen the dreamy look on your face. And she's seen it, too. She's not a fool, that one."

"She's not aware of my existence," I said.

"Like Eva Storr isn't aware of your existence. It was her last time. And Jean Velfrey before that. You divide your time between my father and the woman you happen to fancy —"

"I won't say a word to any woman. Or your father. Not one bloody word."

Susan muttered something which I didn't catch, my attention having been transferred to negotiating the turn into

Brown's drive; the entrance was so narrow that I had to take the corner wide so as not to scrape the wings. But this was the only instance in which he'd scrimped; the house was the biggest on Poplar Road, which meant the biggest in Warley, if one left out the Wales mansion and Sindram Grange. And the grounds of the Wales mansion and Sindram Grange, though big enough by any reasonable standards, would have been swallowed up, even in combination, by Brown's. And their builders had only run to sandstone; for Brown only the best Bolton Woods ashlar had been good enough.

I parked the car outside the main entrance, just behind a dusty Vauxhall Wyvern which I recognized as Mark's. As I helped Susan out of the car I said lightly: "My God, it's time he washed his jalopy."

She drew her breath in sharply. "And spare poor Mark those heavy-footed jokes about his car. And try to be nice to Sybil."

"Yes, dear. Sorry, dear. Just as you say, dear," I said, parodying meekness.

I pressed the doorbell. Harriet, the Browns' resident treasure, let us in. As usual, her greeting was appreciably warmer for Susan than for me; she had worked for the Browns for twenty years and was as much their creation as the house. But I liked the look of the house, even if people like Larry Silvington did call it pure Wimbledon Jacobean; and I even liked the feel of it and would always, before I entered it, surreptitiously stroke its closely textured stone. I didn't like Harriet: she had a very large and, for someone who couldn't be much more than forty, curiously withered face. The face never smiled for me; but I always fancied that if it did it would be a smile of derision. Harriet, Mrs. Brown frequently said, was a real snob, with her own ideas about what constituted a gentleman.

The drawing room smelled of flowers and cigar smoke. It hadn't altered in appearance since I first visited the house ten years ago; the Browns bought only the best, only what was made to last. Mrs. Brown had good taste, or at least talked a great deal about good taste, and was a regular habitué of sales-rooms and antique shops; but none of her acquisitions ever seemed to make their presence felt. It wasn't the Hepple-white love seat or the Sheraton china cabinet that one noticed, but the thickness of the dark green fitted carpet, the depth of the armchairs, the profusion of flowers and silver boxes and cups and statuettes; and when you looked at the walls you didn't see the two eighteenth century hanging cup-boards or the very pleasant set of sporting prints which was about all that had been salvaged from the St. Clair family for-tunes, but only the heavy embossed wallpaper. It was, I re-flected, for what must have been the seventieth time, the drawing room of a public man; it would have made an ad-mirable hotel lounge or Lord Mayor's parlor.

Rose, the junior treasure, came to me with a tray of drinks. I didn't dislike her quite so much as I did Harriet, but she'd only been with the Browns for ten years. She'd learn; this morning I had the impression that she was observing my movements with special attention. I looked away from No-rah, whom I'd just seen in the far corner of the room, and asked her how her niece was. She smiled, her square red face almost pretty for a moment. "She's grand now, thank you, sir."

The niece, Mrs. Brown had once told Susan, was actually Rose's daughter. The old bitch had her good points. But they didn't make me dislike her any the less.

I glanced round the room; Susan was talking animatedly to Mark and Sybil. I walked over towards Norah. Mrs. Brown, deep in conversation with Canon Tintman, didn't, for once, notice me.

Norah was standing by herself. She didn't seem to be distressed at being on her own or to be attempting to cover up the fact by inspection of the pictures or furniture or bric-a-brac; she was enough in herself, she neither flinched away from others or ran towards them.

"We meet again," I said. "Can I get you something?"

"No, thank you." I saw that there was a full glass of sherry on the table beside her.

"This is your first visit, then." To my astonishment I could think of nothing to say.

"In a sense," she said. "It's really impressive."

"Ten bedrooms," I said. "Four bathrooms. A tennis court, a swimming pool, four acres of grounds —"

"Four acres?" she said, incredulously.

"Nineteen thousand three hundred and sixty square yards." I put my hand lightly on her arm; her flesh felt warm and soft under the thin cotton. She didn't move her arm away, but her lips parted slightly. I stared at her; I would remember this. My mind was full of things I didn't want to remember; now there was something I wanted to remember, even down to the serrated glass buttons on her dress.

"I never know things like that," she said. "I'm the wrong person for a journalist, I'm afraid."

"I'm sure you're not," I said. "I like your work." Her dress was short-sleeved; I wanted to move my hand down to stroke her bare skin. Her arms were beautiful, not fat or heavily muscled but strong and rounded. I moved over to the window, my hand still on her arm; she could easily have shaken it off but she kept close to me. "Look," I said. "All that's just about one sixth of the grounds."

"Those roses would be enough for me," she said.

I let my hand drop from her arm; we had only been together for a few minutes but there were other people in the room. I knew them all and they all had long tongues. And Larry Silvington, the longest tongue of all, was approaching us.

He was resplendent in a light blue Italian silk suit and a pink hand-painted tie. Larry, rather surprisingly, was a woolman; he'd come to live in Warley some ten years ago and now had become part of the place. He was a gossip and a scandalmonger and the sort of man who was never described in conversation simply as being a bachelor but always as being a bachelor of course, with heavy emphasis on the amplification. But everyone liked him; without having any special party accomplishments he was always the life and soul of the party. Even Mrs. Brown liked him; I expect that she felt that having so exotic a creature in her house was proof she was a woman of the world, a role which occasionally she enjoyed as a relief from the star part of Lady of the Manor.

Larry took Norah's arm. "Admiring the roses, dear? I can tell you all about them. Albertine and Crimson Conquest on the arch and those yellow ones are Sutter's Gold. And those light red ones are my favorite. Mrs. Henry Bowles. I wonder what *she* was like."

"They're pink," I said. "The red ones are probably Monte-zuma."

"It's a mere detail," he said. He looked at me intently. He had a flat smooth face with heavy-lidded green eyes that gave the impression of being set at a slant.

It was not a face that had ever looked young; nor was it one that would ever grow old. He transferred his gaze to Norah; I wondered exactly what sort of relationship his imagination was creating for us. He shook his head. "Details are Joe's business, Norah," he said. "He's absolutely of the earth earthy."

"Don't be too sure of it," Norah said. She smiled at me. Her dress was the color of her eyes, a gray with a blue tinge, and a good two inches shorter than the other women were wearing. Some would have been embarrassed at being different from the rest, some exultant; but she wouldn't care. She was grown up. I hadn't met a grown-up woman in ten years, and for ten years hadn't felt the need to be with one. And Alice, even Alice, had been broken somewhere, she had lost the habit of happiness. *She'd have eaten you up alive;* and what else could she have done, having been hungry all those years? But she'd given me something, too; more than I'd given her. I smiled back at Norah; it would be the same with her, it would be the same with any grown-up woman. Even now I was somehow in her debt.

Susan was talking animatedly to Mark and Sybil; I hadn't noticed her looking in my direction yet but very soon I'd be giving her the excuse for another fit of tantrums.

"You haven't met my wife yet," I said.

"The pretty girl in the white dress," Larry said. "Talking to the matron in purple and the man in the blazer." He giggled. "Sybil's keeping a tight hand on him today," he said.

"Be quiet," I said.

"I'll tell you after they're gone."

"I don't want to hear it," I said stiffly.

Larry giggled again. "Not much you don't, Big Ears."

He wasn't the sort of person one felt angry with, but for a moment I had a strong desire to hit him. I didn't want Norah to bracket me with him, I didn't want Norah to see me as other than grown up. Then I saw that she was amused, not coldly but indulgently, that she already had Larry's measure. There was no harm in him; he gave people pieces of gossip in the same way that he gave them drinks or cigarettes or flowers or chocolates.

To my surprise, Norah took his arm. "You like to give pleasure, don't you?" she said. I stared at her; it was the continuation of my thoughts.

"I do my poor best," Larry said.

We joined Susan and Mark and Sybil; to my relief Susan seemed so engrossed in her conversation that it seemed unlikely she'd noticed that I hadn't been circulating. All traces of the scene in the car had vanished from her face, she seemed full of gaiety, distributing it recklessly around her, like a queen throwing gold coins to beggars. And Mark and Sybil were certainly the beggars; he was looking at her as if it were only the overflow from her vitality that was keeping him on his feet; and Sybil, looking more than usually dowdy in her purple dress, was looking at her not so much with envy as with a sort of greedy love.

Her face was blotchy under its thick layer of powder; Susan and I weren't the only ones who'd had a scene that morning. She'd found out something about Mark's goings on, as she always did. Normally I would have taken sides with one or the other. I should have been maliciously glad at the discomfiture of one or the other; it served Sybil right for not giving Mark what he wanted, it served Mark right for seducing silly little girls who seemed to get younger every time.

But this morning I was sorry for them both. It was an odd feeling, an unaccustomed feeling. It wasn't a feeling that would be comfortable to live with. I introduced Norah; the flat formal statements of name, the repetition of the inquiry to which there was no answer but the repetition of the inquiry, seemed more than usually unreal. I should at least have told them that a grownup was here, it was a fact worth announcing.

Mrs. Brown was still talking with Canon Tintman. She would have been beautiful once, with finer features than Susan; but all those years of playing the Lady of the Manor had set her lips too firmly, had brought the flesh too close to the bone. Canon Tintman murmured something about a worthy cause and setting an example.

"I'm well aware of it, Canon," my mother-in-law said. "But he really can't undertake any more . . ." She looked at me speculatively.

It wasn't beyond my ingenuity to reconstruct the whole of that conversation, or to guess what she was going to ask of me. I was a councilor now, and it was useful to have councilors on committees. Soon I'd go over to her or the Canon would bring me over; I'd be asked to sit on whatever committee it was, and I'd have to accept. And she'd use my Christian name just once, with a great effort, and she'd continue, more than once, to remind me of my origins and of where my bread was buttered. It was difficult not to hate her, and then, listening to Norah saying something about roses to Susan, the hatred left me. Mrs. Brown was a child; you couldn't hate children.

"I adore them," Susan said. "Why don't we have more in the garden, Joe?"

"They're not easy flowers to grow," I said.

"Nonsense," Mark said. "They're very hardy."

"I expect they are," I said. But the words didn't seem to mean anything, none of the words which I might use would mean anything; all that mattered was that you couldn't hate children. They were all children here, even Brown himself, booming away about the bus strike to Julian Farney, the headmaster of St. Alfred's.

"It's a very responsible job," Julian said. "I wouldn't care to drive a bus myself." He laughed nervously. He seemed more than usually thin and pale beside Brown, who was resplendent in a new hound's-tooth check suit with a pink carnation in his buttonhole.

"*My* job's responsible," Brown said. "But you don't see me going on strike. You don't see me asking for double pay and time and a half and tea breaks and this break and that break and the other break . . ."

He went prattling on, a child with a glass of Bristol Milk in one hand, and a big cigar in the other; I moved a little closer to Norah so that our shoulders at least might touch. I wanted to tell her what I felt, quickly and concisely as in those plays where ten seconds whispering informs the hero that the Countess is really the Field Marshal's illegitimate great-niece and the firing squad used blanks and that the plans which were burnt were blank paper and the Countess's daughter who is really a British agent will be waiting with the real ones at the east gate of the Château de Crapaud at sunset. There should be some way, I thought resentfully, of communicating my message as easily; and then I realized, with a mounting joy, that no words were necessary. What I had to tell her, she knew already.

Brown crooked his finger at me. "Come here, Joe," he said. "Come here and set Julian right."

"I'll try," I said.

A child, I told myself, a child. And at sixty you're nearer the night; how could I have forgotten that?

eight

I suppose that Sybil bathed as often as anyone else we knew, and certainly her conversation was full of references to her daily bath. But she always smelled of stale sweat: I caught a whiff of it now as I patted her shoulder.

"Don't cry, love," I said. "It may never happen. What's the matter, anyway?"

"I can't tell you," she said. "It's too much to bear. It's too much to bear."

"All right," I said. I went over to the cocktail cabinet and mixed myself a whisky and soda. This was the second time this week that I'd come home to find Sybil weeping in the drawing room; my question had been merely a matter of form. I was well aware of the reason for her tears; she'd found out about Mark and Lucy Harbutt. You stupid fat smelly old cow, I said to myself, why are you cluttering up my drawing room?

"I've been such a fool," she said. "Such a blind fool. How they must have laughed at me, the poor blind fool!" She uttered the phrase with a grotesque relish.

"You'd better have a drink," I said.

"You men think that's an answer for everything. Have a drink, have a cigarette, here's some flowers, buy yourself a new hat —" She laughed. "I'm not a baby, Joe, I'm a woman. I'm a woman who's been hurt and humiliated and I can't bear any more of it. If it weren't for the children, I'd put an end to it all."

Her stockings were hanging loosely on her legs; I looked away distastefully. I couldn't really blame Mark: Lucy Harbutt was a cheap little teenage tart, but at least she kept her stockings pulled up tight. I wouldn't have objected to having Lucy in my drawing room; she was silliness, she was selfishness, she was trouble and ruin, but she smelled of hayfields and pleasure.

"You mustn't talk like that," I said with no real conviction.

"I must think of the children," she said. "Poor little scraps, they've only got me."

And Susan too, I thought gloomily; who else do you think is looking after them now? There was a yell from the dining room; it was Barbara.

"Give me it back, you naughty bad!" She started to scream. "I'll slap you!" she shouted. Then there was the sound of two slaps. Dead silence followed and then a confusion of voices. I wondered who had been slapped; it sounded, I thought approvingly, as if it was Barbara that was doing the slapping. She'd told me, tearfully, on Monday that Helen had taken her golliwog and Vivien her panda and Linda wouldn't stop riding her bike; they were all naughty bads and I had to slap them.

"Slap them yourself," I'd said.

"They're bigger than me," she'd said.

"Never mind," I'd said. "Get your blow in first."

I grinned at the recollection. That's my daughter, I thought; she won't let anyone push her around.

"Poor little scraps," Sybil repeated. She didn't seem to have heard the noise from the dining room. "I'm afraid they suspect something's wrong."

"They're too young," I said.

"Linda's seven. And the twins are five. Children are terribly *advanced* these days. And mine are terribly bright, though I says it as shouldn't." She gave me a watery smile. "The twins are full of life, they're at the question stage. You know?"

I poured myself another whisky. I would like to have yawned in her face. "I know," I said. "It's very tiring."

"Ah yes, don't I know it? But rewarding, Joe, deeply rewarding. And Linda — she's the thoughtful one. She doesn't say much but she notices all that's going on."

"She feels things more," I said. "You've got to handle Linda with great care."

Sybil took up her cue instantly.

"She's terribly sensitive. Because she's so big for her age, people often think she's just a tomboy. But she's not. Oh no." She shook her head slowly. "Linda's thinking all the time, step by step. And when she's worked things out, when she's thought the problem *right through* — then she announces the solution. Now, the twins are more impulsive . . ."

The monologue continued; I listened impassively, from

time to time making noncommittal noises. At least she'd stopped crying, she wasn't making any demands upon my sympathy. The children she was talking about didn't seem the same ones who were making a din in the dining room. It seemed as if they were all crying at once. Harry called them the Pudding-faced Bawlers; that, now that I came to think of it, summed them up pretty accurately. I looked at my watch; in half an hour I was due at the Health Committee meeting. At this rate I wasn't going to get anything to eat at all.

Susan came in, her face flushed. She was holding Barbara by the hand. Barbara was clutching the panda and the golliwog with her free hand and was smiling broadly. Her face was smeared with tomato sauce.

"Speak to your daughter, will you?" Susan said. "She's been an absolute little fiend."

"I believe you," I said. "I've heard the sounds of conflict. What's she done?"

"She hit Helen and Vivien. And now she's pushed Linda off her chair."

"Come here," I said to Barbara. "Now listen to me. You've been very naughty. Helen and Vivien and Linda are your guests. You mustn't be rude to your guests."

"You told me to," she said. "You told me to."

"I didn't, darling. I told you not to be so soft."

But that wasn't what I had said; I was telling a lie. It was a small lie, but it was still a lie.

"I love you," I said. That, at least, was the truth. "So be a good girl for Daddy. Tell your cousins you're sorry. Promise? Just for Daddy?"

"Yes, Daddy." The smile had gone now.

"Run along and play, pet."

"It's nearly time for her bath," Susan said.

"So it is," I said. Barbara was beginning to cry; I put my arms around her. I was trying to give her comfort, but I realized gratefully, as I had done before, that it was I who was being given comfort, it was she who stood between me and harm. I was clinging to her, not she to me. I was clinging to my small daughter because I was frightened. But of what I didn't know. I pushed her away from me gently.

"You're a dear little girl," I said. "Now don't let me catch you misbehaving again."

She nodded vigorously and ran out of the room.

"One word from him and she does what she likes," Susan said. "She can twist him round her little finger and she knows it."

"Don't talk like that," Sybil said. "You don't know how lucky you are." She looked at me with a faint flirtatiousness. "My dear, I'll swap husbands with you any time. Joe lives for his children and his work. Mark just lives for his pleasures. His sordid pleasures, his low rotten pleasures."

"I can guess," Susan said.

"No, you can't. Your husband doesn't run after everything in skirts, your husband loves his wife and children, your husband has always had a sense of responsibility. Mark's shifted all his life. From place to place, from job to job, from mess to mess — he doesn't care. Oh, he could be a success if he chose to — he's very clever and very charming. But he can't be bothered. So the painstaking dull people get ahead of him. Oh God, I wish sometimes he weren't so damned clever and charming. I wish things had been more difficult for him, I wish he were just a steady plodder like Joe."

"Thank you," I said. She didn't appear to hear me.

"Do you know what he's doing tonight? Playing in a darts tournament. He'll have been home by now, he'll have read my note but it won't have bothered him. He'll eat some bread and cheese and stroll down to the pub and drink beer and play darts and be matey with every Tom, Dick and Harry and they'll all love it. They'll be thrilled, he's such a *gentleman*."

She pronounced the last word with the same scornful emphasis that I would have employed once.

"Don't be bitter and twisted, love," I said. "He's not as bad as all that."

"You always stick up for each other," she said. "I've stuck up for him myself hundreds of times. But it's over now. I've seen right through him. Oh God, I don't know where to turn . . ." This time there was a note of real desolation in her voice.

"You really do need a drink," I said.

"I need oblivion," she said. "A long, long rest. I'm so tired of being hurt."

"You can stay here, if you like," Susan said. "Harry's not here now, so we can put up the camp bed —" She outlined the sleeping arrangements rapidly and cheerfully as if it would be great fun for me to sleep on the sofa and to share the house with Sybil and the Pudding-faced Bawlers; she hadn't been so eager the last time that I suggested we should have Uncle Dick and Aunt Emily stay the weekend.

"You don't mind, do you, Joe?"

"Not at all," I said.

"And Gerda doesn't leave until Friday, so there's enough of us to look after the kids."

I opened the tin of peanuts. "Of course, dear. Glad to be of help."

"All right, then. That's all fixed."

"You'd better ask Sybil if she wants to stay, first."

Sybil looked almost coy. "It's sweet of you, Susan . . . But I'd better not. I want to think things out in the cold light of day . . ." She stood up.

"I don't know what I'd have done without you these past few days. Bless you. Bless you both."

She burst into tears again. "I wish I were dead!" she cried. "I wish I were dead!"

Susan put her arm around her. "Poor Sybil. Don't worry, darling, we'll look after you —"

I put a handful of peanuts in my mouth; it was too late for a meal now.

"I'm going," I said to Susan. "I won't be late."

She nodded absently. All her attention was on Sybil. Sybil's noisy and untidy sorrow was filling the room; it even seemed to follow me into the dining room where Gerda was undressing Barbara.

"Where are the other children?" I asked Gerda.

"They're in the back garden," Gerda said. "I think they're all crying . . ."

"I hit Linda again," Barbara said, emerging from her vest. "She runned away. And Vivien and Helen runned away too, they did."

"That's very naughty of you," I said. But I couldn't keep

the smile from my face. Barbara smiled back at me, quite un-afraid; I picked her up and held her wriggling, shoulder high. "You're very very naughty," I said.

"I'll sing you a song," she said.

"Daddy must go now, pet."

"Summer's suns are glowing, Happiness is flowing —" She stopped, scowling.

"Go on," I said.

"I'll hit them again if they take my panda and my golly and my bike."

I started to laugh. "That's my daughter," I said. "No one'll push you around."

She looked puzzled. "What say, Daddy?"

I kissed her. "It doesn't matter. We understand each other, you and I."

She nodded; and it was as if the room were bigger and the table set with plenty. Suddenly, hungry and disgruntled though I was, I wanted to cry with happiness.

nine

MARK's house always smelled of fish. It wasn't like the smell from a fish and chip shop, coarse but warm and cheerful, nor was it the seafood smell, sharp but fresh and sweet. It was as if every day for every meal they'd been eating boiled cod. No one else but I — and once Barbara, at the top of her voice — seemed to have noticed it. I've often wondered whether it actually existed physically, whether what I thought I smelled wasn't, quite simply, unhappiness.

But that evening the smell shouldn't have been there. Mark and Sybil had made it up, they were going to make a new start for the sake of the children. The dinner was to be a feast of reconciliation, we were, in Sybil's rather embarrassing words, to break bread together in love and friendship.

As we took our places at the dinner table, she put her handkerchief to her eyes.

"What's the matter, dear?" Mark asked.

"I'm so happy," she said. "Here we are in our own home, having dinner with our friends — I can hardly believe it."

There wasn't much one could say in reply to that; I gave her what I hoped was an encouraging smile, and took a spoonful of soup. It was lukewarm and had a curiously gritty texture; its taste was vaguely of chicken fat.

Sybil patted my hand. "Forgive me," she said. "It's ridiculous of me to be so weepy even now. But we women are queer kittle-kattle, aren't we, Mark?"

Mark nodded. He was looking a little glassy-eyed; I wondered if he'd been fortifying himself with something rather stronger than the sherry the rest of us had had.

"You feel things more," he said. "We're coarser-grained creatures altogether, aren't we, Joe?"

"Speak for yourself," I said. I took a second spoonful of soup; it wasn't any better than the first.

"I'm so grateful to you and Susan," Sybil said. "But for you, we wouldn't be here now. Bless you, darlings."

"And especially Susan," Mark said.

"We ought to drink their health," Sybil said.

She was enjoying herself enormously; she was center stage with the spotlight full on her face. And, for a moment, seeing the happiness on her face, it didn't seem to matter that the dining room was so cramped and drafty, that the bright blue wallpaper and the green curtains and the red carpet all quarreled with each other, that the first course of dinner had been unpalatable and the following courses would be even worse. Nor did it matter that her new dress was far too fussy and frilly and that its color — a dull oxblood — might almost have been deliberately chosen to accentuate the fact that she was approaching forty-five and had never taken enough care of her figure and complexion. It didn't matter; she had come to life, poor fat silly Sybil had come to life. Most human beings are hurt all the time, even in their sleep the hangmen and the tigers chase them; one never sees them as they really are. And I hadn't seen Sybil until now; it was as if I'd judged her by her behavior in the dentist's chair. Now she wasn't being hurt, for once; she even believed, perhaps, that Mark had changed his ways and she wouldn't be hurt again. She was happy; so I was released from the irksomeness of pity and, against all expectations, found that I was enjoying myself. The underdone veal cutlets were almost entirely without taste, the peas had a strangely glutinous texture, the ice pudding was soggy, the Yugoslavian hock had been frozen to death; but they tasted to me as they would to Sybil: they were the materials of the feast, they were the symbols of reconciliation.

Susan talked very little and hardly touched her food. Despite this, she too seemed caught up in the spirit of the occasion; it seemed a long time since I'd seen her face so illumined by gentleness. I had never seen her look so young; her white organdie dress, décolleté though it was, had a First Communion look about it. It was impossible to believe that she'd borne two children, I thought with possessive pride; and then, almost with fear, I recognized the gentleness for what it was. Susan was maturing, Susan was being Mother, Susan had helped Mark and Sybil, Susan had brought them together again. I felt my respect for her growing into something like veneration; she'd become a better person than ever she'd allowed herself to be and suddenly — to admit it gave me a curious sense of release — she'd become a far better person than I was.

Sybil sighed. "I'm very happy, sitting here with my husband and my friends. I feel we've weathered one hell of a storm. Don't you, darling?"

"Yes, dear," Mark said. "Yes, indeed."

I saw with amusement that he had only just taken his eyes away from Susan's breasts.

"There's some port," Sybil said. "But you mustn't sit too long over it." She wagged her finger at us.

"We won't," Mark said. "In fact, it's a foolish custom. I've always been against it, haven't you, Joe?" He winked heavily.

"Yes. Ah yes. Absolutely."

"That's what you say. I know better."

She wagged her finger at us again. Her face was flushed; she was, if not drunk, mildly tipsy. I rose and drew her chair back for her. I caught a whiff of her scent. It was a light floral scent, not heavy enough to mask the smell of her sweat. I'd never known her to use scent before; Mark would have a big night tonight. She was excited; and try as I would, I couldn't find the notion anything but distasteful, nor feel anything but a half-amused contempt for Mark.

As the women went out of the room, his eyes were on Susan. I saw again on his face that expression of desperate longing which I'd noticed before.

"You're a very lucky man," he said.

"I know," I said.

"Susan's been a jewel. I don't know what Sybil would have done without her. She's been here every day, helping out. Sybil — well, you know how women are. They're very tough, and then they just cave in. Only another woman can help."

He was speaking rather as if what had happened in the past

ten days had had no connection with him; and as he detailed all the ways in which Susan had helped Sybil out, my temper began to rise.

"Be more careful next time," I said. "Why the hell had you to pick on Lucy of all people?"

He grinned. "You don't pick girls to have affairs with, old man. They pick you." He straightened his tie in the mirror. It was a blue polka-dotted bow tie and would have made me look like an out-of-work actor; on Mark it gave the impression of gaiety and prosperity. He was wearing a double-breasted gray suit; double-breasted suits hadn't been worn for ten years, but Mark somehow made me wonder uneasily if it weren't I in my new single-breasted suit who was out of fashion.

"I wouldn't know about that," I said. "But I wish you'd play away from home."

"Don't throw the first stone," he said. "I've been a bad boy, I know. Look, you don't really like port, do you? It's bloody awful port anyway. And you've got to decant the stuff and pass it round —" He went to the sideboard and took out a bottle of White Horse.

"That's more like it," I said. I thought of what Susan's help of Sybil had resulted in for me: ten days of snatch meals, ten days of listening to the account of the woes of Sybil either from Sybil herself or from Susan; ten days of having the Pudding-faced Bawlers in and out of the house . . .

Mark poured out two big measures of whisky. "You won't have had a very comfortable time of it lately," he said, as if reading my thoughts. "I'm sorry."

"It's pointless to worry about it now," I said.

"I've been a fool," he said. "I really have. But you need a change after ten years. Just a change, that's all. Believe me, I love my wife."

It was obvious that he didn't; he uttered the words very quickly and on his face for the first time in our acquaintance I saw a genuine guilt.

"Women don't really understand," I said.

"Too true. But you've got to have them." He took a gulp of whisky. "You're a good type, Joe, but maybe you don't understand either. Lucy's a silly little bitch — but she — she renewed my youth."

He sat down astride his chair, one hand on its back. It was a musical comedy pose, the way the handsome Hussar sits in the tavern scene; it was not the sort of pose, I thought, that I could get away with.

"You can spend the whole of your life not doing things you want to do, then suddenly you're old. Children are great fun when they're young, but they don't stay young. And you don't do things you want to do, for the sake of the children, and then you find out that they don't care. They only care about leaving you as soon as they can. You've got to have them if you're normal, if only because women turn queer if they don't give suck. But don't love them too much."

"You can't avoid it," I said.

"You have to avoid it," Mark said. He emptied his glass. "Help yourself, Joe, it's the only cure for what ails us." He refilled his glass.

"I'll just freshen mine up," I said. I went over to the sideboard and took out the soda syphon. The sideboard, like the chairs and table, was in what furniture shops termed Jacobean reproduction with bulbous turned and fluted legs and a great deal of carved decoration on the front. The top was scratched and there were several white rings to mark the spots where people hadn't bothered to use table mats. As I closed it I noticed that the paper lining the inside was stained and wrinkled. I thought of the dining room of Harling Crescent with a sharp nostalgia; it was as if every moment spent in this room was a kind of betrayal. There was a confused picture in my mind of my home being besieged, of the ugliness and untidiness of Mark's house somehow invading it.

I took my drink to the table; as I sipped it the mood passed. After another drink the heavy bosses and curlicues of the back of my chair would cease to bore into my spine; or else I would follow Mark's example and sit the other way round. And there was even some satisfaction, though not of a kind I was proud of, in comparing Mark's home, and his life, with mine. But he didn't look as if he knew I was more fortunate than he; a broad grin had appeared on his face, a grin of unmistakable self-satisfaction.

"What's the joke?" I asked.

"Nothing, old boy. I was just thinking how odd life is."

"You're lucky it's not a damned sight odder," I said. "Lucy's father has a very nasty temper."

I offered him a cigarette. Mark shook his head. "No, thanks, old man. You know I prefer my own brand of poison." He took out a cigarette and tapped it against his cigarette case. It was one of the mannerisms, like his keeping his handkerchief in his sleeve, which I found intensely annoying. And the smell of his cigarette — like Susan, he always smoked Turkish — seemed unbearably cloying.

"I'm surprised he didn't beat you up," I said.

Mark laughed. "Not him. He hinted he should get some compensation, though. Don't ask me for what."

"Did you give him anything?"

"My dear chap, I can't give him what I haven't got. It's one of the advantages of being flat broke. Besides, what the devil should I pay him for? She's over sixteen."

"Only just," I said.

He got up and opened the window. "Don't remind me," he said, his back to me. A cool breeze blew in the scent of lilac; he took a deep and noisy breath.

"That's good," he said, lost in the pleasure of the moment. "That's very good. That makes the sap rise."

"One of these days that sap of yours is going to rise too far," I said.

He went back to his chair. "I know. But what's the use of worrying about it? Believe me, Joe, I was the world's greatest worrier once. Christ, I used to join every demonstration there was. I didn't just worry about myself, I worried about everyone else. And then the war came and I found out what really mattered. You live for the moment. It won't come again. I wanted to poke Lucy so I poked her. If I hadn't, then I'd be kicking myself for missing the opportunity. Why, you're envious of me now. Aren't you?"

"I don't fancy her," I said. I drank the last of my whisky and soda. "We'd better join the ladies."

"Not yet," he said. "They'll be quite happy in there, tearing us to shreds over the coffee. Have some more whisky, and don't drown it this time —"

I let him fill my glass. "You're quite wrong about Lucy," I said. "You're welcome to her."

"I wasn't thinking about Lucy," he said. "I was thinking

about you. Here I am, forty-six years old with three children and a dogsbody's job which I only got through my mother-in-law's influence. I live from overdraft to overdraft, and the only reason they'll allow me an overdraft is because my mother-in-law won't live forever. And here's you, with a damned good job and a wonderful wife . . . a pillar of the community, on top of the world — you're lucky, aren't you?"

"Not especially," I said.

"Ah, you've worked hard. But you've had a little bit of luck, too, haven't you?"

From his intonation of the phrase I knew what he had in mind.

"I expect someone has told you that Harry was very big for a premature baby," I said. I looked out into the garden; there was nothing much to look at there but the lilac bush and a few rather dejected lupins, but I didn't want to look at Mark's face.

"I didn't really mean to bring that up, old man," he said softly. "But you *are* lucky, you know. And yet — this is the remarkable thing — you're envious of me. Why is that?"

I turned my gaze to him with an effort. He wasn't angry with me, but he was accusing me. The conversation was going out of control.

"Let's drop the subject," I said. I smiled at him. "I'm sure Lucy's gloriously pokable, but once and for all, I've never fancied her."

"I never said you did." He was grinning again. "But is there no one else? No one else you fancy? And what are you going to do about it?"

He started to chuckle; to my surprise, I found my face reddening.

ten

THE KNIGHT had his foot on the dragon's neck. He was wearing yellow armor with a red cross on his shield and his sword was nearly as tall as he was. There wasn't any blood on the sword, but the dragon was obviously dead. It was navy blue with a long corkscrew tail; it looked pathetic rather than dangerous. The knight had pushed his visor back; he looked very young and serious. In the other window he'd taken his helmet off and was kneeling before a young girl with long black hair and a jeweled crown. Though the colors were on the crude side the windows weren't without charm. Barbara would have liked them, though perhaps she would feel sorry for the dragon. But perhaps it would be a mistake ever to take her to Sindram Grange. It was better that it should remain a castle for her just as, to judge from the suits of armor and swords and tapestries and the rest of it, it had always remained for Tom Sindram. He'd made his money in the twentieth century in Leddersford; but here at Sindram Grange he'd been a robber baron of the Middle Ages or, which was more likely, a handsome young knight who killed dragons.

I was losing the thread of my talk; I paused and took a sip of water. "And at that one might almost leave it," I said. "Particularly on a fine summer's evening. I've outlined the structure of local government. I've tried to give you a picture of what the councilor actually does to justify his existence. Or her existence, as the case may be. But there's just one thing I must say to you in conclusion . . ."

I looked at Norah, who was sitting at the back row with a young man in a bright red shirt, and lost the thread again. I looked away from her and for about three minutes told them that I could say much more about local government but that I was going to say just one thing more. I smiled at the audience and took another sip of water. They were looking fidgety: I would have to end and quickly.

"There's a great deal wrong with local government. It's far less than perfect. It could be immeasurably better than it is. Well, ladies and gentlemen, the remedy is in your hands. I don't care if you've heard this before; now you're hearing it again. I don't only ask you to take an intelligent interest in local government — in any case by attending this course you're doing that already. I ask that each one of you who feels himself capable of doing the job of councilor should do his best to become a councilor. I don't care what your politics are: your duty is plain." I heightened my voice. "I address this appeal especially to the young people in the audience. You know what the definition of an idiot is — the real definition. An idiot is a person who takes no interest in public affairs. Don't be idiots, please. Yes, watch us like hawks. Yes, question us. Yes, criticize us. Yes, even abuse us if we deserve it. But, best of all, join us. Join us in working for the public good, join us in making democracy work. Thank you."

I sat down, wondering, as I always did, just what I was thanking them for. The Warden rose and said the usual things: I was refreshing, I was down to earth, I was practical, I had an unusually comprehensive experience of local government . . . I looked at Norah again. Her dress was a bright blue with a pattern of golden birds; the neck was high but the skirt scarcely covered the knees. She crossed her legs; there was the faintest of rustles and the sound of nylon rubbing against nylon.

It was that sound which undid me; it wasn't loud, it couldn't have been heard had I not been listening for it, but it was of the same order of sounds as a finger rubbing against glass. It hit a raw nerve, it awakened a sensuality which I had thought was tamed. I began to understand what makes a man rape a woman. It wasn't the need for sexual intercourse, it was the need for rape.

The trouble with cunt, Mark was fond of saying, was that the women have all of it. Norah had all of it now as far as I was concerned; I wondered if she knew it, if that revelation of rounded knees had been deliberate, if that faint smile wasn't because she had no intention of giving me what I wanted because for her I didn't exist as a man at all.

"And now," the Warden said, "Mr. Lampton has very kindly agreed to answer your questions . . ."

There was an awkward silence. It seemed as if the room had tied everyone's tongues, as if the oak paneling, the huge empty fireplace, even the stained glass windows had intimidated them all. Or had they detected the fact that I hadn't wanted to come here at all, that I didn't particularly believe in what I had been saying, that at this moment all that I cared about was whether I might see another fraction of a young woman's legs?

Then a young man in a blue sports shirt — only the Warden and I appeared to be wearing jackets — mumbled his way through a long statement about politics and local government. He appeared to think that politics could be kept out of local government; briefly and firmly I told him that it couldn't be. I went on answering questions in a daze of boredom; hadn't Councils too little power, hadn't Councils too much power, were big administrative units really efficient, how long would Warley retain its independence; towards the end I had to struggle to keep the bad temper out of my voice. They were young, they were presumably well educated, but they didn't know, they wanted justice, they wanted the dragons killed. Then I saw that Norah was looking at me. She whispered to her companion.

He rose. There was a smile on his face which I didn't like. He had sallow skin and blue jowls but his teeth were very good. He seemed to be showing them in more ways than one: this question, I sensed, would be a stinker.

"If I may," he said, "I'd like to be very specific. Mr. Lampton has made great play with the fact that English local government is essentially conducted in public, that councils have nothing to hide, that they're always delighted to inform citizens exactly what they're doing."

I nodded.

"You're not prepared to go back on this, Mr. Lampton? You're sure that you really mean it?"

Norah was smiling now. I felt a sense of betrayal. It was as if I were on trial, as if they were in league against me.

"Of course I mean it," I said.

"How do you explain that council meetings have been closed to the public and to the press on no less than three occasions during the last twelve months? And always when a certain matter had to be discussed, I may add. And that isn't all. The Housing Committee —"

His rather harsh voice ground on; after he'd been speaking for four minutes I ceased to take any notice of what he was saying.

He'd lost his audience by not sticking to one point; when he started to refer to the much delayed public baths scheme I looked pointedly at my watch and then appealingly at the Warden.

"I'm afraid I must cut you short, Mr. Graffham," the Warden said. "It isn't that Councilor Lampton isn't willing to answer your question. But it does seem to be developing into a kind of general survey . . ."

I smiled at him.

"I almost feel that I'm in the wrong place tonight," I said. "I warned you of my inadequacies as a public speaker at the beginning of my talk, and now, after Mr. Graffham's most lucid and searching exposition of the shortcomings of Warley Urban District Council, I wonder at my temerity in speaking to you at all. But Mr. Graffham did ask a question. It was a very good question indeed. It was a question which needed to be asked and, frankly, a question which I hoped wouldn't be asked. Because I find it very difficult to answer . . ."

But I answered it somehow, making heavy play with the

notion of the members of the Council being one and all devoted to the public good. It didn't in any case matter very much, for I could sense that the evening had ended, that everyone had had as much about local government as they could take. I had known this; Graffham, I reflected with satisfaction, hadn't. Then I remembered that he was with Norah and I wasn't; the satisfaction disappeared.

After the meeting had been closed, I asked the Warden who Graffham was.

"He's very Left," the Warden said. He filled his pipe. He had, I noticed, a face which didn't really go with a pipe, curiously metropolitan and sleek, with a sallow skin. It was like Graffham's face, now that I came to look at it. There wasn't any real worry there. He lit his pipe: it smelled unusually strong and acrid. "Black shag," he said. "The only tobacco left with any taste . . . Yes, you handled him extremely well."

"What does he do for a living?"

"Ah, that's a real West Riding question. And most apposite. He teaches somewhere in Leddersford. That's an uncommonly pretty dress Norah Hauxley's wearing, isn't it?"

"She's an uncommonly pretty girl," I said.

He gave me a sly look.

"She's very ambitious," he said. "I don't think she'll stay in the North very long."

"No one does," I said.

"Peter's very ambitious too. They're much alike —" He broke off as Graffham and Norah approached.

Graffham held out his hand. "You know Norah, I believe. My name's Graffham, in case you hadn't caught it."

"He has caught it," the Warden said. "He really was impressed by your question, Peter."

"I was impressed by his answer," Graffham said. "He's quite a nice Tory, I think."

"A cunning one," I said. "The most dangerous kind."

"He's a thirsty one, I'm sure," the Warden said. "We'll adjourn to the Staff Room."

"Jolly good," Graffham said. "Do you know why I come to each and every weekend school here, Councilor Lampton? The Warden serves beer. And he always ends the meeting an hour before closing time . . ."

He started to talk about the merits of beer in warm weather; as we walked down the long terrazzo-floored passage to the Staff Room he proceeded to the subject of English licensing laws and then, smoothly enough, to the Warley Council's plan for a new public bathhouse. Norah said very little; and though he addressed all his remarks to me, I noticed that whenever I moved nearer to her he would interpose himself between us; at one point he actually took hold of my lapel.

"It's as plain as a pikestaff," he said. "And if you want to know how plain a pikestaff is, look at the walls of this monument to a pseudo medievalism. Everyone in Warley wants the swimming pools —"

"There's the river," I said. "Not to mention the canal."

"Dead dogs and currents and weeds," he said. "Would you have *your* child bathe in the river or the canal?"

I pushed the thought of Barbara from my mind. More and more often lately the mere thought of a possible danger to her would make me almost physically sick with fear.

"We're speaking beside the point," I said. "The plans for the baths are being considered now."

"Are they really," he said.

"Norah can confirm that," I said. I moved over to her. Suddenly the poky little room with its oak panels half covered with notices seemed once again a room in a private house rather than part of an institution.

"Aren't we going to have the swimming pools, Norah?"

There was a pleasure that was nearly sexual in speaking her first name; and now that I was nearer to her I could smell more distinctly her lily-of-the-valley perfume.

"The Council's discussing it," she said. "That's not the same thing as doing something about it."

"That's not fair," I said. "It's gone as far as discussion of the site."

"The Palace," she said. "Yes, I can see it would be ideal. It's central, you've got the shell of your main building, and it's just an eyesore now anyway. But what if Amborough doesn't want to sell?"

She seemed to know a lot about it. Amborough, the owner of the Palace cinema, didn't in fact want to sell it to the Council.

"I'm not the whole Warley Council," I said. "I can't tell you what it will or won't do. But if it's decided that the Palace is the only possible site, then there are ways and means of acquiring it. But don't quote me."

Graffham snickered. "You're being very cautious, Councilor Lampton. You mean compulsory purchase?"

He took a swallow of beer. He had a scrawny neck; I could trace the progress of the drink. He hadn't the physique or the complexion to wear a red sports shirt; I wondered jealously what Norah saw in him. I imagined his sallow blue-jowled face next to hers in bed: when I answered him it was difficult to keep the anger from my voice.

"If it were absolutely necessary," I said. "Or rather if the Council decided it was absolutely necessary. Though as you're aware, my party isn't exactly enamored of the device."

"We'll see," Graffham said. "But if I were a betting man . . ."

Norah shook her head slightly. He stopped.

"Norah's reminding me," he said. "We promised to have supper with the Hewleys."

It was quite easy to work out. Hewley was the leader of the Labor group on the Council. And Graffham had been talking to him. And Hewley thought that the compulsory purchase wouldn't go through. Hewley was the sort of person who was always on the lookout for sinister Tory plots, he liked to feel that nothing was hidden from his keen and fearless Left Wing eyes. He couldn't believe that our promise to build the bathhouse was anything but an election trick and in consequence his imagination had enlarged a rumor into fact.

It would give him great pleasure to show off in front of Graffham and Norah; when I came to think of it, about the only kind of pleasure the poor devil ever enjoyed. His family had lived a long time in Warley but had never accumulated any money; and his wife, who didn't share his love of the underprivileged, made it a constant reproach that at forty-five he was no more than a senior assistant at Warley

Secondary Modern and was evidently never going to be. She was bitter and twisted. Bitter and twisted; why did that phrase so often recur to me?

"I'm going that way," I said to Graffham. "I can give you a lift if you like."

"I've got transport," he said.

"Fine. Give my regards to Councilor Hewley. I'm sorry he couldn't be here tonight. Tell him not to worry about the swimming baths."

To my surprise Norah looked angry.

"You sound a little patronizing," she said.

"I've an enormous respect for Councilor Hewley," I said. "I know how much this project means to him. I know that he didn't want the Palace there in the first place. He wanted the site for a public bathhouse. And now that the Palace has closed down, he naturally can't think of any other site. It's absolutely understandable."

"Is there another site?" she said.

"I honestly couldn't tell you, but it's possible that there could be."

"That's the answer I'd expect," she said. "You're very clever, Councilor Lampton."

"Don't call me that," I said. "Please don't call me that. It makes me feel a hundred years old."

To my surprise she colored a little. "I'm being rather rude," she said.

"I don't mind. Pretty girls in pretty dresses can say what they like to me."

"You don't really care, do you?"

She was standing against the window: the sunlight now

seemed stronger than it had been all day. I looked at the shape of her legs through her dress and felt a lunatic certainty that I had willed the earth to move westward so that the material of her dress might become less opaque, that I might see her, if only briefly, as a woman and not as a set of opinions. I had an idea of what those opinions were; they bored me as much as my father-in-law's opinions bored me. I didn't care about the swimming baths or indeed about local government; but not for the reasons which she supposed. She was the only one in the room who would understand my reasons for not caring; but I couldn't give her those reasons now. For she saw me as a sleek cynical man in a new mohair suit, a man who possessed power as he possessed gold cuff links, not obtrusively but not displeased if the rich glitter showed.

I became aware that everyone was waiting for my answer. I was tempted to give her the sort of answer she expected, if only to jerk them into some semblance of life. I glanced round the room: they seemed a drab lot, neither young nor old, with a tendency towards sweaters and cardigans and flat-heeled shoes. Then I saw Mrs. Fulwood, plump and drab in a faded cotton dress which sagged at the hem. Mrs. Fulwood was Warley's most indefatigable joiner; member of almost every organization except the Freemasons and the Oddfellows, she was also the self-appointed guardian of the taxpayers. At the Town Hall they called her the Watch-bitch. She didn't like me, or indeed any Tory councilor; the Tory Party had twice refused either to nominate her or to let any of their candidates stand down to give her a clear run as an Independent. In fact, she didn't like any councilor;

the other two parties felt much the same about her as we did.

She was waiting now for me to say something flippant or cynical, something to provide the ammunition for one of her attacks on the Council. She didn't matter very much; but our majority wasn't so big that we could afford to expose ourselves in even the smallest degree.

"What don't I care about?" I asked Norah.

"The baths, for one thing. You don't really think it's important. Or where they're sited. Or politics — that's something you've hardly touched upon —"

Graffham put his hand on her shoulder. "We really must be going," he said. "You're very cruel, Norah. Can't you see the poor man's tired?"

I saw what he was trying to do.

"You needn't try to rescue me, Mr. Graffham," I said. "Norah hasn't even begun to ask me any real questions yet. But just let me say this: I care very much about the swimming baths. I care very much about anything appertaining to the welfare of Warley. Let's leave it at that. We'll argue about politics some other time." I held out my hand.

"I'll look forward to it," he said. His hand was sweaty: I imagined it on Norah and felt a spasm of jealousy.

Mrs. Fulwood had turned her attention from me to the Warden; the tension had relaxed as quickly as it had tightened.

"I didn't know you felt so strongly about things," I said to Norah. "It makes a pleasant change. Don't forget you must come and see us soon. I'll show you the roses . . ."

"Thank you," she said. "We'll enjoy that, won't we, Peter?"

He took her arm possessively, more in the manner of a

policeman than a lover. As he opened the door for them to go out the draft from the corridor molded her skirt to her hips for a second; I saw that she was not as slim as she'd first appeared. She hadn't boyish hips; she had childbearing hips.

The door closed. I finished my beer and went to the table to open another bottle. But even as I opened it I knew that I didn't want any more to drink. I would drink it, but I didn't want it. I strolled over to the window; the courtyard was empty except for half a dozen cars and a Volkswagen minibus.

Except for my own Zephyr and a shiny red MG Midget the cars looked old and battered. I tried to extract some feeling of superiority from the fact of mine being the newest and most expensive there, but succeeded only in thinking of Norah again.

The Warden came up to join me. "My God," he said. "Are there many more like her in Warley?" He glanced behind him at Mrs. Fulwood, who had now transferred her attentions to a young woman whom I recognized as being the deputy librarian of Warley.

"She's one on her own," I said. "When they made her they broke the mold."

Graffham and Norah got into a Ford Popular. I turned away from the window as the engine started up. This was what I'd been waiting for; but now that the moment had come I couldn't bear to see them together.

"This is a fantastic place," the Warden said. "Just look at that courtyard. All that stone — God knows what it cost to bring it up here."

"He didn't like tarmac or concrete," I said. "When he was

riding high there used to be as many as a hundred cars parked there, all chauffeur driven. When Tom Sindram entertained he did it in style."

"I thought he was mean," the Warden said.

"He was. But entertaining his business friends was a different matter. He called it casting bread upon the waters."

"A hundred cars," the Warden said. "Fantastic."

"He walked on the battlements every evening," I said. "And had the portcullis lowered at night."

"It's been taken out now. My decision, I'm afraid. By the way, Councilor Lampton, I hope you weren't offended by those, shall we say, rather *spirited* questions . . ."

"The more spirited the better," I said.

"It was very good of you to come at such short notice. I don't want you to feel that it's not appreciated."

"I'm always glad to help out," I said.

From the passage came the sound of music. It was an old Vera Lynn tune, "Auf Wiedersehen"; I felt a not unpleasant melancholy. The room began to empty.

"We're having a little social," the Warden said. "Would you care to join us?"

"No, thank you. It's getting rather late."

We'll meet again, we'll meet again, my dear. It would be better if we didn't, but Warley was a small place. I would see her in church, I would see her at the Thespians, I would see her at other people's houses, I might even if I wanted to bring grief upon myself, see her at my own house. And now I wouldn't be able to look at Sindram Grange again without thinking of her.

I made my farewells and slipped out of the room quickly

before Mrs. Fulwood could see me. It was growing dark now; as the car clattered over the drawbridge I began to feel, with an absurd intensity, a sense of adventure. I was not finishing something, I was not escaping, I was setting out from the castle on the hill, swooping down the narrow winding road into the valley. Norah was there, just as the poplars which bordered the road were, just as the silver birches at the next bend were; she would be at the Hewleys' this very moment. And I would be in her mind; we remember those we disagree with rather than those with whom we're in perfect accord.

Then I thought of Mrs. Hewley. Not so long ago, I'd heard through devious channels, she'd referred to me as a superannuated gigolo. She'd be telling Norah my life story now; she'd certainly say nothing to my credit. I would be the villain of the piece, the smooth false-faced villain who'd risen from the working classes, not by brains, not by hard work, but by getting a rich man's daughter in the family way. And the story of Alice would once again be dragged up; but in Mrs. Hewley's hands it would be turned into something even worse. It was probably Mrs. Hewley, when I came to think of it, who was responsible for the rumor that I'd told Alice I was sick of having an old woman hanging on to me and her best way out of the mess was to kill herself.

Even if she hadn't been responsible for the rumor it would still be fresh in her memory. And her husband and Graffham wouldn't exactly leap to my defense.

I stopped to adjust my mirror and glanced back at Sindram Grange. It was in the worst of bad taste, it occupied enough space for a hundred Council houses, it was the wildly, almost cruelly ostentatious monument to one man's greed and egotism, the stone realization of a childish daydream. But it was still well worth looking at and I felt happy looking at it now, its bulk melodramatic against the setting sun.

I started the car again. Sitting in the Hewleys' little pebble-dashed box of a house Norah would be hearing my life story. She wouldn't be hearing anything good of me; but she wouldn't be hearing anything boring.

It might even happen that her curiosity would be aroused; a gigolo may not be a praiseworthy type of human being, but he does possess a certain glamour. I hadn't got as far as I wanted to go, I was much fatter than I ought to be, Susan had started to nag me again, I wasn't as clever as Graffham nor was I going to be as rich as young Hethersett; but women had wanted me. I was well aware that my lecture at Sindram Grange had been a shoddy performance, smooth and coherent and delivered in a loud clear voice but without one scrap of originality and I was well aware that I had both bored and infuriated Norah. But in bed it would be a different matter.

It was as if she were beside me, the wind from the open window rippling her close-cut curls, her hand carelessly on my knee. If I wanted her then it wasn't possible for me not to have her; desire is catching if it's strong enough. It was time for a change, time for my life to take a new shape. Mark had hit the nail on the head: I was envious of him. I could hear the mockery in his voice. *Is there no one else? No one else you fancy? And what are you going to do about it?*

And then, slowing down to cross the river at the hump-backed bridge which led into Squirrel Road I knew what

I was going to do about it. I had been using the direct logic of my bachelor days. I had been wishing the last ten years away. I fancied Norah, if that weren't too mild a word: but I wasn't going to do anything about it, just as, when it came to the point, I hadn't really done anything about Jean.

In one minute I'd reach Market Street, in two minutes St. Clair Road, and in five minutes I'd be home and my wife would be making supper. And after supper I'd have a whisky and go to bed; I'd be able to imagine then that the woman beside me was Norah. I wasn't Mark, I never could be Mark; but there at least I had it over him.

eleven

As I walked along the corridor to my office, Hillington, who had recently been put in charge of the computer room, was very much in my mind. He was a pale young man with brilliantined hair parted in the middle and a breast pocket crammed with pens and pencils, who always wore unfashionably high collars and a rather raffish tie clip in the shape of a hunting crop. For some reason he never failed to depress me and I went to some effort to keep out of his way. I rarely had much success in doing so; I felt gloomily certain that he would buttonhole me very soon. There was never any legitimate reason why he should; he was Middridge's appointment, not mine. In fact, I reminded myself sharply, everything connected with the computer was Middridge's responsibility. And that was something for me to treasure. Middridge had spent his whole life passing on the can: now at last he was carrying it and it was full of trouble.

The corridor smelled agreeably of fresh paint; I had an absurd desire to touch the gleaming cream walls to ascertain whether they were still wet. For five years I'd been pestering Middridge to brighten up this part of the works; a month ago, quite unexpectedly, he'd given way. He'd even consented to have a glass door put in at the end of the corridor. Through it I could see sunshine; I quickened my pace. Then, at the moment I drew level with the door of the computer room, Hillington came out. This was the third time this had happened recently; I wondered how he always knew exactly when I was in the vicinity.

"I'd like a word with you, sir," he said.

He was wearing a black jacket of shiny alpaca; together with the center parting and the high collar, it gave an impression that he had somehow slipped back three decades. He might have been the model for one of the illustrations to the textbooks on office methods that I studied before the war. As I followed him into the Computer Room I felt the familiar depression take hold of me. He was Middridge's subordinate; and through him Middridge would somehow draw me into his mess, would somehow pass the can on to me.

"I'm in a hurry," I said. "But fire ahead, old man. Get it off your chest." I always found myself using this outdatedly breezy idiom with Hillington."

"It's serious, sir. I've thought about it very deeply. I'm going to resign."

"We all feel like that sometimes," I said. "What's the matter?"

"I'm not going to be sworn at," he said. "But it was worse than swearing. Much worse."

"How much worse?"

He didn't seem to hear my question. "The computer

will do exactly what you tell it to do, Mr. Lampton. No more, no less."

"I know," I said gently.

"There's always teething troubles, Mr. Lampton. I didn't design the machine, after all. There's things that should have been done initially and haven't been done . . . It's no good Mr. Brown swearing at me." His face was reddening and his eyes suspiciously moist.

I patted his shoulder. "Now, now, don't work yourself up about it," I said. "Mr. Brown's very quick-tempered but his bark's worse than his bite. Haven't you told Mr. Middridge about it yet?"

"I did, yesterday. But he's been taken ill. I don't think he had time to see Mr. Brown."

"Then it looks as if I'm elected, doesn't it?" I knew Middridge's illnesses; whether genuine or not, they always afflicted him at the most convenient time and always lasted exactly the right period.

"I had my resignation written out," he said. "But my father said not to be hasty."

"That's right," I said. "Always take notice of your father. Don't worry, old man. I'll explain about the teething troubles." I looked over his shoulder at the cabinet which housed the computer. The Computer Room was dismally plain with battleship-gray walls and a floor covered with cheap linoleum. Middridge's false economy again; a brighter color scheme would have cost no more, and one of these days someone would trip over a hole in that lino and we'd have a compensation claim besides being a typist short.

"It's not just teething troubles," Hillington said. "You

can't run a project of the sort Mr. Brown has in mind with only two or three months planning."

He knew more about it than Brown but he too was humanizing it; there was a note of genuine indignation in his voice, as if the computer were a human being driven too hard. It was only a machine, and an unusually anonymous-looking machine at that. The control panels with the array of dials and switches and buttons could have been for any purpose one cared to think of. Or didn't care to think of; this computer hadn't come into the market until 1955 since the firm which manufactured it had been busy with defense contracts. And there was no point in thinking about *that* on a sunny June morning. The control panel was the means of obtaining information about steel alloys and not the dropping of H-bombs and the four girls sitting around it wore library-green overalls and not RAF blue. But it was with an effort I reminded myself of this. I offered Hillington a cigarette; rather to my surprise, since he had the look of a nonsmoker, if not also a teetotaler and a vegetarian, he accepted it.

"Look," I said. "Supposing you tell me what all the fuss is about?"

"Mr. Brown had me come to his office. About the scrap figures. He was furious. He said first of all that he couldn't offer me a seat because the office was piled ceiling-high with scrap. The whole works were, he said —"

"I can imagine it. What was the figure?"

He handed me a slip of green card. I glanced at it and burst out laughing.

"Well, if that's correct there really wouldn't be room for

you to sit down," I said. "A billion tons is an awful lot of scrap."

"It's not the machine, Mr. Lampton."

"I don't see what else you can blame," I said. The suspicions I'd been entertaining ever since the installation of the computer were now being confirmed. I knew enough about production to be aware that it wasn't only a question of having the necessary labor, machines and materials, but also of being given accurate information. It didn't at the moment matter very much about the scrap; even I, though that side of the business wasn't officially my concern, could estimate roughly how much we had in stock. It would matter in the future; and if the computer had given the wrong figure for scrap it could give the wrong figure for anything else.

Hillington assumed a sorrowful expression and shook his head slowly. "No, Mr. Lampton. No, no, no. The machine isn't the culprit. You must blame your system. Even the teething troubles are merely a minor consideration. If you don't put the right information in the machine you can't expect to get the right information out of it. You see, it's like this . . ."

He went on to explain; I listened with a mounting exultance. It was all exactly as I had foreseen. Brown was first and foremost a man who knew how to produce steel. He had had no metallurgical training whatever; but he could tell you all about a casting from the look of it, from the feel of it and sometimes, I used to think, from the smell of it. And there wasn't any process of steel production which he hadn't learned by practical experience. Otherwise, as Susan's old flame had said, he was a throwback to the nineteenth century. It had taken a long time to persuade him to install the computer, just as it had taken a long time to persuade him to install a punch-card accounting system. But, once persuaded, he wanted to be off with the old and on with the new immediately. He was not a patient man. The change-over from punch card to computer couldn't be managed in less than three years; he'd expected it in three months. Consequently he was in a mess, and it was a mess that had cost the firm ninety thousand pounds. And it was going to cost the firm a great deal more than that if something wasn't done about it. It wasn't going to be Middridge, sound reliable old Middridge, who would save the day, either. It was evident now that he'd ducked out of trouble pretty quickly. Hillington was no fool; he'd known whom to come to.

He was beginning to repeat himself now; I looked at my watch. "My God, the conference!" I gave him what I hoped was a winning smile; computer operatives, or indeed office staff of any kind, weren't easy to come by these days.

"I'll have to dash, Mr. Hillington. I'll take the matter up with Mr. Brown, believe me."

"Thank you," he said. "There's just one thing though." He looked at the computer almost lovingly. "I'm not complaining about the machine. It's wonderful, it really is, Mr. Lampton."

"So is an abacus," I said.

"I don't follow you, Mr. Lampton."

"We couldn't do anything about an electronic brain," I said. "I'm only an accountant. But abacuses are easy."

"I see what you mean," he said.

"Good. Now, don't worry any more. We'll soon get the beads shuttling up and down again."

"What's that about beads?" Ralph Hethersett asked, seeming to emanate from behind Hillington.

"Nothing of any consequence." He was wearing a light fawn suit in hound's-tooth check; it looked more suitable for the golf course than a steelworks. Although I had more right to be in the Computer Room than he had, yet he somehow made me feel as if it were no longer part of A. Z. Brown and Co. but a room in a club of which I was not a member.

"I've just been telling Mr. Lampton my troubles," Hillington said. There was an expression on his face which might have been fear. "I didn't hear you come in, Mr. Hethersett. Excuse me." He went over to the filing cabinet at the far end of the room and began to talk in a low voice to the girl who was sitting at the desk beside it.

"I pad about the place like some great jungle beast," Hethersett said. "Great muscles rippling, great nose twitching . . . Actually, once again your father-in-law has sent me home empty-handed. Whenever the Board has a bright idea that my papa knows damned well the customer won't wear, my papa always agrees with them and then sends me. He doesn't hold with sending the clever ones. Says it discourages them and wastes their precious stock of self-confidence. Acute psychologist, my papa. Even finds a use for fools like me." He yawned. "Well, I'd better have a peep at this clever little machine, hadn't I? Do you think that chap with all the fountain pens will show me round?"

I glanced at Hillington who seemed to have moved even

closer to the girl by the filing cabinet. I couldn't see her face but she had a long slender neck and a great deal of black hair; from the way she carried her head I could tell that she was very young.

"He's busy now," I said. "But I'm sure he'll tear himself away for you. If you really want to know about the thing . . . Haven't you got one at your place?"

"Not the same kind," he said. "Ours goes click-click-click-clickety and yours goes clickety-click-clickety-click. Highly significant." He strolled over to Hillington. "I'll be seeing you, old man," he called to me over his shoulder.

"Cheerio," I said absently. He was out of my mind almost as soon as I went out of the room; I was busy recapitulating the information which Hillington had given me. The conclusion was obvious. There was going to be a huge snarl-up very soon. Someone would have to untangle that snarl-up. Someone who had worked his guts out for a seat on the Board. Someone who had no responsibility for the mess, but who, on the contrary, had from the beginning warned Brown against the dangers of too hasty a change-over from punched cards. Even that was a sloppy way of putting it; just as a wheel had to be round in order to function, so the work of the computer had to be organized to a certain pattern. Now that pattern would have to be changed and yet, basically, it would have to remain the same. Someone, if he wanted a seat on the Board, would have to learn a great deal more about computers very quickly. I opened the glass door and went out into the sunlight, happily chewing over the problem.

twelve

I was still chewing it over a fortnight later in London. It wasn't as easy a problem to solve as I had supposed; for the first time I felt a sneaking sympathy for Middridge. Even a visit to the Flamville Computer head offices, made after a long lunch at l'Epicure with Tiffield, did nothing to clear my thoughts: I went away with an armful of brochures, an aching head, and ten pages of notes which I couldn't decipher.

The day after my visit to Flamville's I decided to go home. At the moment I made it the decision seemed clear cut and reasonable. I had successfully concluded my business with Tiffield, the hotel I was staying at this time was far below the standards of the Savoy; and, above all, my return a day earlier than expected might do something towards mollifying Susan, whose complaints about this trip — undertaken at precisely three hours notice — had been more than usually vicious.

Despite all this, as I went over to the reception counter, I found myself seized by a curious inertia. I didn't want to stay; I didn't want to go. I had again the sense of too many burdens, of too many decisions; I wanted to let go, to sleep, to drink tea on waking and sleep again. It didn't, a whining voice inside me said, seem much to ask. One day . . .

The voice faded away; it was not a voice which I had ever listened to very much. I pressed the bell.

"Can I have my bill, please? Two hundred and one."

The receptionist looked up from a pile of typewritten sheets. Her harlequin spectacles didn't make her expression any less severe.

"Just a moment, sir."

The moment extended into five; then she consulted a card index and came over to me.

"You're not due to leave until tomorrow," she said. Her expression now was one of suspicion.

She was wearing a navy blue dress; when she lifted her hand to adjust her spectacles I could see a patch of sweat at the armpit. She wasn't bad-looking; but her face was too tired and her hair too mousy.

"I finished my business earlier than expected," I said. "So I'm returning to the cool breezes of the North."

She didn't take any notice of this; but the suspicion now, I fancied, was specific; I wanted to abduct her. I mopped my face; the handkerchief was soaked with sweat, and it didn't help very much.

"I'm afraid you'll have to pay the full amount, sir. It's most clearly stated —"

"Yes, yes. Of course. Just give me my bill, please."

I thought of the train journey ahead of me and for a moment was tempted to change my mind. I didn't really care about paying thirty shillings for a room I wouldn't use; but it seemed a shame to give whoever owned the hotel a double profit. For, whatever the receptionist might say, my room wouldn't go begging tonight. London was full as it always was. And Jean was back in Kensington, having just taken a small part in a revue. I'd taken Tiffield to see the revue last night; Jean had been given a solo spot, a song about, as far as I could gather, the crying need for men who could do it more than once a night. Remembering the song and Jean's costume I felt the city and the summer bearing down upon me; the strip clubs, the whores, the couples in Hyde Park, the girls in bikinis at the Lido, all added up to one thing, and I wasn't feeling so pleased with Susan that I was disposed to refuse the invitation which was now being made to me.

"We can't possibly fill the room at such short notice, you see," the receptionist said. "At this season we can fill the hotel twice over but people don't expect there to be any vacant rooms tonight."

"Naturally," I said. The sweat seemed to be stinging my eyes; I took out the clean handkerchief from my breast pocket.

"It's the rules," she said, and began to make out the bill.

I looked at the notice on the wall to my right. There seemed to be a great many things one wasn't allowed to do in the hotel. There was a notice by the lift for good measure.

"You're certainly not short of rules," I said. I took out my checkbook.

"Would you mind putting your address on the back, sir?"

"If it makes you happy," I said.

She smiled. "It's the rules, sir, not me."

She'd been sizing me up; the smile was one of invitation, an invitation which I'd not expected to find here in this neutral-tinted hotel lounge. Or else I was imagining it, it was time I was home.

I brushed off the hall porter's offer to get me a taxi; I had only my briefcase with me and saw no sense in paying half a crown for him to bellow one word. The small economy, the small victory over the forces represented by whatever anonymous group ran the hotel, pleased me momentarily; but I couldn't get rid of the feeling that I was leaving the party before it ended, that there was something waiting for me in London that I was frightened to take.

There was no reason why I shouldn't stay; Susan wasn't expecting me until tomorrow. And it didn't matter, I thought as I paid the taxi driver at King's Cross, that I'd vacated my hotel room; I'd find a bed for the night easily enough. I stopped, irresolute, by the booking hall entrance and spun a penny. It was childish; but I was tired of being grown up, tired of being the model husband, tired of behaving well.

I wanted only to please myself for once, to demonstrate to Jean that there was no truth in her little song; heads I stayed, heads phone Jean as I'd promised, watching the revue this time with a different kind of pleasure, knowing I was to have what everyone else wanted but couldn't get . . . And waiting for her backstage, and supper at Prunier's . . .

The penny came down heads. I put it in my breast pocket with the idea of keeping it as a souvenir of my liberation. And then as I picked up the telephone I realized that it was ten years too late for me to enjoy Jean. I'd grown too accustomed to taking into account the consequences of every action, I'd grown too accustomed to weighing the pros and cons, I was too sensible to do anything foolish.

Jean's evident delight in hearing me and her fresh almost schoolgirlish voice, embellished now by a not unpleasant trace of stage cockney, tempted me away from caution for a moment.

"I want to be with you," I said. Then I had a picture in my mind of Susan picking up the telephone in our bedroom. It was yellow to match the curtains; I could see it now, just as I could hear the receptionist's voice saying with great satisfaction that I'd checked out of the hotel at four o'clock. Susan rarely phoned me when I was away; but that didn't mean she never would. I could think, though I didn't like to, of at least one good reason.

"I want you too, pet," Jean said. "I'm feeling homesick."

It was suffocatingly hot inside the phone booth; I put my foot in the door to open it.

"I'm afraid I've got to go back," I said. "Barbara's not well. Nothing serious, but she's fretting for her daddy."

"I'm so sorry. Poor little darling. What is it?"

"I don't know exactly," I said. "She'll live though. It's some infection that's going the rounds —" I went on, trapped by the lie into giving Barbara what were, I realized as I left the phone booth, most of the symptoms of an illness there was a scare about at the time; an illness which I dreaded above all others. Not but what there weren't plenty to choose from: if God loved little children He had a peculiar way of demonstrating it.

A voice from the loudspeaker said something about the

Leddersford train; as I stood there, sweating and grubby, it seemed to have an admonitory note. The four forty-five for Leddersford, stopping at Peterborough, Grantham, Wakefield and Tanbury, had now arrived at Number Ten platform. There was a message for Mr. Joe Lampton of Warley. Mr. Joe Lampton of Warley. His lie had been detected. Mr. Lampton would suffer for it. Mr. Lampton would suffer for it.

I remembered Barbara when I'd said goodbye to her early on Monday morning. I'd slipped into her room quietly as not to wake her but as soon as I opened the door she'd awakened and held out her arms. "Earn a lot of pennies this time, Daddy," she'd said. "A big lot of pennies."

"Why?" I'd said.

"Then you won't have to go away again, Daddy."

I smiled at the recollection and the voice from the loudspeaker diminished into an ordinary statement of time and destination. It could well have added that despite his many faults Joe Lampton loved his daughter; but it didn't matter. He knew it and she knew it and he told the lie only to be with her the sooner.

And, I reminded myself as I settled down in the dining car, though I couldn't be said to have earned any pennies for myself this trip, I had certainly saved Barbara's grandfather a lot of pennies. What I had predicted a fortnight ago had happened far sooner than I had anticipated. Several of our big orders had fallen behind schedule, among them Tiffield's. I had been sent to London to apologize humbly — but not too humbly — for the fact that delivery of both the KL 51 and XA 81 alloys would be at least a month later than promised and also, even if it meant giving him rather better terms, persuading him not to cancel either order. To my surprise Tiffield, though he had made no attempt to conceal his delight at Brown, through me, having been forced to plead cap-in-hand, had been more reasonable than I had dared to hope. There would be slightly less profit on the KL 51, but it was only to be expected that he'd extract some concessions. He was in a position to do so; though there wasn't, in the usual sense of the word, a time clause in the KL 51 contract, he would have been within his rights in refusing to accept a later delivery. Our only bargaining counter was the XA 81; and Tiffield Products was so large an organization that this didn't really matter. The new process depended upon XA 81 and naturally Tiffield wanted to start production on schedule; but a few months' delay wouldn't break him and we weren't the only firm capable of making the stuff.

It had all been settled quite casually; over the apéritifs I had outlined the position to him and before the coffee and brandy he had accepted it. Even the price reduction had been almost an afterthought; he had mentioned the figure as he was watching the waiter cook his steak, and I had simply nodded my assent. It was difficult to believe now that I had succeeded so easily just as it was difficult to believe that he had been serious about his offer of a job with Tiffield Products. I tried to remember his exact words, spoken just before I dropped him off at, of all places, a supermarket.

"Don't worry, my boy," he'd said. "Don't worry. You're bringing home the bacon. Your father-in-law will be delighted with you. Or should be." It was then that he made the offer; muzzy with food and drink and triumph, I found myself interpreting his words as if they were referring to some other clever and energetic young man, who wasn't perhaps sufficiently appreciated by his present employer, a young man who would give himself heart and soul to the Company and who in return . . . Perhaps a seat on the Board . . .

It didn't hang together; jobs were not offered in that offhand manner. I decided to treat the incident as if it had not occurred; if he was serious I should hear from him soon enough. There remained the problem of what should be done about the abacus, as I'd now christened the computer. I took the notebook out of my case and looked at the figures I'd jotted down after my visit to the Flamville head office. Once again the figures didn't seem to have any sort of coherence; but after a couple of gin and tonics my brain forgot about my body's sweaty fatigue and began to extract the hard inescapable facts from the scrawled figures and abbreviations. By the time when, with a start, I discovered myself at Leddersford Victoria I'd written the first draft of a report which I knew would be the best thing I'd ever done. I left the train with a kind of reluctance; I had done good work there. I wanted to stay there to put the finishing touches.

I remember now the feeling of impregnable happiness which seized me as I walked out of the station. I took a deep breath and for the first time that day felt cool and clean. The hills were there beyond the city and the huge central archway of the station entrance was the city's answer to the hills. And I had made my answer to the city, I would bring order out of chaos, I knew my job. I was an intelligence, a human brain. I was better than any abacus.

I felt a hand hit me gently in the back and turned to see Larry Silvington.

"My dear," he said. "What a lovely surprise. I've just returned from Manchester; what hellhole have you been to?"

"London," I said.

"You're a lucky thing," he said. "I can't find any excuse *at all* to go to London."

"It's no treat at all this weather," I said.

"London's always a treat," he said. "Have you seen the new revue by the way? Your chum's in it."

He leaned closer to me; I caught a whiff of eau de cologne and whisky. "She does a strip tease," he said.

"If you mean Jean, she doesn't. But all her wares are on display."

He nodded in the direction of the station hotel. "Let's have a little drinkie and you can tell me all about it."

He had a pleading expression; it wasn't a drink he wanted, it was company. There were no lines on that smooth face, no worry in those narrow eyes; but there was loneliness. The pink tie and the biscuit-colored linen suit seemed to make it even more evident: he had no home, he had lost his way.

"I'd love to, Larry," I said. "But I've had the hell of a day. I just want to crawl into bed —"

"All the more reason for a reviver," he said.

"I can't," I said. "I promised Susan."

He wagged his finger. "You married men," he said.

A taxi came into the station yard. "Come and have a drink at my house," I said. "Susan'd love to see you."

"No, love," he said. "She won't welcome company at this hour. I'll be seeing you."

As the taxi was going out of the station I looked back. He smiled and waved; I felt an overpowering pity. It wasn't fair that he should have so little, it wasn't fair that I should have so much; but then, I thought complacently, I didn't make the world.

When I reached Harling Crescent there was a light on in the drawing room. I paused at the front gate for a moment; that lit window seemed the epitome of home. It was a good exchange for a night with Jean — and the guilt the morning after and the thick head and the exhausted loins. Now I was back among the hills; they enclosed Warley and they enclosed me.

I opened the gate and went through into the back garden; once again I could look at Sindram Grange through Barbara's eyes, once again I could see it as the magic castle on the top of the hill overlooking the river. Norah had nothing to do with it, I wouldn't let her spoil it for me; or for Barbara.

She would be sleeping now under the dark blue ceiling with the silver stars, not knowing that I was standing out here in the moonlight. And when she saw me she would say she was glad to see me first and ask me what I'd brought back for her later; if indeed she asked me at all. She wasn't a greedy child.

I took out my packet of cigarettes and then put them back in my pocket again. The smell of tobacco would spoil the smell of the night. The striking of a match would disturb its silence. I leaned back against the wall and let the night and the silence take over. My future was clear at last; I'd stopped being frightened.

Far down in the valley I heard the sound of a train. It would be the ten-twenty for Leddersford. With a shock I realized that I'd been standing in the back garden for a full twenty minutes. Warley would still be there tomorrow and the night was growing cold. I took a last lingering look over the valley and let myself in quietly by the front door.

The drawing room was empty. I put my briefcase down, feeling vaguely irritated. I had wanted to surprise her both with my news about the Tiffield contract and the gift of a blue nylon negligée; she knew how important the contract was and she'd had her eye on the nylon negligée ever since she'd seen it advertised in the *Observer*. And now she'd gone to bed early leaving the light on to burn my good money away. And the ashtray was overflowing.

I remembered my mood of only a moment ago and my anger subsided. I took the negligée from the briefcase; it seemed to weigh no more than the eight pound notes I'd bought it with. I imagined Susan's face when she unwrapped it. I would give her it now, I decided; and went upstairs, holding the small flat parcel behind my back.

Barbara's room was at the far end of the landing, with Harry's room next to it. I stopped and opened the door. She was in deep sleep, her arms around her panda. I closed the door softly.

The smile was still on my face when I heard Susan's voice from our bedroom. It didn't startle me as it once used to; she often talked or rather babbled in her sleep. Then as my hand was at the door I heard her speak.

"Go on. Go on, darling. *Go on* . . ."

Then I heard a deeper voice, but it was saying nothing, only, like hers now, moaning as if overtaken by some unendurable pain. I held my breath; but they had heard nothing; I walked slowly downstairs; my feet made no noise on the fitted carpet, but they wouldn't have heard me if I'd been wearing Army boots and walking on corrugated iron.

The drawing room seemed strange to me when I returned. It was as if all the furniture had been changed round in the few minutes that I had been away. It reeked almost unbearably of Turkish tobacco; I went over to open the window then stopped myself. They wouldn't hear it being opened; but I wouldn't risk any unnecessary sounds.

I poured myself a large whisky and sat in the armchair in the far corner of the room. When they came down they wouldn't notice me immediately. But perhaps it would be better for me to go upstairs again. One charge would force the bolt of the bedroom door; if indeed they'd bothered to fasten the bolt. One kick between the legs would settle Mark; if I was lucky I wouldn't kill him but do something much worse.

I was six feet and he was five feet seven. I was clothed and he was naked. I knew he was there and he thought I was two hundred miles away. It was almost too easy, too delightfully easy. And I wouldn't kill Susan either. There are worse things to do to a pretty woman than to kill her.

I was on my feet and halfway up the stairs before I remembered Barbara. There would be a scream, at least one scream; she would wake up and run into her parents' bedroom, holding the panda tightly to her. And what she would see in her parents' bedroom would crack her world from side to side. That was it precisely; the mirror would crack, there would be no repairing it. I had her life in my hands.

Slowly I made my way downstairs, the long way downstairs, sixteen dark-gray carpeted steps downstairs past the

Dufy seaside scene, past the Douanier Rousseau jungle scene, into the hall where dark gray carpet gave way to dark red carpet, back into the drawing room.

I sat down again in the armchair at the far end of the room. I took a sip of whisky but it seemed to have no taste. There was no way of easing the blow. There was nothing to do but wait. I contemplated having a cigarette; but the effort involved in taking out the packet and striking a match seemed frighteningly enormous. I needed all my strength to wait. They wouldn't be long now; he wouldn't dare stay out too long after closing time.

I looked up, fancying I heard footsteps overhead. But there was no sound. Suddenly I became aware of something soft and slippery on my left hand. It was as if someone had put it there. I had within the last five minutes unwrapped the negligée and crumpled it into a blue ball. I let it fall to the ground to lie with its torn blue candy-striped wrapping.

When they came hand-in-hand into the room I felt nothing but a curious shyness. I didn't want to look at them and, idiotically, I didn't want them to look at me. But I looked at them long enough to appraise their blatant physical delight in each other; enviously, hopelessly, I almost felt an intruder.

Mark was the first to see me. He dropped Susan's hand; she gave him a puzzled stare.

"What's the matter?" she said.

Then she saw me. Her mouth opened as if to scream but there was no sound. She fell rather than walked into a chair and sat with her legs apart, a hand on each arm of the chair. But there was no tension in her arms, everything about her seemed slackly askew. I went over to her.

"Don't sit there like a whore," I said, "even if you are one."

She closed her legs, her expression unchanged.

Mark seemed to recover himself. "Steady on, old boy," he said. "You mustn't jump to conclusions. I've only just come in. The window catch —"

"I've been here half an hour," I said. "Get out."

"It wouldn't fasten . . ."

"Get out before I kill you."

He looked uneasily at Susan. "I shouldn't leave you with him," he said. "If he has this stupid idea in his head —"

"You'd better go, Mark," she said. "He really will kill you if you don't. Look at his face."

She spoke with no more emotion than if she were asking him to look at my tie or my shirt or my shoe.

I went up to him. Even as I did so I was aware that I had made a mistake: the desire to kill him had ceased to be hot and wild and now it was a cold and reasoned choice of methods which filled my thoughts.

"Don't let me see you here again," I said.

His eyes widened. They were a tawny color, nearer gold than brown; I had never noticed their shade so exactly before.

I remembered a barroom brawl between two G.I.'s I had seen in Wapping during the war. It had turned me sick then, but it didn't now; I smiled and clenched both my fists, leaving the thumbs to protrude. It seemed to me that no price was too high for the pleasure that was in a few seconds going to possess me, a pleasure more intense than ever I had known; I brought my hands up very slowly and then in the very moment of action he turned his head away.

"Jesus Christ," he said, half sobbing. "Jesus Christ," and ran out of the room.

The front door slammed. I sat down feeling dizzy.

"Give me a drink," I said to Susan.

She brought me over a glass of whisky then returned to her chair.

"I feel like a pimp," I said. "I don't know why I didn't kill the filthy little bastard."

"You were going to do worse than kill him," she said in a flat voice. "Were you not?" She started to giggle hysterically.

"Stop it," I said. "He was safe, and you're safe, as long as my daughter's in the house. But I still feel like a pimp."

She continued to giggle. I went over and slapped her face.

The giggling stopped.

"Do you want a divorce?" she asked.

I sat down and took a drink of whisky. "I don't know," I said. "I don't know. How long has this been going on?"

"It wasn't the first time tonight."

"How long has it been going on?"

"Since May."

"That fits," I said. "And he gave you that horrible cheap scent, so you wore it. I expect he gives a bottle to all his whores. You haven't much pride, have you? He'd just finished with one woman, and you had to be the next. What was the attraction? Is he better in bed than I am? Is he?"

"It isn't that," she said. "You think that's the answer to everything." She stood up. "Joe, I'm sorry, but I can't keep awake any longer. I'm too tired to make sense of anything you say. We'll talk about it tomorrow."

I grabbed her arm. "Why did you go with him?"

"He listens. He always listens. And he's not so —" She searched for a word — "so damned *triumphant* as you . . . He was in a mess, he'd reached rock-bottom, everyone despised him. He needed me. You don't need anybody. You just use people."

I released her arm. "I never was unfaithful to you," I said.

"You have been this ten years."

I looked at her uncomprehendingly. "I swear to God —"

"Do you think I'm a fool, Joe? I was when we first married, but I've had my eyes opened since. Do you think people don't still talk about it?"

"Alice is dead."

"That's it. That's exactly what I'm complaining about." She lit a cigarette. "At least I was unfaithful with a live person. I had that much decency. So you think you've the right to abuse me now, you think you've the right to call me a whore."

"She's dead," I said, helplessly. "She's not in my mind at all."

"If she isn't some other woman is," she said. "I only know that I'm not and never have been."

She looked at me accusingly; suddenly I had a lunatic impulse to kneel at her feet and ask her forgiveness.

thirteen

THE FOUR fledglings' mouths gaped so wide as to be ridiculous; they were parodying themselves, as was the mother sparrow, whose head was drooping despondently as if she'd given up the struggle to feed them.

Harry had borrowed my Zeiss Ikon to take the photo; it was a pretty good effort for a boy of nine. I wondered what it was doing on our bedroom wall and how the gray and primrose wallpaper had changed to plain cream distemper and the light gray fitted carpet to black linoleum and a tatty oatmeal rug at the bedside.

Then I realized that I was in Harry's room, lying on top of the bedclothes in my shirt. My trousers and jacket were on the floor; I couldn't see my shoes and socks. I got off the bed and walked over to the window, the clammy cold of the lino striking my bare feet. I parted the curtains a little and saw that it was a fine morning. The view was better from here than from our bedroom; this morning I could see as far as the spire of Gilden Parish Church to the north.

Near the church a little stream made its way down to the

river in the valley; Harry had fallen into it one day during the Easter holidays and come home soaked to the skin. It looked pretty and harmless from here, sparkling in the sun as it ran into the woods alongside the church, but at the point in the woods where Harry had fallen in it ran deep and a little boy had been drowned there last summer.

I let the curtains fall back into place and went back to the bed. I didn't go back under the sheets but pulled Harry's Indian blanket over me. It wasn't actually Indian but Norwegian, soft and thick and with a pattern of stylized fir trees in bright green against a scarlet and black background. It was, in fact, the only bright and cheerful object in the room; why had I taken such trouble over my daughter's room and so little over my son's? Why had I been angry with him for falling into the brook? Why was I so often angry with him?

When he came home for the holidays we'd have this room redecorated. We'd go together to the shop to choose the wallpaper and the paint and even, if he wanted it, some more civilized floor covering than lino. Or he might fancy a sheepskin for a bedside rug, an undyed one with the aura of the outlaw's cave in the mountain hideout. He was only ten, after all.

I reached down and took my cigarettes and matches from my jacket pocket. There was a cup and saucer on the bedside table; Susan had made tea last night after Mark had gone. That had been the most peculiar event of all; wearing her dressing gown, she'd come into the room with the cup of tea, put it down beside me and she'd stood waiting silently. I hadn't said anything; I'd said enough when they came downstairs.

Even now, despite the understanding Susan and I had

finally arrived at for the sake of the children, I felt as if I couldn't live with myself. No matter what the consequences I should at least have left my mark on that sleek olive face. I should have made him look a bit less like a matinee idol. I'd been taught once how to shatter a man's eardrums, how to gouge out his eyes, how to make him a eunuch with one kick; I put my hand to my mouth and bit until it hurt, thinking of all the ways in which I could have hurt him and then trying not to think of them.

Suddenly I remembered Tom Larriman's hair. Tom was a widower of seventy and very proud of his mane of white hair. He wore it long and washed it three times a week; there were some people in Dufton who said that he blue-rinsed it a little. He died of cancer; for a week before he died you could hear his screams right across the street. He tore all that beautiful white hair off, scalped himself piecemeal. The pain of it was a distraction from the larger pain and it was, I suppose, a pain which he chose and could control.

I understood him now as I had not done in Dufton, closing the window of my bedroom to keep out those high-pitched screams. I bit my hand harder; it was beginning to throb. Then I took it away from my mouth, feeling sick. Slowly and with extreme care I eased myself out of bed; it seemed that if I changed position too abruptly I should be sick on the floor. I pulled my trousers on, sitting on the edge of the bed, and walked slowly along the landing.

I was cleaning my teeth in the bathroom when Barbara came in. I dropped the toothbrush and kissed her. For the first time since I'd stood outside the bedroom door last night I began to feel myself readmitted to the human race.

"Somebody was sick in the toilet," she said.

"You dreamed it," I said. I lifted her up to look at herself in the mirror. "There's a cheeky face there," I said. "I haven't any presents for a cheeky face."

"I'm a good," Barbara said. "Daddy, you were away a long time, weren't you?"

"Too long," I said.

"We went to tea at Uncle Mark's yesterday, we did."

I put her down. "I hope you enjoyed it, darling."

"The cakes tasted funny. And Linda drinks tea. And the twins drink tea. Why do they drink tea?"

"I expect it's because it's cheaper than milk," I said. I half filled the basin with cold water and dipped my head into it. I dipped my head five or six times, making a great noise and sprinkling Barbara as I shook the water from my hair.

She squealed with laughter. "Daddy, you're not to! Mummy says it's naughty!"

"We mustn't do it then, must we? Hand me the towel, pet."

The towel was clean and dry and warm from the electric towel rail; it was bigger and more expensive than the towel I'd been given in the last hotel I'd stayed in.

I was home, home to the pink tiles, the pink bath and double washbasin, the electrically heated towel rails and the bathroom cabinet crammed with eau de cologne and talcum and bath salts. And that was the only difference between my house and the hotel; the greater comfort, the greater amount of buyable things.

Then I looked at Barbara in her blue pyjamas with the pattern of yellow ducks. I could leave this house but I couldn't leave her. There was a certain relief in knowing that, there was a certain relief in facing the facts. I couldn't take Barbara away from her mother, so I had to stay. We would move to a new house, a house with no associations, we could start afresh; but the voice that had whispered those shameless words last night, the body that had lain naked in Mark's arms, would still belong to the same person.

Once a whore, always a whore; no matter what she'd said last night the itch would come again. She wouldn't always bother to bolt the bedroom door; lust and foresight don't go together. And Barbara might not sleep through it next time: I put my hand to my mouth again.

"What are you doing, Daddy?"

I stroked her hair.

"Nothing, darling. Let's go and have breakfast."

"Why have you got your trousers and shoes on, Daddy? Where's your fuzzy dressing gown?"

"It's in our room," I said. "Do I have to get it?"

She stamped. "I don't like you without your fuzzy dressing gown," she said. "I won't let you be my horse."

"I don't care," I said.

Tears appeared in her eyes. She didn't weep very often but could always weep at will. It was wrong of me to encourage her in this kind of blackmail; but I'd drawn too heavily on my reserves last night to be able to resist it.

"All right," I said. "Wait there. And be as quiet as a mouse."

Susan was asleep when I went into the bedroom. I took down the dressing gown from behind the door but didn't leave the room immediately. Her black hair, unloosened, fanned out over the pillow; she looked very young and I felt against my will what was unmistakably pity. *You've used me,* she'd said last night, *you've used me from the very beginning.*

It was true enough; for a long time now I'd not thought of her as a person.

Mark always listens, she'd said. *You never listen, you don't care . . .*

I put on the dressing gown and went out. I knelt at the bathroom door and Barbara climbed on my shoulders. She stopped me at the window on the landing by pulling my hair. I opened the venetian blind.

"The giant made a big lot of pennies," she said. "A big lot as high as the sky. And he runned up to the castle, he did, and he put the pennies under the castle window . . ." She tugged my hair again; that was the signal for me to move off.

"Go on," I said. "What did the giant do next?"

"I'm hungry," she said.

"Who was in the castle?" I asked, looking at Sindram Grange.

"The princess was in the castle. And they had strawberries. And there was roses. I want Sugar Puffs, Daddy, I do. And yoggy. And cheese."

Yoggy was yoghurt, for which she'd lately developed a passion. And cheese was bright orange Canadian cheese which she ate rind and all.

"God bless your belly," I said.

"God bless your belly too, Daddy. What are you going to have, Daddy?"

"Do you know something? I'm quite hungry."

I opened the drawing room door and drew back the curtains. The negligée was still there on the floor by the armchair; I kicked it into the corner and knelt down to pick up the briefcase which contained Barbara's present.

"What's that blue thing?" Barbara asked.

"A new floorcloth," I said. I took her into the kitchen and set her down on a stool. She stuck her tongue out at me.

"It's not a floorcloth," she said. "It's a nightie. Silly Daddy." She looked down at the briefcase. "Why for have you took that, Daddy?"

"There's something nice there for a good girl."

I opened the briefcase.

"I've been a good girl, Daddy, all of the time."

I gave her the parcel from Hamley's. It was a small white poodle; for some reason she hadn't any dogs in her collection of stuffed toys.

"It's lovely, Daddy," she said, and kissed me. "Now get me my Sugar Puffs, Daddy. And my yoggy. And my cheese. And my juice with ice in and straws."

I put some sausages under the grill and went over to the sink with the kettle.

"Presently," I said.

"If you're very hungry, Daddy, you can have your breakfast first."

"That's noble of you," I said.

I plugged in the kettle and switched on the grill. I opened the refrigerator and took out the orange juice and the ice tray.

"Don't forget the straws, Daddy."

"Give me time, honey," I said.

She jumped down from her stool and caught hold of my knees. "I want to tell you something," she said. "Bend down, Daddy." She put her mouth to my ear.

"When I'm big," she whispered, then looked at the door to see if anyone was coming — "when I'm big I'll make you your breakfast every morning, I will."

"You're a dear little girl," I said.

"I won't ever leave you, not ever."

I handed her the glass of orange juice. She smiled; her teeth were small, white and evenly spaced. "You'll leave me one day," I said. I put my arm around her shoulders; she wasn't undernourished but she was very thin.

"I'll stay here forever and ever," she said.

She clambered back to the stool.

"I'm hungry, Daddy."

"Wait a moment, I've only got two pairs of hands," I parodied an old man wheezing, bent nearly double.

She exploded into shrill laughter. "Oh, Daddy, you are funny! Daddy, do it again!"

"I've only three pairs of hands," I said, shuffling about the kitchen. "I'm a poor old man with only four pairs of hands . . ."

"You've only one pair of hands," Barbara shrieked. "Silly Daddy."

"That's right," I said. "I've only five pairs of hands." I poured the cereal into her dish.

I was free, the sausages were browning on the grill, the kitchen was full of sunlight and Barbara's laughter. I was free and Susan had set me free. Two could play at that game; I would salvage my pride and I would please myself at one and the same time. It was as if I'd been given back the ten years of my marriage.

Barbara was still laughing; sometimes her laughter crossed the border into tears. I shook her gently. "Eat your breakfast or I'll smack you with all my six pairs of hands," I said.

"You wouldn't really, would you, Daddy?" she said.

"You don't know what I'd do," I said. "Your daddy's a most astounding man."

fourteen

"How much longer is the slaughter to continue?" Hewley asked. He pounded the table; this was a gesture which had once made everyone jump, but now it only meant that he was approaching the end of his diatribe. "We have *repeatedly* asked the Ministry of Transport to allow us to install traffic lights at this junction. Since we last asked there have been three serious accidents —"

I closed my eyes so that I might not see his face. Normally it was a quite unremarkable middle-aged face; but now it seemed to have puckered and withered with his own bitterness. It was not only the mouth which seemed to have tasted something sour, but the eyes and forehead and even the long wispy hair.

He sat down and I opened my eyes again. I had agreed with all that he had said, as anyone not actually a certifiable lunatic was bound to; but he had not influenced events in the slightest. He might as well have spent his time in singing comic songs; the traffic lights would be installed whenever someone at the Ministry of Transport got round to the Warley U.D.C. file or, which seemed more likely, drew the name blindfolded from a hat.

I glanced up at Brown, who as Chairman of the Council sat above us on the dais at the far end of the room. The dais was rather too high and rather too far away from the long mahogany table round which the rest of the council sat; generally one had the impression that he considered himself not the first among equals but our absolute master. This evening it was as if he were unpleasantly surprised to find himself in a position of such prominence; he read out the announcements in a lifeless mumble far removed from his usual loud assertiveness, and from time to time twitched his shoulders irritably under the weight of his golden chain of office.

"Three, Sub-Section One," the Town Clerk said. "Three, Sub-Section Two. Four. Five. Six. Seven . . ."

Brown was wiping his forehead with his handkerchief, his mouth half open; I turned another page of the agenda; I noticed that Brown was not even looking at his. The Clerk whispered something to him; Brown shook his head impatiently and took a sip from the glass of water beside him.

The Clerk continued his way through the agenda; the pause after each item was now almost nonexistent. Usually Brown, by a scowl, an upraised finger, or a request for repetition of a number, would make the Clerk go a little more slowly. Apart from the consideration of conducting Council business in a seemly manner, he didn't like Ray Kempett very much; he felt with some justification that Kempett would, if he were permitted, run the whole show. In his own estimation he was, I reflected, doing that now; as he stood there, tall and spruce and fresh-faced, he seemed palpably to radiate energy and competence. We wouldn't keep him much longer in Warley; at thirty-three a small urban district council would only represent the beginning of his career.

I found myself envying him. He was bound to work to a strict procedure, there were more things he was forbidden to do than he was allowed to do; but the same applied to his employer, the Warley Urban District Council. His salary would only amount to half of mine, his expense account would be microscopic, he had even to buy his own car; but he was a free man and I wasn't.

Brown took a little glass tube from his pocket and swallowed two white tablets. The color came back to his cheeks almost immediately. He picked up the agenda and turned over the pages unhurriedly; he was the chairman of the Warley Urban District Council and the king pin of A. Z. Brown and Co. again.

I was the bright and energetic young man for whom a place would always be waiting at Tiffield Products. There was no need for me to endure the boredom of another Council meeting, there was no need for me to endure the frustration of waiting for Brown's decision on the computer report. Tiffield had actually been serious about his offer of a job, and had even in his letter mentioned a figure which was four hundred above what Brown was paying me. It was a week since I'd received the letter; I'd answered it by return, thanking him profusely for his confidence in me, assuring him that to join an organization like Tiffield Products was my dearest wish, and asking him for time to think it over. In short, I hadn't said yes or no; and I hadn't heard from him again.

John Daynton, the oldest member of the Council, was on his feet now, complaining in a high quavering voice about the inadequacy of the compensation made to the subject of a compulsory purchase order. He seemed to be totally unaware that he himself had approved the compulsory purchase order in committee. No one would point this out to him; he wouldn't understand if they did. He was nearing eighty, a widower, and had lost his only son in the war: the only place where now the poor old fool could be happy was the Council Chamber. Here he had attended every Council meeting for the last forty-five years: here, after each meeting, the thick dark hair had thinned a little, the teeth had loosened a little, the back had bent a little, the flesh had fallen away a little further from the bones. In those forty-five years the ceiling would have been replastered, the oak paneling revarnished, the red carpet replaced, and new portraits of past chairmen presented to join those which now covered two walls. And, as long as I kept out of jail and voted as I was told to vote, then one day I'd be up there on that dais. I'd have my portrait on the wall and my name on the tablet under the Warley coat-of-arms.

Daynton had at last sat down. George Aisgill in his capacity of chairman of the Housing Committee had said something smooth and consoling about the balance between the private good and the public good always being maintained by the Housing Committee, difficult though he frankly admitted it could be . . .

Norah, who was sitting in the section of the Chamber reserved for the public, took out her notebook at this point. Graffham, who this evening was wearing a navy blue blazer, dark gray flannels, a white shirt and a navy blue tie — the effect was of a uniform with the insignia of rank ripped off — took out a notebook too.

The meeting was nearing its end now; it had all gone as it had been expected to go, everyone — first and foremost Councilor Lampton — had voted as they had been expected to vote. Graffham scribbled away busily for ten minutes, then stuffed his notebook into his pocket. He touched Norah's hand and whispered something to her; she smiled. I stared at her: she caught my eye and the smile vanished. Deliberately I continued to stare at her: I wanted to disturb her, at least to make her wonder if there was a smudge on her face or her slip showing. A little to my surprise she did not take out a mirror or look down at her skirt: after a while she returned my stare, but the expression in the large gray eyes was one I'd never encountered before. Now it was I who was beginning to feel embarrassment; I directed my attention to the agenda once more.

After Brown had closed the meeting I looked in their direction again. They had gone; I pushed my way out of the Council Chamber, affecting not to notice either George Aisgill, at whose home I'd made a vague arrangement to call, or Mrs. Fulwood, who was making her way towards me with a sheaf of typescript which I knew contained thirty-two questions — or rather complaints — about the Park Ward.

I looked around for Graffham's Ford Popular, then saw it in Horner Place, a little cul-de-sac at the other side of the street. I crossed over and tapped gently at the front passenger window. Norah cranked it down.

"I hope you had a profitable evening," I said.

"It wasn't entirely wasted," she said. "I note you're applying for a compulsory purchase order for the Palace site after all."

"Are we?"

"You voted for it," Graffham interjected.

"I suppose I must have done. It was so damned hot in there that I could hardly keep awake . . ." Norah's hand was on the window sill. I put mine over it. "Except when I looked at you," I said to her.

Graffham started the engine. "May I remind you that you have to phone in your copy, Norah?" he said. "If Councilor Lampton will excuse you."

She paid no attention to him. "You looked your fill, didn't you?" she asked me.

"No," I said. "I'm just beginning. Can't we have a drink somewhere?"

She withdrew her hand gently. "You heard what Peter said. I've work to do."

"You can phone from my house."

Graffham revved the engine.

"Your wife mightn't welcome visitors at this hour," she said. "Goodnight, Councilor Lampton." She closed the window.

"It's Joe," I said; but the car was already moving off.

I crossed the road again and got into my own car. The meeting had taken much longer than usual: as I drove along Market Street the sun was setting. Over Sindram Grange the sky was striped pale pink and white like peppermint candy; the delicate colors seemed to me a confirmation that the evening which had begun so badly was now ending well.

Whether anything came of it or not, Norah had acknowledged my existence: she wouldn't be able to go back on it.

When I reached Harling Crescent I saw with relief that the curtains of the front bedroom had been drawn. Susan had gone to bed early, as she had done for six out of the nine nights we had now slept apart. I wouldn't have to listen to her, I wouldn't have to look at her, I wouldn't have to smell her damned Turkish cigarettes, I wouldn't have to watch every word in order to prevent the continuation of the quarrel she'd begun just before I set out for the Town Hall.

As I let myself in through the back door I remembered snatches of what she had said. *He's himself, he's a real man, he's not afraid of the consequences. You're like one of your bloody calculating machines, you're not a real man at all . . .*

I smiled and went into the kitchen. Suddenly her words had lost the power to hurt me. It was not a calculating machine that had looked at Norah; it was not a calculating machine that had taken the first step towards entanglement with her. And she wouldn't be the woman for a man who was afraid of the consequences. I had my answer ready for Susan, and it wouldn't be in words.

I cut a plateful of cheese sandwiches and took out a bottle of lager from the refrigerator. It was the first food and drink that I'd enjoyed that day; my breakfast had been spoiled by Susan's silence, I hadn't been able to eat any lunch, and our quarrel had made me leave my dinner — or rather high tea — almost untasted.

When I had finished my supper the idea of a large whisky became urgently attractive. I rejected it with no difficulty:

tonight I didn't need again to sit up drinking until the small hours, becoming steadily more and more self-pitying and resentful as one whisky became two then three, then finally half a bottle. It was enough to remember that Norah had a tiny scar on her forehead which I hadn't noticed before, that her hair unquestionably curled naturally, that when she had asked me whether I'd looked my fill at her she'd also, without any further words, asked me if I'd liked what I'd seen. It was enough too that now I could look at Larry Silvington's murals and enjoy them simply as superior pin-ups; they could not hurt me and nothing in the house could hurt me.

I rinsed the glass and the plate and put them in the drying rack. As I was going upstairs it was as if I were absolutely alone in the house. I didn't even think of Barbara but instead felt again, with an almost ridiculous intensity, the warmth of Norah's hand under mine. If I'd known of any prayer of thanksgiving to fit the occasion I would have knelt on the steps there and then. *Show thy pity upon all prisoners and captives;* but I wasn't a prisoner any longer.

As I opened the door of Harry's room I heard Susan's voice.

"Is that you, Joe?"

"Who else would it be?" I said. I grimaced; I would have to remember not to say things like that again.

"Come here," she said.

I went to the door of the room which now, I realized with a queer pang of regret, I could never again think of as ours. It was half open and the light was on.

"What do you want?"

"Don't be an idiot. I can't talk to you like this. Come in before you wake Barbara."

I went into the bedroom. She was lying with her head propped up by two pillows. The bedspread was pulled up to her chin, and her arms were underneath it. The bedspread was of bright yellow candlewick; I didn't remember having seen it before.

"You're late," she said.

"It was a long meeting."

I sat down on the bed and lit a cigarette.

"I was worried," she said.

"That's nice of you. But there wasn't any need to be." I stroked the bedspread. "When did you buy this?"

"Yesterday, to cheer myself up. Have you had something to eat?"

"I cut myself some sandwiches."

"You look after yourself very well."

"I manage." I took the bedspread between my finger and thumb. "I really like this. It makes the whole room look different."

"You haven't been drinking, have you?"

"You can see I haven't. Why should you care, anyway?"

"I know how long Council meetings last. An hour at the most." She frowned. "You look as if you've been with a woman. You smell of it somehow."

"I've told you. I've been at the meeting all evening. I came straight home."

"You look like a cat that's swallowed the cream," she said. "Do you think I'm a fool?"

I stood up. "I'm tired. Goodnight, Susan."

"Wait," she said. "There's something you'd better know. Sybil phoned today."

"What? Has she found out something?"

"No. But she'll suspect something soon. We can't keep on avoiding them."

"*I* can." I sat down again.

"Joe, if you could see your face! It's full of hate."

"What the bloody hell do you expect?"

"Joe, it's all over. We've lived through it. We've got to start again for the sake of the children. Don't you know why I was angry this afternoon? Don't you?"

"Your conscience, I expect." Her hair looked very black against the pillow.

"Oh God," she said. "Haven't you abused me enough? You say you'll forgive me, but it's only words. You're hating me and hating him all the time —"

"Let's leave the subject," I said.

"I would have done anything rather than hurt you. You refuse to understand —"

"Oh Christ. I understand you. I understand you through and through. I'm just a common fat slob and you're sick of me. I'm not even a real man like Mark. You don't want to sleep with me —"

"I don't?" she said. "*I* don't? Who started all this but you?"

"It doesn't matter who started it now," I yawned. "Honestly, I'm dead on my feet, Susan."

"Did you know Jean Velfrey was home?"

"I didn't. I don't give a damn about her, and that's the truth."

For the first time since I'd come into the bedroom she smiled. "You went to a party at her place in London, didn't you?"

"Nothing happened," I said.

"I'm assured otherwise," she said. "Aren't you aware that there's a phone service between Warley and London? And a postal service?" She sat up. "Not that I blame you, darling." She pushed the bedclothes away.

I stared at her naked body for a moment, then started to undress.

She got out of bed and padded over to the door. She bolted it and came over to me.

"Jean isn't a natural blonde, is she?" she asked. She unbuttoned my shirt. I let her help me and then took hold of her by the hair, forcing her head back.

"I've been lonely," she said. "I've been lonely, Joe."

I kissed her. "You deserve to be," I said.

Her eyes dilated. "Hurt me, Joe. I deserve to be hurt. Hurt me, Joe. Kill me, I won't stop you, Joe." She knelt sobbing at my feet.

"I'll hurt you," I said. "I'll hurt you all right."

I had never been so excited in all my life; and I had never hated myself so deeply.

fifteen

HETHERSETT paused when he saw me, his hand on the door of the white Porsche coupé. In his light gray mohair suit and sunglasses he seemed an eminently suitable owner of nearly three thousand pounds worth of sports car. Pound sterling for pound avoirdupois, I thought, it had cost twice as much as Brown's Bentley: as I looked at it my dissatisfaction with myself deepened.

"I thought you were on holiday," I said.

"I am, old man. Off to Spain on the great silver bird first thing tomorrow. I just had a tiny loose end to tie up with your father-in-law, that's all. It hasn't been tied up, but now my conscience is clear."

"That's more than mine is," I said. "I was going to make an early start today."

I checked my watch by the big square clock above the entrance to the General Office. The clock bore the letters of the firm's name instead of numerals, a clumsy advertising device which never failed to irritate me. The hour hand now pointed to L and the minute hand to R; when I calculated the time, as I always had to, my depression deepened. I wasn't obliged to turn up at nine o'clock sharp and my salary wouldn't be docked for my turning up at twenty past ten, but I had never been late before.

"You do look a little fragile," Hethersett said. "Mind you, it was quite a party. It was jolly nice of you to have me. I kept the evening free to do my packing and then discovered I'd got it all done at eight. Leddersford's damned dreary on a Sunday evening."

"We enjoyed having you. You must come again now you know your way . . ."

The party hadn't ended until three in the morning: I ran my tongue over my dry lips and wished that Susan and I had chosen some other way of celebrating the first week of our reconciliation.

"I think I'll look around for a flat in Warley," he said. "My part of Leddersford seems to be full of whores and West Indians . . ."

He looked at the clock.

"What does the Z stand for? I've often wondered."

"Zachariah," I said. "He doesn't use it."

He smiled. "It suits him."

He opened the door of the car. "I must away. Be good, as they say in these parts."

"Enjoy yourself," I said.

The Porsche's engine gave a complacent well-fed cough; I turned away so that I should not watch — or be seen to watch — him going.

As I walked up the steps into the entrance hall I thought of the Tiffield Products house magazine which I'd received that morning. It was the first communication I'd had from him since I'd written him a week ago. The magazine itself was of no great interest; like all magazines of its kind the picture it painted was a little too rosy. What had interested me more was the page describing future developments. On the compliments slip accompanying the magazine Tiffield had put the page number followed by three exclamation marks and his signature. Not content with that he'd written at the top and bottom of the section MORE TO COME! ! ! There was no other message, but he had made the only possible answer to my letter. Tiffield Products was growing, building new factories, rebuilding old ones: A. Z. Brown and Co. was ossifying, and the computer muddle was only one of the things which proved it. For which firm should a bright young man be expending his energies? I toyed briefly with the notion of a new life in a new place, knowing as I did so that it was impossible. There were too many things holding me to Warley and to A. Z. Brown and Co. Susan would never, I was well aware, leave Warley; consequently Barbara couldn't. That was that; I didn't need to enumerate any other reasons for not accepting Tiffield's offer.

But my office, particularly when compared with the sort of office I could expect at Tiffield Products, was one of the reasons for my not having definitely refused the offer. I looked at it with distaste. I had been palmed off with the most cramped and ill-ventilated room in the whole office block. And the title on the door hadn't rated a carpet on the floor but worn coconut matting and a scratched oak desk with drawers that always stuck.

I looked at Hilda, my secretary, with rather less distaste. She was a small round girl in her early twenties with a small round face and a great deal of fuzzy ginger hair. She'd never represented any temptation to me but she was unfailingly cheerful, had some notion how to spell and, most important of all, knew all the office scandal.

"Hello there," I said. "What's new?"

"Those estimates," she said.

I took the folder out of the In tray. There was at least four hours work there; I put my hand to my head.

"Won't they wait?"

"Mr. Rabin wants them for three o'clock. And you've an appointment with Mr. Smithers at half past three."

"He's at Wakefield," I said. "I'll never make it."

"I'll put it back half an hour," she said. She rummaged in her handbag and passed me a bottle of aspirin. "I'll get you some tea." She lifted the phone.

When she'd ordered the tea she gave me a long appraising look, sighed, and returned to her typing.

"All right," I said. "I admit it. I'm a little frayed round the edges."

She giggled. "Mr. Hethersett thought you might be."

"What did he want?"

She puffed out her cheeks and assumed a gruff voice. *"Hello, my poppet. Ai just wondered if Ai could have a little word with Mr. Lampton . . .* I told him you weren't in yet, and he grinned and said he wasn't really surprised, and went along to Mr. Middridge's office."

I took the cup of tea from the office boy.

"He told me he was seeing Mr. Brown."

"He didn't," she said.

I swallowed four aspirins and washed them down with a mouthful of tea.

"You don't seem to like Mr. Hethersett," I said.

She pretended to retch.

"He's slimy," she said. "He's one of those men who seem to have an extra hand and you're never quite sure where it is . . ."

"He's none the worse for watching," I said. I yawned. "Oh God, I hate this time of year. I'd do with my holiday right now . . ."

"You're going to Cornwall, aren't you?"

"We've got a cottage."

I unfastened the folder of estimates, then glanced impatiently at the copy of my report in the Out tray. I reached out for it.

"Don't," Hilda said. "It's perfect. An absolute jewel of a report. You've summed up the whole situation and you've told A. Z. Brown and Co. precisely what to do. Now you can only wait."

"I've been waiting for a fortnight now," I said. "He hasn't asked for me this morning, has he?"

"I'd have told you if he had."

"Get me him."

"Mr. Brown?"

"Who else?"

"Honestly, I wouldn't if I were you."

"Goddammit, Hilda, don't argue the toss. I've put too much work into that report to let him forget about it."

She put out her tongue at me. "He won't be in his office just now," she said.

"Never mind. Track him down for me, wherever he is."

She stuck out her tongue at me again, but within one and a half minutes I was speaking to Brown.

"What the devil do you want?"

"It's about the report —"

"What report?"

"My report about the computer situation."

He snorted. "Did you disturb me for that?"

"It's important."

"The business I'm doing now's important. I'll attend to your report when I find time."

"You've had it a fortnight," I said. "The situation's not growing any better, either."

"That's not for you to say, young man. And the computer's Mr. Middridge's responsibility, not yours. Got that clear?"

"You don't understand —" I said despairingly; but he had hung up on me. I slammed the phone down.

"I might just as well tear the bloody report up," I said.

"I did warn you." She put her hand on my forehead. It was a cool hand and smelled pleasantly of scented soap.

"Don't worry," she said. "Think of your holidays. Are you taking the children?"

"Both of them," I said.

The hand stroked my forehead gently; I closed my eyes. I had no designs on her; but the smallness of the hand, its softness and coolness and its smell of jasmin, momentarily abolished my growing sense of futility.

"That'll be nice," she said. "You'll enjoy being with Harry."

I opened my eyes. She took her hand away and went back to her desk.

"I don't see much of him except in the holidays," I said.

With her back towards me she said: "He's a lovely little boy."

"He'll pass," I said absently. My mind was not on Harry but on Tiffield; suddenly I remembered that Brown didn't have the power to humiliate me any longer. Whether or not I could accept the offer, it had made me realize my own value; I could never be frightened of Brown again. I smiled at Hilda; perhaps, I thought, if ever I do accept the offer, I can persuade her to come with me . . .

"He's very sensitive," she said. "My little brother's like that. He needs careful handling."

"Harry? You mean Harry?"

"Harry feels things very deeply —"

I laughed. "My dear, Harry's a real little tough. Self-sufficient, hard as nails. Believe me, he's well able to take care of himself."

"He's lucky then," she said. She swiveled round in her chair to face me and I was taken aback by the pity in her eyes.

sixteen

THERE WAS rain and a high wind the next morning. As I drove along Market Street to Forest Bridge a curious resignation came over me. I had driven this way thousands of times, past the Town Hall, past Vintrip's the jewelers, past Finlay's the tailors, past Ingett's the florists, past Priestley's the grocers, past the hundred buildings which made up the street; today I was driving a little more slowly because of the rain, but that was the only difference between yesterday and today.

My wife had been unfaithful to me but there was still the same number of traffic lights to obey; the computer report seemed to have been received with indifference, but I should still have to take the turning to the left past the Christadelphian Chapel. And after a thousand more journeys I should cease consciously to count the journeys or to care whether Mark was invited to my house or whether other men got ahead of me at A. Z. Brown and Co.: after a thousand more journeys there would only be one more. I had never hoped for much from people, except one; and now she was dead. And perhaps she was dead because she was my kind of person, because she should never have relied upon other people for happiness.

I glanced at the Leddersford bus queue. Once, when I had first acquired a car, it had been one of my most reliable pleasures to see someone whom I knew there, whether they noticed me or not. Now everyone I knew had a car; it had ceased to be the wonderful glittering symbol it was just after the war. But this morning I was petty enough to look into the faces of the queue for some mark of envy so that I could console myself that even if I were making the same journey as them, at least I was making it in considerably more comfort.

Then I saw the one face that would never know envy, serene and rosy under a blue umbrella. I stopped the car and pushed open the nearside door.

"Going to Leddersford?"

"Into the center," Norah said.

"So am I. Hop in before you get any wetter."

"I'm glad you came by," she said as she settled down beside me. "But are you sure you're going into the center? Brown's is off Birmingham Road, isn't it?"

"Of course it is. But we're not going there. And we're not going into town either. In one second, when we cross the bridge into Forest Road, a pad will drop over your face and the next thing you know —"

"I'll wake up in Buenos Aires." She laughed. "I must say you're much more cheerful than when we last met."

"I'm never very cheerful at Council meetings."

"Or anywhere else," she said.

"I didn't know it showed."

"It does, Councilor Lampton, it does. I'm sure you'd love to be able to conceal your thoughts, but you've the wrong face for it."

"Don't you like my face?"

"Not very much," she said. "I don't really like anything about you."

"That's a shame. What especially don't you like?"

"You stared at me all through the Council meeting. Everyone must have noticed. And then you spoke to me as if Peter weren't there at all."

"He wasn't there," I said. "I could only see a notebook and a pair of spectacles. Are you angry with me?"

"Why should I be angry?"

"I showed that I wanted you. I didn't behave very well, did I?"

"I don't suppose you ever have behaved very well."

I glanced at her; she was smiling. I looked back at the road.

"You didn't mind my not behaving very well?"

"Don't be so bloody arch," she said, sharply. "And give me a cigarette."

"In my right-hand pocket," I said. "And light me one, please."

I felt her hand in my pocket.

"You always make me want to smoke," she said, putting the cigarette in my mouth.

There was no lipstick mark on the cigarette but it seemed already to taste of her scent. I remembered a story in one of my Latin textbooks; there had been a treasure chamber, and a cunning thief. The treasure chamber was dug deep and lined with lead but the cunning thief broke through in the end. In the story he was punished; but after all, it had been a story for children, not for grownups.

We were out of the forest now and traveling down the hill into Harcombe village. Soon, at the sign, just beyond the parish church, we'd pass from Warley into Leddersford, soon the air would lose its freshness, the high wind would be lost in the sodden fields, the ruler-straight Ring Road would change the journey into the wrong journey, the journey I had been resigned to before I met Norah. And soon the chimneys of Leddersford would remind me that responsibilities were beginning again, that common sense would rule my actions; but now, still in Warley, still in my own country, was the only time to speak.

"Do I make you nervous?" I asked. It wasn't what I wanted to say; but suddenly I was overcome by a kind of pity for her.

"You made me nervous from the first time that I met you. You're so completely the opposite of what I'd want in a man. I feel it's unfair of me to be *against* anyone so much —"

"Go on," I said. "Build me up. Say some more nice things."

"I'm tired of talking," she said. "If we talk all day you'll be just as awful at the end of it." She took my hand and kissed it.

"I won't wash it again," I said. "Why did you do it?"

"I like your hands. It doesn't mean anything."

Now we had passed the Warley boundary; but there was no change. I had no responsibilities except to myself, there was nothing that mattered except to extract from her the answer that I wanted.

"It does to you," I said.

Suddenly I thought of Mark with Susan; but now it had ceased to hurt, I had for them both a contemptuous tolerance. I threw away my cigarette and then put my left hand briefly on Norah's thigh. I felt her shiver.

"I wish you weren't so awful," she said. "Not that anything can be done about that. I wish just that you weren't married —"

"Oh God," I said. "Can't we stop the car?"

"There isn't anywhere to stop it. And this isn't the time." She put her hand in my breast pocket and took out a fountain pen. "I'll give you my phone number."

I looked at the fields beside the Ring Road. There were no winding lanes, no high walls, no hollows, only a great open flatness in the rain.

"When will the time be?"

"I don't know," she said. "Perhaps never. When are you going on holiday?"

"Next Monday for three weeks."

I put my arm around her shoulder.

"No," she said. "People will see us."

"All right. But touch me for a moment. I only want to feel your hand."

She squeezed my knee. "Ah God, you're terrible. No good will come of this."

"You can keep the pen."

"I intend to," she said.

seventeen

"WE SAW Auntie Sybil this afternoon," Harry said at tea the next day. "She asked when you and Mummy were coming over to see them."

"You'll have to ask your father that," Susan said. She frowned at Barbara. "Barbara, for goodness sake do eat your bun and not mess about with it."

"I don't like Auntie Sybil," Barbara said. "She's scowly-faced. And she smells, she does."

I suppressed a smile. "That's very naughty, Barbara."

"Why for does she have to be my auntie?"

"She isn't really," Harry said. He smeared his sausage with tomato sauce. "Grandma says it's vulgar to call people your aunts and uncles when they're not."

"Sybil's your cousin," Susan said. "It's a commonly accepted mark of respect and affection for older people. And, much though I hate to nag you on your first day home, please don't put that sausage in your mouth whole." She lit a cigarette and stared gloomily through the kitchen window. It was still raining as it had been since daybreak.

Harry swallowed the sausage with his mouth full. He said: "She does pong a bit though, doesn't she?"

"Shut up!" Susan shouted. "Don't be such a horrible little oaf!"

Barbara began to cry. "Don't shout, Mummy. Please don't shout, Mummy."

I put my arm around her shoulders. "Turn off the waterworks, Barb," I said. "If you're good I'll read to you."

Susan took a drink of tea; I noticed that the cup was rattling against the saucer. "That's right," she said. "Encourage her. And encourage Harry, too. Don't mind about me. I'm just the poor old drudge."

"Take it easy," I said, still holding Barbara. I would like to have held Harry too; he had a frightened look. But his prep school had long since taught him that all physical expressions of affection between parent and child were — as he'd told me when unthinkingly I tried to kiss him when I came home — sloppy and embarrassing.

"Take it easy! I've been at it every minute of the day. You know Mrs. Morlatt's off and I've to do it all myself, you know I've not been well, and what do you do to help?"

Barbara began to howl.

It was a high-pitched animal sound, half anger and half misery. I held the small body tight.

"Ah don't sweetheart. Don't, my darling, my precious . . ."

Harry continued to eat his sausages. "Silly little baby," he said. "You cry for nothing."

Barbara looked at him as if somehow betrayed; Carruthers suddenly appeared on his face and her howls redoubled, ending in hiccups which left her face dark red.

"Leave her alone," I said. "You know she hates being called a baby."

I patted her back gently. "She's tired," I said to Susan.

"You put her to bed, then," Susan said. "If you love her so much, you look after her for a bit and see how you like it."

"Get me a bloody pinny," I said, "and you can go out to work. Believe me, I wouldn't mind. You'd probably be better than me, anyway. My face doesn't fit, you see —"

I stopped; I was whining, I was whining in front of the children, I was doing what a long time ago I'd sworn I'd never do.

"I'm sorry," I said. "Leave the kids to me. Harry, help wash up, won't you, Harry?"

Susan stared at me, her face twitching, then ran out of the room. I turned back to my plate, but put it aside, half eaten. Sausages and chips and beans were Harry's favorite meal, but not mine.

I lit a cigarette. This was the way a marriage ended. I had felt no pity looking at Susan's white, twitching face; I had only wanted, genuinely and soberly, to hit her.

The rain had washed the color from the sky and the laughing peasants on the wallpaper were dancing at an auto-da-fé not a fiesta, they were laughing at someone writhing in the flames, they were dancing round a blackened figure — its mouth jerked by agony into a grotesquely symmetrical oblong — in the center of the cobbled market square. And now that I came to look at it, the wallpaper never seemed to show the square in its entirety. The pattern was incomplete; but if I looked at it long enough I should see the missing piece.

"Where's Mummy gone?" Barbara asked.

"Not far," I said.

I began to gather up the plates.

"Come and help Daddy. Harry, too."

"I want my mummy," Barbara said.

"She'll come back soon," I said. "I'll read you a story."

"I don't want a story." She started to cry again. "I just want my mummy."

Her lower lip was pushed out, her eyes red, the usually pretty face strangely adult, its soft but pure lines lax and monkeyish; for the first time in my life I felt genuinely angry with her, seeing her as Susan's daughter rather than mine.

"Then want must be your master," I said. "Shut up or I'll give you something to cry for."

The tears stopped. She had never heard that tone in my voice before.

"Darling, you must be told. Daddy loves you, you know that . . ." My voice, to my surprise, was weak and quavering.

"I want my mummy," she said.

"I'll fetch her," I said.

Later, after Harry had gone to bed, Susan looked up from her sewing and said quietly: "Joe, we can't go on like this."

"It'll adjust itself," I said.

"I'm afraid that Barbara has guessed something."

"Don't be stupid. She's only four."

"She's not stupid. And you're making your feelings about Mark and Sybil pretty obvious."

"Am I?" Again I felt the desire to hit her. "Perhaps it's not my *feelings* which upset the child. Perhaps she's seen something —"

Susan stood up. "You promised," she said. "You promised. You're not being fair."

"All right. I shouldn't have said it. But tell me what's on your mind, for Christ's sake."

"Joe, you're full of hate. You can't hide it, Joe. It's twisting you, can't you see it?"

"I'm bitter and twisted, is that it? What the hell else do you expect?"

"The child sees it. She doesn't know, she can't know, what causes it, but she sees it. And so can Harry."

"What am I supposed to do about it? Should I feel grateful to Mark? Should I send him an illuminated scroll expressing my profound gratitude? Shall I tell you what I'd like to do to him?"

I told her, making it as ugly as I could in the hope of shocking her into an admission that she still cared what happened to him; but disappointingly her face remained undisturbed. She wasn't even disgusted, because she wasn't listening; my voice trailed away into a repetition of obscenities.

"Have you finished, Joe?"

"I haven't begun. You'll find that out one of these days."

"What's the use of talking like that?" she said, wearily. "It's only your pride that's hurt, not you."

"I don't see the distinction." I poured myself a large whisky.

"That's your trouble, Joe. That's what will destroy you if you're not careful. You're full of pride and hatred.

You always were. You hate my father, you hate my mother, you hate almost everyone you work with, and you always did."

The wallpaper in the drawing room had no definite pattern, but cream predominated slightly over gold in vertical stripes. There was no sharp difference between the two kinds of stripe; that was one of the reasons for its being so expensive. I found myself suddenly resenting it, suddenly finding it too much in good taste. It was as if it were in someone else's house; like the parquet floor, like the Grundig radiophonograph, like everything else in the room, it cost more than I could afford. I put the drink down untasted.

"I'm going out," I said.

"That's what I expected," Susan said. Her voice was consciously calm. "You're very good at running away, aren't you?"

"What do you want? In Christ's name what do you want? Haven't I done enough for you? Haven't I eaten enough dirt? What more do you want?"

She put her hand on my arm. "Joe, be calm. Be calm, honey, be calm. You're shouting. You'll wake the children."

The kindness in her voice made me feel inexplicably guilty. I wanted to put my head in her lap, to weep safely and warmly; yes, I thought with astonishment, I am sorry, I want to tell her that I'm sorry, but for what am I sorry?

"I'll be reasonable," I said. My throat felt constricted; the words were difficult to utter. "I promise I won't be angry. But tell me what you want."

"Joe, we can't go on not seeing Mark and Sybil. Warley's too small. People will talk. It's odd to see a great deal of someone and then just cut them off. Sybil must be suspicious already. I can't put her off indefinitely."

I rose. "I'm going out."

"Joe, it's all over between Mark and me, you must believe that."

"It seems like it," I said.

"Where are you going?"

"For a walk."

She muttered something.

I grabbed her shoulder. "What did you say?"

"Nothing," she said. "I was a fool to expect you to behave like a gentleman."

I spat on the floor. "I'm not a gentleman," I said. I let go her shoulder.

I turned at the door; she seemed struck dumb by fear, her eyes dull with shock.

"Don't wait up for me," I said. "I'm not a gentleman. I'm not worth it."

Her mouth moved, but she didn't speak; again I was seized by the inexplicable guilt.

I snatched up my coat and hat and rushed out into the rain.

After about half an hour of fast walking I began to enjoy myself. It was a long time since I'd walked in the rain, a long time since I'd walked around Warley; and longer still, it seemed, since I'd been alone.

I found myself standing by the bridge in Snow Park watching the river. It was swollen with the last two days of heavy rain; another day like today, I thought dreamily, and it would burst its banks. I pulled my hat down further over my eyes. There was something profoundly satisfactory about the idea of a flood, of the black cold water engulfing first the park, then the town. It wouldn't happen; it couldn't happen because the town was too high above the river, but it ought to happen; the river had its rights as the town had, the black cold water eddying and swirling under the iron bridge was alive as the town was alive.

The guard rail was waist-high; I leaned over it, the iron cold under my hands. There was a gas lamp at the entrance to the bridge; I could see the rain dimpling the water. To my left I could see only the vague outline of Warley Forest; to my right the trees on the skyline hid the bandstand and the tennis courts. I was alone watching the river, the trees around me, and now, by some trick of light, the water appeared not black but silver. It was flowing, flowing between the trees, flowing away from the town, flowing to wherever rivers flow to, but flowing away. And now the wind was stronger; I could catch the smell of the river, rank, canine, a mastiff coming out of the darkness.

I put my feet on the trelliswork beneath the guard rail. A gust of wind caught my hat; I automatically grabbed its brim. I turned away from the river and walked back into Market Street. The water had turned black again and I was not by myself; I hesitated outside the Great Western Hotel for a moment, then walked on towards St. Alfred's.

As I approached it the clock struck ten. I looked back in the direction of the Great Western. I knew what I would be given there in exchange for a few coins; it wasn't exactly what I wanted, but it was better than going straight home. The alcohol didn't matter; what mattered was that there I should be among other people without the necessity to talk to them. For half an hour I'd have the sort of solitude that I'd gone out for, for half an hour I'd be, if not happy, anesthetized.

It wasn't enough, I decided. I turned left into Carmel Street. Standing outside the door, my finger on the bellpush, I began to feel self-conscious. Carmel Street was a street of red brick terrace houses, built at the time when the local stone had been worked out; it was a quiet street, a respectable street, a street of retired people and hands drawing aside curtains just far enough to see and not be seen.

For a married man to call on a young woman at ten o'clock wasn't discreet anywhere in Warley; but particularly not here. Norah would hardly be pleased to see me. I pressed the bell again.

The door opened creakily. Norah stared at me.

"Joe. What on earth —"

"You might ask me in," I said.

She put her finger to her lips and beckoned me to follow her. There was no light in the hall and only a dim light on the stairway; the house smelled of damp and camphor and after my own house seemed cramped to the point of claustrophobia.

She ran up the stairs; when we reached the top landing she had to wait for a second so that I could catch her up. She half pushed me into the room, her finger still on her lips.

I sat down in the nearest chair, breathing heavily. She closed the door and stood over me frowning.

"My God," she said. "You're in dreadful shape."

"In a worse state than China."

She touched my coat. "You're soaking wet. Take it off. You'll ruin the beautiful Turkey carpet."

She knelt by the gas fire. As she put a match to it I noticed again the strong curve of her back and the broadness of her hips, which the gray checked skirt she was wearing did nothing to conceal. The thought occurred to me that unlike most women she would look better naked than clothed.

"I've been for a walk," I said.

She took the raincoat from me, shook it out at the door and hung it over a chair in front of the fire.

"So I see. Take off your shoes."

"They're quite dry," I said, overtaken by an odd panic.

"Take them off." She held out her hand. "They're sodden. You are an idiot, aren't you?"

"Yes," I said. "I shouldn't come here at this hour."

She took the shoes from me and began to stuff them with newspaper. "You shouldn't have come here at all," she said. "Not by yourself."

"There wasn't any reply when I phoned you yesterday," I said.

"I told you I wouldn't be back until late. Why didn't you phone me tonight?"

"It wouldn't have done," I said.

"Why? And for heaven's sake look at my face."

"I will in a moment," I said. "But I don't want to talk just now."

"You really are the strangest man I ever met. You come bursting in on me at ten o'clock, soaking wet, then you don't want to talk but to stare at my midriff. Can't you bear looking at my face?"

I rose and went to the dormer window. I parted the curtain a little; it was still raining and the street was empty. Over the roofs of the houses opposite I could see the spire of St.

Alfred's. I had not seen it from that angle before; for a moment I didn't recognize it. And from here the street itself was different, its red brick more mellow in color, the unbroken parapet line seeming the consequence of a desire to please the eye rather than the necessity to cram the maximum amount of houses into the space available.

I went back to my chair. It was a long time since I'd been in a room like this, since I'd had threadbare carpet and dark stained deal planks under my feet.

The furniture was all dark and massive: a double-doored wardrobe, a chest of drawers which reached nearly to the ceiling, a table which took up a quarter of the floor space, two armchairs and a sofa covered in greasy-looking black leather. It was an oppressively ugly room; but now it was the one place where I wanted to be.

"Have you seen everything?" Norah asked. "There's a bathroom and a bedroom, too, and a kitchen. Don't miss those."

I lifted my head. "It would be nice if you'd just let me sit here. I don't want to talk."

She came over to me and sniffed. "You've had something to drink but you're not drunk. What is it? Are you in trouble?"

"Not now," I said.

"Do you want a drink?"

I shrugged my shoulders.

"Even if you don't, I do. Stay there — no, come with me." She looked at my feet. "There's some slippers in a red box in the bottom of the wardrobe. They should fit you."

The kitchen was tidy; the presence of the gas washer, a large deal table and the sink made it impossible to occupy it with anyone else without touching them. I put my arm around her waist. She sighed and moved closer to me then pushed my arm away.

"I'll break the glasses." She sighed again. Her whole body suddenly seemed to have gone rigid. I looked at her. Her face had gone very pink.

I took the tray from her and followed her back into the sitting room. As I watched her pouring the drinks I suddenly realized that a problem had been solved. It had been solved because I wasn't a gentleman, because I had no scruples about compromising Norah.

I lit her a cigarette.

"Thanks," she said. She handed me a glass of whisky. "Do you want water?"

I shook my head.

"I don't think I do, either." She sat down on the chair opposite me.

"I love you," I said.

She took another sip of whisky. "I'm glad you can talk," she said.

I went to the sofa. "Come over here."

"No. You'll have to go very soon anyway."

"I like it here. This is the right place for me. Isn't it the right place?" I stood up. "Why don't you want me to come near you?"

"I never did. I don't like you. If you weren't so conceited, you'd understand that."

"Why did you invite me in?"

"Because I was sorry for you. Because it's so obvious you've taken a beating." She crossed the room to the chest of drawers and brought out a towel. She threw it over to me.

"Your socks are wet, too, Councilor Lampton. I've told you where the slippers are."

I opened both doors of the wardrobe. The slippers were brand-new blue morocco.

"These are very opulent," I said.

"They're a present for my father. They'll have to be a present for you now, won't they?"

"Keep them here for me."

"You're not going to come here again, Councilor Lampton."

My back still towards her, I put out my hand to touch a neatly folded white slip, then drew it back again. "I wish you wouldn't call me that."

"It seems to keep the situation manageable. What are you staring at inside the wardrobe?"

"I was looking at your clothes." I closed the doors.

"There aren't many," she said. "I travel light."

"I'll buy you some," I said. I sat down and took off my socks and began to dry my feet.

"I know you will," she said. "If I let you." She knelt down, taking the towel from me, and rubbed my feet vigorously. "You have corns," she said. "And your little toes are crooked. There's nothing right with you at all."

I stroked her hair gently. It had a reddish tinge I had not noticed before, and the tight curls were springy, electric with life and, almost contrary to my expectations, soft and fine-textured.

She let the towel fall and put her arms around my waist.

"You won't be sad any more, will you, Councilor Lampton?"

"Joe," I said. I stroked the nape of her neck; the hair, my fingers confirmed with pleasure, began high up and the skin was smooth, smoother even than her face which my fingers now started to explore.

"You won't be sad any more, will you, Joe? It was funny seeing your face at that meeting. The other faces weren't there. They weren't bad or even particularly silly, but they just didn't count. You were sweating, you were so miserable, you kept staring at me. It was as if at the top of your voice you were shouting *Here I am, what are you going to do about it?* You wanted me, you see. It's a very rare thing."

"No one could look at you and not want you," I said.

Her hand moved downward. It was a square, capable-looking hand with filbert-shaped nails that were cut very short. It was trembling now. "You won't be sad again, Joe. You'll never be sad again."

When I returned at half past eleven, Susan was sleeping on the sofa in the drawing room, a book lying face downward on the coffee table beside her. I went into the kitchen and made a pot of tea. I set out the tea things on a tray and then, as an afterthought, sliced up a lemon and arranged some chocolate biscuits in a pattern on the plate. The problem had been solved, I thought contentedly. Even if I never made love to Norah again, I had got back my self-respect. I could now afford to remember that Susan liked lemon in her tea and that she liked biscuits to be arranged in a circle instead of piled anyhow upon the plate; I could now afford to behave as I had behaved before I discovered her unfaithfulness. It didn't seem to matter very much now; all that mattered was that she had always liked tea to be made for her at bedtime.

I set the tray down on the coffee table and very gently pulled open her eyelids.

"Joe. Where've you been?"

"A walk. I've made you some tea."

She smiled. "It's a long time since you made me any tea, Joety."

"I've been walking off my bad temper." I went over to the cocktail cabinet. I had scarcely touched the drink Norah had given me; but I needed one now. Looking at Susan's face, so pale in contrast to Norah's, so childishly delighted at the tea and lemon and biscuits, I felt again unreasonably guilty. I sat down at the foot of the sofa.

"You'll be wet," Susan said.

I took off my shoes. "I called at the Great Western. But I still felt bloody minded so I walked up Gilden Lane and back through the park."

"We won't have Mark and Sybil here if you really can't bear it," she said.

"It's no use dodging it," I said. "I've been thinking about it, and you're right. She certainly will suspect something if we keep on avoiding them. But if we just see them occasionally, there'll be nothing to start her busy little brain working . . ." I yawned. "We'll think of something."

"Joe, come here."

"What, darling?"

"Joe, I've been very silly. I've hurt you very much. But I'll make it up to you. I swear I will."

"Don't think about it now," I said. "The first ten years are the worst. I'm not blameless, you know."

"Kiss me," she said.

Her hands round my neck were very hot.

"You know why I was so horrid," she said. "It *would* have to happen today."

I felt vaguely embarrassed. "I should have remembered," I said.

"You don't expect a man to understand."

"I'll try harder," I said.

"Joe, just be kind, that's all. I don't care even if you don't understand, as long as you're kind."

"I'll be kind, darling."

"We'll have a good holiday, won't we? I wasn't looking forward to it at all, but I am now."

"I feel the same," I said. "But I've got over the bitterness now, honestly I have."

She tightened her grip around my neck, clinging to me like a child, clinging to me as Barbara would often cling to me. I looked longingly at my glass of whisky out of reach on top of the cocktail cabinet. It wasn't true: I hadn't got over my bitterness and never would. But now there was something to sustain me over the next four weeks; now there was something to look back at and forward to: I had begun to avenge myself.

"I'm tired," Susan said. "I'm so tired, Joety."

I thought of Norah, whose body even when quite still after love, the arms and legs spread out wide, held down as if by nails, nevertheless exuded an almost blustering well-being.

"You'll be better after the holidays," I said. "We both need a holiday."

I kissed her again.

eighteen

WHEN I saw that it was Mark and Sybil standing at the door my first impulse was to slam it in their faces. In the six weeks since I'd last seen him Mark had, in my imagination, grown larger than life, had become a figure of positive malignance; deep down I felt that he'd slept with Susan not out of desire for her but out of hatred for me, to prove that always and in every way the sahib class was effortlessly superior. Then as he came into the light I saw only a middle-aged man with a white shirt that too much washing had given a faintly yellow tinge.

"Hello, old man," he said. "Long time no see."

"We've been playing Box and Cox," I said. "When we came back from our holidays you went on yours."

I kissed Sybil.

"And how are you, love? And the children?"

"Full of beans," she said. "We all are, except Mark. He picked up some horrid bug in Majorca . . ."

"I'm sorry to hear that," I said.

Mark rubbed his hands together nervously. "It's nothing," he said. "Just Spanish stomach, that's all. And it stirred up the old trouble."

The old trouble was a tropical illness which he'd picked up in Burma; he always managed to mention it at least once in conversation, just as less subtle men would manage to mention their decorations. But tonight he looked genuinely ill; his eyes were bloodshot and his tan failed to hide his pallor.

"You want to watch that, old man," I said.

"I'm always telling him," Sybil said. She put her arm around him.

"He shouldn't really be out of bed but he couldn't bear to miss Susan's birthday party."

She looked at me angrily as if I had personally dragged Mark from his bed. "I told him Susan would understand but he didn't want to disappoint her . . ."

I smiled. "Well now, that's a genuine tribute. And we *would* have been disappointed if Mark hadn't come."

"For heaven's sake, Sybil, I'm not dying," Mark said. "You're making Joe feel uncomfortable."

"She's only thinking of her husband's welfare, old man," I said. I ushered them into the drawing room.

"That's what wives are for, isn't it, Sybil?"

She gave me a puzzled look. I burst out laughing.

"Well, isn't it? You have a drink, honey, then you'll feel better. And Mark, too. You name the drink, we have it."

I looked around the room; the party had begun. Only five minutes ago there were twenty separate people making conversation, drinking rather slowly, helping themselves to the buffet supper in a queerly surreptitious way, as if the food weren't meant for them; and now there was a party, a collective entity eating and drinking and, if not actually making love to its neighbor's wife, contemplating the possibility.

I brought Mark and Sybil two large whiskies.

"You know everyone, don't you?" I asked.

"I don't know that curly-haired girl over by the window," Sybil said.

Mark looked over at Norah. His face seemed to brighten for a moment. "Of course you do, dear. We met her at the Browns'. Norah Hauxley."

"You *have* a good memory, dear. She's quite pretty, isn't she? Your father-in-law seems quite taken by her, Joe."

Amid the general noise I couldn't hear what Brown was saying; but it was evident that it was amusing Norah. He took her hand and turned it palm upward. He studied it for a moment, quite unabashed in his enjoyment of holding it. There was a brief lull in the noise around him.

"I'm never wrong," I heard him say. "Now look at your life line."

There was a burst of laughter from the corner where Larry Silvington held court; I turned back to Sybil. I still didn't like my father-in-law; but I was glad in a disinterested kind of way that he should still take pleasure from a mild flirtation with a pretty girl. And wasn't it, after all, an endorsement of my own good taste? He had picked the best-looking woman in the room. Anne Rogers' nose was too big. Eva Sykes had grown too plump. Sally Timbal's legs were too thin. Coral Smith was shortsighted but wouldn't wear glasses and in consequence always either squinted or frowned. And my mother-in-law and Sybil didn't count; though it was hardly fair to bracket them together. With all her faults my mother-in-law would never wear a dress in such a violent shade of purple or one which showed so much of her legs . . .

Mark was shivering.

"You look a bit rough," I said. "Can I get you anything?"

"Some more whisky, old man." He rubbed his hands together again. "It's been damned cold lately," he said.

I took his empty glass.

"It's only autumn yet," I said. "It hasn't really begun to be cold."

I refilled his glass.

"Would you like to lie down for a moment, Mark? Use Harry's room —"

"Use Harry's room what for?" Susan asked.

"Mark doesn't feel very well."

"Poor darling," Susan said.

She swayed a little as she stood over them; it was obvious that she'd been fortifying herself in anticipation.

"Don't stand up," she said, and kissed each of them in turn. The kisses were loud and moist.

"It's lovely to see you both again," she said. "We've kept missing each other . . ."

"Box and Cox," Sybil said. "Many happy returns, Susan." Mark rose.

"Many happy returns from us both, dear. And please accept this little present with all our love."

It was a blue nylon negligée. "It's lovely," Susan said. "Just what I wanted."

"You've me to thank for it, dear," Sybil said. "Mark wanted to buy you something useful."

I held the negligée up against the light. "This'll reveal more than it conceals," I said. "Are you sure you chose it, Sybil? I think Mark did and he won't let on. You're a dark horse, aren't you, Mark?"

It wasn't the same as the negligée I'd brought Susan back from London; having been chosen by Sybil, the trimmings were overfussy and its color curiously dark and metallic. I had never seen exactly that shade of blue before.

The second whisky had brought the color back to Mark's cheeks.

"I didn't choose it, Joe," he said.

"I was only joking," I said. I saw that he was frightened; he wouldn't have wanted to come to the party, but he wouldn't, even with the valid excuse of his illness, have dared to put it off.

"It's just what I wanted," Susan said. "It's very sweet of you both."

"It was Sybil's idea," Mark said. He looked at me appealingly. "She just went out and bought it."

He watched my face as if expecting a blow to which he couldn't retaliate. He knew that that particular kind of garment had some special significance, he knew that the wrong choice had been made, but he didn't know why. He was up against the ropes, he wasn't resisting any more. At some time in the last six weeks he'd cracked. I didn't know why or how, I only knew that before me was a badly frightened man.

"It was a very good idea, too," I said. I put my arm around

Susan's waist. "We'll have a second honeymoon, won't we, darling?"

She giggled. "Wicked!" she said.

My father-in-law made his way over to us, holding Norah by the hand.

"It's too late for an old man to be up drinking," he said. "I must be off as soon as I can drag my wife away."

"You're not old," Norah said. "You're a good-looking man and you know you are."

He took out his cigar case, opened it, looked at it longingly, and then closed it again. It was true enough; with his heavy eyebrows and bold features which as yet didn't sag he was what is called a fine figure of a man.

He smiled at Norah.

"A few more compliments like that, young woman, and I'll take *you* home instead of my wife."

"I hope you enjoyed yourself," I said. "Do you really have to go?"

"I'm afraid so, Joe." He turned to Norah. "You must come to our sherry party next Sunday," he said. "And mind you tell your brother to see me about that job."

"You've not met him yet," Norah said.

"If he's as bright as his sister, he'll do very well." He kissed Norah's hand.

Suddenly I was astounded by compassion, compassion for the old man who dared not smoke a cigar, who had to leave a party at half past nine; and compassion too for Mark, still frightened, still expecting a blow. There wasn't anyone left to hate. I tightened my arm around Susan's waist.

nineteen

THERE WAS a moment when it didn't matter where we were, when comfort and pleasure and even tenderness were elbowed aside by her whispered then screaming demands; we were each traveling out of ourselves, out of ourselves as separate persons, now out of ourselves even as one person: we were the act itself and the act was blind and big as death.

And then we were in the back seat of my car in the turning off Gilden Lane; it was night, it was cold, and a white mist was rising as if exhaled by the fallen leaves. I stroked her back gently, my face against hers. I did not know whether I was happy or not, only that I could not be sad; for now tenderness was beginning, a tenderness which overflowed even to the garments she'd thrown onto the back seat: they weren't prosaic, they weren't the components of a pornographic picture, but part of her as the smooth strong back was, as the close-curling hair was, as the serenely smiling face was. There had been no betrayal between us; there could be no sadness after the act, and even nylon and lace and cotton could be involved in tenderness, could be even endearingly comic, as her disarray was at this moment.

"Your hands are warm," she said. "As if you didn't know."

She sighed.

"Could we stay like this all night, do you think?"

"We may have to," I said. "I think there's a fog coming up."

"We could stay somewhere," she said. "We could drive northward before the fog gets really thick —"

"No, darling. I want to as much as you do, but it can't be done. Susan'd smell a rat straight away."

Abruptly she moved off my lap and sat down beside me.

"It makes me wild when you say things like that," she said. "What the devil does it matter about Susan?"

I pulled up my trousers. "Let's be sensible, darling," I said. "She's the guilty party now, legally anyway. Let's not stick our neck out." I tugged at the zip of the fly; it stuck halfway. "Goddam the thing," I said.

She laughed. "Let me do it," she said. She leaned over me. "There. Skill, not brute force."

"I love you," I said.

"Do you, honestly, Joe?"

"I can't live without you. If we couldn't meet, if we couldn't see each other, I'd go mad. That night I came to your flat I'd nearly reached the end of my tether. And then it all became different."

"It became different for me too," she said. She shivered.

I put my arm round her. "You're cold, darling."

"I'm not," she said.

I looked at the little pile of clothes on the seat beside me;

suddenly I didn't want her breasts to be uncovered any longer.

"Hadn't you better put some clothes on, Norah?"

She moved away from me.

"Why are you always making me get dressed, Joe? Don't you like looking at me?"

"You know I do. It's not often I get the chance, is it?"

"Four times. Four times since August and it's nearly the end of October now. And I didn't count that damned party either, watching you with your arm round your wife's waist, making polite conversation to her boy friend. I don't think much of her taste, by the way."

"It hardly matters now," I said.

"No, it doesn't. Because you've got a nice mistress to console you."

"Ah God," I said. "How often do I have to tell you? I love you. Why do you have to go on about being my mistress!"

"I love you, too," she said. "I loved you from that night." She put my hands to her breasts. "You made everything different for me, too. You were like a big animal bellowing in a trap."

"It's sweet of you to say so. I wouldn't like to have any illusions about myself."

She kissed me. "But you *are* like that, Joe. You think you're awfully subtle and cunning, but any woman can see right through you. But you're dangerous just the same. You've messed up all my plans without even trying."

I took my hands away from her.

"I don't seem to be making you very happy, do I?"

"Baby," she said. "Big fat baby. Of course you make me happy. But I'm not very good at being a mistress —"

She screamed. There was a face at the window. For a second it seemed to fill the window, grinning toothily, then disappeared. I pushed past Norah and opened the door.

A man in a dark-colored raincoat was running towards the woods. He was already out of my reach: this stretch of Gilden Woods ran for more than two miles uninterrupted. He stopped at the entrance to the woods, waist-high in white mist.

"Filth!" he shouted. "I saw you, filth."

As he was telling us exactly what he saw, I picked up a stone. It thudded against a tree a hundred yards away from where he was standing; he flung up his arms as if to guard his face and disappeared into the woods.

When I got into the car Norah was putting on her brassière.

"You might have killed him," she said.

"He wouldn't be much loss."

She pulled her sweater over her head.

"It was a silly thing for you to do, just the same," she said as she emerged from it.

"Don't nag me."

She took a packet of cigarettes from my jacket pocket.

"Mistresses mustn't nag," she said. "That's a wife's prerogative, isn't it? Mistresses are humble creatures, grateful for what they can get, aren't they? Once a week, in the back of your car, with a lunatic goggling at us —"

"Steady on," I said. "That's the first time."

"And the last." She lit two cigarettes and handed me one.

"We'll go somewhere else," I said. "I'll find somewhere."

"Not with me, you won't."

For a moment I couldn't speak; there was a dry sensation in my throat, gritty and choking as if I were swallowing sand.

"You're tired of me," I managed to say. "You want to finish it, don't you?"

"No. Oh God, you are a fool. I wouldn't be here with you now if I wanted to finish it, would I? I'm going away, that's all."

"To London?"

"That's where I've been intending to go all along. I've just been marking time here."

"Do you have to go?"

"Don't you understand?" There was irritation in her voice. "The job's fallen vacant that I've been wanting for years. I turned it down once because my husband didn't want to leave Leddersford. I won't get the chance again."

"When are you going?"

"Next Friday."

"You mean, they've only just told you? It's short notice, isn't it?"

"I've known since September."

"You might have told me," I said. I looked out at the woods. A breeze was pushing the mist away; far away on the left I could see the outline of Gilden Hill. The breeze strengthened and a flurry of leaves struck the window; I could smell them now, damp yet acrid, faintly smolderingly metallic. I had liked this kind of landscape once, even down to the bare trees and the smell of the dead leaves: I was not going to like it any more.

Norah kissed me. "You'd have only tried to stop me," she said.

"I couldn't," I said. "Of course you must go to London if that's what you want. Why are you crying?"

"You've messed everything up," she said. "You're making me feel absolutely wretched. I knew you would, I knew you would from the first moment I saw you."

I gave her my handkerchief. "You'll forget me," I said. "You'll find someone else and you'll forget me."

"That depends on you, doesn't it?"

"I want to marry you." I paused, thinking of everything that stood in the way. I looked at Norah; she was smiling now. The smile unaffected, untroubled, triumphant, settled it. "I want to marry you," I repeated. "I can't live without you. It won't be easy —"

"That's enough." She opened the door. "We'd better be going. There'll just be time for a drink if you want one."

I followed her, slightly puzzled.

"D'you mind if I drive?" she asked.

"If it gives you any pleasure."

"I'm going to buy a car when I go to London. It's something I've been looking forward to for a long time. I could have bought one before, but I wanted to wait until I could buy it in London."

She turned the ignition key; the car jerked forward convulsively, then stopped.

"Put it in neutral first," I said. "Don't you want to marry me?"

"Of course I do."

"It won't be easy. I shan't be able to join you straight away."

She turned the ignition key again.

"You won't be long," she said. The car moved away smoothly into Harp Lane. "You've nearly made up your mind now."

"I'll have to get a job first," I said.

"You won't have any trouble," she said. "Wouldn't Tiffield do anything for you?"

"I doubt it," I said.

"You told me he was very much impressed with you."

"That was the effect of a good lunch. I haven't heard from him since." As I spoke the words I wondered whether it was a proper caution or a weak-kneed fear that prompted me to lie; I decided unhappily that there wasn't much difference between the two. "There's the children too," I said. "I'd leave Susan tomorrow but for them."

"I know how you feel, darling, particularly about Barbara. But you've forgotten something."

"What?"

She smiled. "I'll give you children."

twenty

"I WANT to see you," Brown said. "Now."

There was a peremptory tone about his voice which I didn't like.

"I cleared up that trouble at Bradford," I said. "Do you need to look at the file again?"

"It's your report I want to see you about. *The* report. The masterpiece."

"I'll be over," I said, and hung up before he could hang up on me.

"You don't seem very pleased," Hilda said.

"I've waited too long." I tugged at the drawer where the report had lain undisturbed for nearly three months; suddenly it came free and shot out onto the floor. I picked up the report from a pile of catalogues and newspaper cuttings.

"I'll put them away," Hilda said. "That drawer's overdue for tidying, anyway."

I opened the report. She frowned, and pointed at the door. I grinned.

"O.K. If there's anything wrong with it, it's too late to do anything about it now. Wish me luck."

She smiled. "I told you he'd come round in the end."

As I left the room I blew her a kiss; she put two fingers to her lips and then, surprisingly, colored a little. I made a resolve to keep a tighter rein on myself; particularly since Norah had left Warley a week ago, these gestures of affection between Hilda and myself had become more and more frequent. This was no time to become entangled with my secretary, or indeed anyone else.

Middridge was standing by the desk when I went into Brown's office. He didn't speak, but gave me a brief nod. He was wearing a light gray suit which seemed to make him taller than usual, to bring him up from the diminutive to the merely small. He had worked for Brown's for more than thirty years, never doing anything not in accordance with the principles of sound accountancy and never doing anything original or farsighted either. In addition to everything else he lived in Warley and was a lay preacher and consequently not only knew all about me but was bound to disapprove of all he knew.

I nodded back to him and drew up a chair to the desk. Brown looked up from a page of handwritten figures. They were neat and small and in green ink; even upside down I recognized them as Middridge's.

"I agree," he said to Middridge. "But our young friend here had me worried for a moment."

Middridge smiled. He had a small pursed mouth in a large square face; there was so little of the mouth that you had to watch carefully for the smile. But this morning it was so broad that it was as if it had been doubled to half the normal size. There was no doubt that he was pleased with himself.

"Mr. Lampton is a little impetuous," he said. "We older ones have learned to look before we leap."

His voice had two tones: one was the professional man's, quiet and precise, the other the lay preacher's, booming and unctuous. He was using the preacher's voice now.

"We've been working out costs, Mr. Middridge and I," Brown said. "I worked out some figures myself at the week-end, and they seemed a bit different from yours. But I'm not an accountant, I may well be wrong. I go by my instincts, you see. I'm just a rough ignorant businessman . . ."

"Those figures aren't final —"

He slapped my report down on the desk.

"Not final? Then what the hell's the good of this document?"

He opened the report. "All normal clerical work — that naturally includes stock control — to be put onto keyboard machines. That's what you say here. You recommend buying six of the damned things — do you know how much they cost? Nearly two thousand pounds. There's the delivery difficulty too. Have you thought of that?"

"Of course I have," I said. "If you'll look at page ten —"

"I've read it. It does seem to cover the point at first sight. Mark you, I only say *seems* to cover it. For one thing, you've underestimated the number of clerks we'll need until we get the machines."

"And most emphatically overestimated the salary that they'll be paid," Middridge said.

He went over to the sofa and sat down. Ordinarily he sat down stiffly and bolt upright when he sat down at all; now he was positively lolling back, his eyes on the cocktail cabinet as if for once he was prepared to make an exception to his own rules.

"Clerical staff aren't easy to get in this part of the world," I said. "And we aren't exactly offering them security, are we?"

"Security!" Brown looked as if he were going to spit. "We're not an extension of the bloody welfare state! How many keyboard machines would you say we needed, Mr. Middridge?"

"Four at the very most. At the outside, I assure you."

"That's different from your estimate, isn't it, Joe?"

"I still think that six is the minimum," I said.

"I'm glad you're obstinate," Brown said, "though you *are* wrong." He handed me the sheet of calculations. "We've got some more, too."

I looked at the spinsterishly neat figures. For a second they meant nothing; it was as if I had lost the power to count. Then I realized that I was defeated. I had not taken enough trouble over the report, I had taken too many short cuts.

I knew that I was right, but I could not prove it here and now; and that was all that mattered. When I should have been thinking of the report, I had been thinking about Susan; and now when I should be arguing about the report, defending its rightness in essentials, I was thinking about Norah. Suddenly nothing mattered except the need to be with her; after ten years I had reached the point I swore I'd never arrive at again, the state of hopeless dependence on another human being. I put the sheet of paper down.

"I could still argue about it," I said. "But I won't."

"You argue, lad. Go on. I told you, I like to see a man stick up for what he believes. I don't mind a chap being a bit pigheaded; you should know me after ten years. Shouldn't he, Mr. Middridge?"

"Mr. Brown doesn't like his employees to give way easily," Middridge said.

I lit a cigarette. "I didn't give way easily about the computer project originally," I said. "If what I suggested and what the computer people had suggested had been done from the start, we wouldn't have had all this trouble."

"That's what I mean." He glared at me. "Why the hell didn't you argue me out of it?"

I looked at him incredulously. Then I began to laugh.

"You've left me speechless," I said. "I haven't any answer to that."

Brown permitted himself a smile. "I can manage them all, can't I, Middridge?"

"Wait a moment," I said. "It's a question now of getting the computer to do the right things for us. We've got to re-think the whole business and we need some help."

"We're coming to that, Joe," he said.

"You can't deny that I'm right on that issue."

"You are. Flamville are the only people to do it. They made the damned thing and they're the only people who can do the allover programming." He paused. "Programming. Why the hell don't they call it planning? However, they're the people to do it, and they're the people who *will* do it. But they're not getting five thousand pounds out of us."

"That's their figure," I said.

Middridge smiled again. "Excuse me, Mr. Lampton, but you weren't given the authority to ask them for a figure."

"That's immaterial," Brown said. "Joe asked them and they told him. Joe had a pretty good idea of what the figures would be before he asked them. It's fair enough, too. As Joe's just pointed out, we wouldn't have had all this trouble if we'd done what he suggested in the first place."

"And what they suggested," I said. "There isn't any way out of it."

It was hardly possible, I thought: I had lost all the skirmishes and was going to win the last battle.

I leaned forward.

"We can ask them officially," I said. "And then —"

"And then nothing," Brown said. "We're sending someone down to put it to them straight. If they can't do the programming for us free then I'm scrapping the computer. And I'm telling everyone that I'm scrapping it because it's no use to me. They're a small firm; if I do that it'll cost them more than any five thousand pounds. They'll be ruined, won't they?"

"The laws of libel —" Middridge began.

"Don't be such an old granny. There's no law to forbid me scrapping the computer and no law to forbid me saying I've scrapped it. You've realized that, haven't you, Joe?"

"It's obvious," I said.

"Well, not instantly to old fogies like Mr. Middridge and me. But a bright young man like you can see it a mile off. Or Ralph Hethersett."

"Ralph Hethersett? He doesn't work for us —"

Brown burst out laughing. "He does, Joe. There's going to be changes here. Hadn't you guessed?"

"What was I supposed to guess?"

"There's going to be a merger with Hethersett's. We're moving with the times, Joe."

I threw down the pencil I had in my hand. "You always said you'd never do that. You've deliberately made a bloody fool of me. Hethersett. That cunning, scheming sod. And you let me go on all these months, hoping you'd do something about the report . . . Well, you have, haven't you?"

"Hoity-toity, what a tizzy we're in," he said. "We shall be crying in a moment if we don't take care. Now, get the muck out of your ears and listen. As you've noticed — and I'm well aware with just what satisfaction you've noticed — my health's not been too good lately. I've been ordered to take it easy. I can't run the whole show any more. And apart from that, a firm of our size isn't what they call a viable unit any more. It used to be before the bloody taxman got the bit between his teeth, but it's not now. Anyway, you have a nice long talk about it with Mr. Middridge sometime. You'll explain it to him, won't you, Donald?"

"It will be a pleasure," Middridge said.

"Don't feel too badly about your report," Brown said. "Parts of it are useful even now."

"The merger makes most of it waste paper," Middridge said.

"Don't discourage the lad too much, Donald. I'm just making it plain that there's going to be big changes here."

"New faces," I said. "And they won't be junior to me, will they?"

"The old faces'll still be there," he said soothingly. "There'll always be a place for a sound reliable man like you, Joe. There'll always be a job for you, I promise you that."

I reminded myself that Tiffield's offer of a job still stood; at first the thought had no reality, but then it began to assert itself more and more strongly. Later it would restore my self-esteem, later it would make me free; but now I knew that I had reached rock-bottom. I couldn't take any more. I stood up. "Have you finished?"

"I think we have," he said. "You and Mr. Middridge can take the report away with you now."

I put my hands on the back of the chair. "Hethersett's definitely going down to see the Flamville people then?"

"It was his idea," he said. "Fair's fair."

I mopped my forehead. When I took one hand away from the chair I felt suddenly dizzy; I swayed and put the hand back with the handkerchief still in it.

"You look a bit poorly," he said. "Hadn't you better sit down again?"

I took a deep breath. "I'll be all right," I said.

"I'll get you something, if you like. Brandy? Whisky? Gin? Vodka? Sit down, lad. You look as if you need a drink."

I took my hands away from the chair. "It's nothing serious. I think I'll go home."

"You do, lad. It's no use forcing yourself on when you feel sick."

He looked every inch the father figure sitting there behind the big walnut desk, his face contorted into an expression of concern that didn't really suit it. I turned away from him and walked slowly towards the door. As I reached it he called out my name. I turned my head towards him.

"You tried, Joe," he said. "You tried hard."

twenty-one

"I TWISTED his arm until he screamed," Hethersett said.

"You've told me."

I looked gloomily at the letter on top of my In basket.

"You wouldn't like to twist the arms of some of these keyboard people, would you?"

I handed him the letter.

"You'll note the tone," I said. "Real shock. We want the machines not next year, not the year after, but now. Don't bother looking at the other letters, they're all the same."

He dropped the letter back in the basket.

"That's how it goes," he said. "After the spectacular coup comes the hard thankless drudgery." He patted my shoulder. "What I did was easy, Joe. You're the chap who has to follow it up, you're the chap who has to look after the details. On the broad backs of men like you British business is founded."

"That's very nice of you," I said. "But it isn't going to make them deliver those keyboard machines any faster."

"Engage more clerks," he said. "Middridge will enjoy that. He has a broad back, too. Solid man, Middridge."

"Didn't you say something about seeing him this afternoon?" Hilda asked.

"So I did, love. And so I will. Keep at it, Joe." He strolled out, whistling.

"I hope all his rabbits die," I said. "That's the seventh time since September that he's reminded me how clever he was about Flamville's. If he does it just once more I swear to God I'll bash him."

"He's got a Judo belt," Hilda said. "I can't remember what color."

"The people I want to bash always have Judo belts. Or else they're small-arms experts or boxing champions. But why did he tell you? Is he afraid of you? Is he indicating that he'll sell his honor dearly?"

She giggled. "I expect he means that resistance is hopeless." She pulled the sheet of paper out of her typewriter. "Here's the list you asked for."

"Add it to the pile on the right," I said.

"Mr. Middridge said he'd like a decision on it today."

"I can't give him a decision until tomorrow. Besides, he's busy with Superman, isn't he?"

"That won't take long. You really had better look at it. And then you've just got time to have a word with Varney."

"What has he to do with it?"

"It's as much a personnel matter as it is anything else."

"Or anything worth bothering with at all."

I picked up the list: the information it contained seemed on the face of it absolutely essential but had in fact never been used. It seemed to me sometimes that as fast as I cut out one unnecessary piece of paperwork Middridge dreamed up two new ones.

"Your desk is an awful mess," Hilda said.

"It's my own system; today's work on the left, yesterday's in the middle, Middridge's lists on the right."

Normally I took some pride in keeping my desk clear; but for three weeks now the pressure of work had been so high that it wasn't possible even when I took a bulging briefcase home every night to keep abreast of it. It was four-thirty and I'd have to see Middridge very soon; there wouldn't be time even to begin to deal with the papers in the middle of my desk. And so tomorrow which would be no less busy than to-day I'd be another day behindhand with the hard thankless drudgery . . .

"You've taken a bit too much on," Hilda said. "Most of that stuff isn't your responsibility at all."

"I'm well aware of it," I said. "It's one of the consequences of having a broad back."

She shrugged. "It's your funeral," she said. "Are you still going to Leeds tomorrow?"

"I haven't much option." Even as I said it I was aware that it wasn't true: what was true was that in the three weeks since Norah had left Warley I had deliberately drugged myself with work. There was already as much on my plate as I could manage; after my visit to Leeds there would be far more. So much more, in fact, that I would forget Norah without even wishing to, that I would be forced into acknowledging the impossibility of my ever marrying her, indeed of ever seeing her again.

Hilda looked at me curiously. "That's a phrase you're using a great deal recently," she said.

"I've stopped trying to make things happen," I said. "I just let them happen."

I went over to her and put my hand on her arm. The sun was already setting; in the half-light her face lost some of its plumpness, became more sad and mature. Her forearm was bare; I stroked it gently. "I let things go over my head now," I said.

I heard footsteps coming down the corridor; I took my hand away and went over to switch on the light. She screwed her eyes up against the light for a moment, her face faintly resentful as if suddenly disturbed from sleep.

I lit two cigarettes and handed her one.

"Sorry," I said. I looked at Middridge's list again. "Ask Varney to step in, will you?"

It's all over, I thought with increasing despair, it's all over. I stood up. "Don't bother about calling Mr. Varney, Hilda. And cancel my appointment with Mr. Middridge. I'm going home." I put on my raincoat.

"What shall I tell them?"

"Anything you like. Tell them I'm drunk. Or ill."

I opened the door. She caught hold of my hand. "What is it, Joe?"

"Nothing," I said. "I'm going home early, that's all."

"Will you come in tomorrow?"

"Yes," I said. "And the day after that and the day after that." She released my hand.

But when I reached Warley Forest I found that I didn't want to go home. I pulled the car into a little clearing on the verge of the road and switched off the engine.

I sat there for about half an hour. It was quiet except for

the rustling of the trees, and the quietness was no different from the quietness that had always been there; but it was not what I needed. There was no moon and in the distance I could see the lights of Warley: I looked from one to the other but had no pleasure from either. It was all over, it was all finished. Norah hadn't represented a new life but my last fling. I would answer her letters, I might even snatch a meeting with her in Leddersford or London; I would never marry her, just as I would never take the job with Tiffield Products. It was settled now. Warley held me, Brown held me, Barbara held me.

For ten years I'd wanted to stop on this particular stretch of road; for ten years I had driven past it, waiting for the moment when I should most need what was to be found here. And now I'd stopped the car and everything was still the same: I'd broken open the box of emergency rations and found it empty.

twenty-two

"You didn't tell me you left work early last Tuesday," Susan said.

"Didn't I?" I yawned and settled myself more comfortably upon the sofa. "It hardly seemed worth mentioning."

"Not to me perhaps."

She gave me a coldly mirthless smile.

"Are you quite sure you've enough cushions, by the way? Or would you like me to bring you a rug?"

I sat up. "For God's sake, won't you even let me lie down on the sofa for a minute? Can't you see that I'm tired?"

"Not just tired," she said. "Worse than tired. You're heart-sick, aren't you, Joe? Your life hasn't any meaning any more, has it, Joe?"

I stood up. "What the hell are you driving at?"

"You're not very quick on the uptake tonight, are you? You'd better lie down again. Why don't you?"

She lit a cigarette from the stub of the previous one.

"Lie down, Joe; you look so charming, it's just the finishing touch to the drawing room . . ."

"I'm going," I said. "I don't know what's making you so bitchy, and I don't care. But I'm not putting up with it."

"I thought you were tired. But you're not too tired to go to the damned Council Meeting, are you? You couldn't cancel it to be with your wife, could you?"

I sat down. "Please, Susan, stop it. I don't want to quarrel with you." My voice rose despite itself. "Jesus Christ, can't you see, you stupid cow, *I don't want to quarrel with you.*"

"You'll wake the child," she said. "Not that you're worried about your children."

The mirthless smile appeared again. "She's going to give you some more children, isn't she?"

"She?"

"Come off it. Norah." She opened her handbag and handed me a letter.

"You don't take much care of your property," she said.

I stuffed the letter into my pocket, feeling for a moment oddly shamefaced.

"I can't help what she says," I muttered.

"I see." She poured herself a glass of brandy. "You mean she's a head case? You haven't slept with her? You haven't promised to marry her?"

"I haven't done any worse than you've done. Did you expect me not to get my own back? And how the hell did you get hold of the letter, anyway?"

"Your secretary posted it on when you were away in Manchester. Don't blame the poor girl. It was marked Personal and Urgent."

"You shouldn't have opened it," I said. "It was a pretty filthy thing to do, wasn't it?"

She looked at me incredulously.

"My God, that I should live to hear you say it. Aren't we becoming gentlemanly? Go on, Joe. Say it wasn't cricket."

"I leave that kind of remark to your ex-lover," I said. "If he is your *ex*-lover."

She finished her brandy.

"It's all over. Whether you believe me or not. He's in the hospital, in any case."

"Good. I hope it's cancer."

"That's more like it. That's more like the real you. It might well be cancer from what Sybil says. But he'll still be a gentleman. And that's the real reason for your hating him."

"Spare me the penetrating character analysis, for God's sake. What do you want to do?"

"I don't propose to do anything. Because I know that you're not going to marry her. You haven't got the guts, Joe. You're not going to throw up a good job and all this —" she made a sweeping gesture — "to live with Norah Hauxley. You would if you loved her. You've never loved anyone but yourself. I used to think that you loved Alice Aisgill. I even used to be jealous of her. But I'm not now, I'm sorry for her . . ."

"I'm surprised that you want to keep on living with me."

"I haven't said I did. But perhaps I don't want to divorce you. Or if I do, I'm going to choose the time. Perhaps I've still got my pride, too. Perhaps I don't like my husband being taken from me by that big fat cow Norah Hauxley. It's funny how history repeats itself, isn't it? You always go for big fat cows, you always go for the mother type, don't you?"

I saw her eyes moisten. I went over to her. She moved away from me.

"I'm all right," she said. "You go to your meeting. Don't

forget to call at the club to get your final instructions from Father. By the way, have you told him yet about Tiffield offering you a job?"

I stared at her. I had known her angry, I had known her hysterical, I had known her, after being hurt, to fling at me the wildest of accusations in order to hurt me back; but I had not known her before to sustain for so long this tone of calm, icily amused superiority. For the first time — acknowledging it I felt a kind of respect for her — she was reminding me that I'd married a rich man's daughter.

"No," I said. "I don't know whether I'm going to take it."

"You're not," she said. "Just as you're not going to marry Norah Hauxley. But I didn't expect that you'd tell Father about it."

"Why should I? He doesn't tell me everything."

"He certainly doesn't. He kept you in the dark about the merger, didn't he?"

I put my glass down with a bang, slopping whisky over the table. "Shut up."

"It's still going through even if you don't like it." She lay down on the sofa. "I think I'll have a lazy evening," she said. She looked at me coldly. "What are you waiting for?"

Brown was sitting at a table next to the window when I went into the bar of the Conservative Club.

"Hello, lad," he said. "You look a bit flustered. Been having an argument with Susan?"

"We had a slight difference of opinion," I said.

He chuckled. "Wait till you've been wed thirty years and you won't let it bother you. Want a drink?"

"No thanks," I said.

"Nonsense. Just because I can't drink any more it doesn't follow you young chaps can't." He ordered me a double whisky. "Drink that up," he said when the whisky arrived. "It'll put a bit of life into you." He rubbed his hands. "You're drinking it for me," he said. "I'm going to enjoy myself tonight, just watching Hewley's face, by God I am."

George Aisgill came over with Arthur Wincastle, a small timid man who ran a chain of draperies. Drapers, as if to assert that they don't use their wares, seem to tend towards a beefy mustached masculinity; Arthur was the exception that proved the rule.

"Excuse me for butting in," George said.

"We've finished," Brown said. "Why's Arthur looking as if he'd wet his britches?"

George sat down. "He's bothered about the compulsory-purchase item."

"I've been away," Arthur said.

Brown laughed. "By God, you certainly have. There's money in corsets, eh? You're never in Warley these days, Arthur. What's up, anyway?"

Arthur shifted uneasily on his chair. "I don't think it's right," he said. "We even made it part of our program this year. We've given our word —"

Brown held up his hand.

"Just a minute, Arthur. The baths are part of our program. We've agreed that they're needed. And those baths will be provided as soon as possible. But who said anything about the Palace site?"

"The Health Committee agreed —"

"We can change our minds, can't we? There can be a better site than the Palace, surely."

"You mean that all the arguments put forward for compulsory purchase of the Palace site were nonsense?"

Brown sighed. "You're an awkward devil, Arthur. Why can't you just take your chairman's word that we're doing the best thing for all concerned? Why do you always want to know every in and out of every bloody item on the agenda?"

"It's my duty," Arthur said. "I'm not going to vote blindly."

"All right," Brown said. "I'll explain it to you. But don't have any brainstorms when the item comes up. George's abstaining because he's declared an interest, and every vote counts."

He sighed again. "Why can't you be like the rest of them? Why can't you be like Joe here?" He patted my back. "Joe doesn't rock the boat, do you, Joe?"

"If I do it might sink," I said.

"If any of us do it'll sink," Brown said. "But you won't, Joe. You appreciate that the party's decisions are always right. Otherwise why be in the party?"

He patted me on the back; I felt that the gesture was the equivalent of patting an obedient dog. He began to explain to Arthur why it had been decided not to apply for a compulsory-purchase order after all; I didn't bother to listen, I knew all about the block of luxury flats which were going to be built on the Palace site. And I knew the difference between the amount that Amborough would receive for the site from the Council and the amount that he would receive from the company which was going to build the block of flats.

My opinion on the ethics of the matter was irrelevant: I was a sound reliable man who wouldn't rock the boat, I wouldn't have the guts to, I had never had the guts to do anything that I wanted to: I had sold myself to the first bidder, I would never be any more than a sound reliable man obeying orders without question. I had betrayed Alice, I had betrayed Norah: I had been given two chances of freedom and I hadn't had the guts to take either. I hated the room, I hated the green and buff country; but I would live in it until I died.

I thought of the first time that I had met Norah. A wind and night; she had worn a white trenchcoat and a blue headscarf, she had stood for a moment outside this building. And then she walked away. She had walked away. I had walked up the steps of the Club, across the terrazzo flooring of the entrance hall, and into this room. It was all over; why did I torture myself?

George Aisgill looked at me sharply. "You're not very talkative, Joe."

"My father-in-law can talk for both of us," I said.

He chuckled. "Do you know, I feel rather sorry for Hewley."

"*He* doesn't," I said, nodding towards Brown.

George lowered his voice. "He's an old tartar, isn't he? He always gets his own way."

"He has so far."

"I only hope Hewley bows to the inevitable. I'm not in the mood for one of his long speeches." He looked out of the window. "It's a lovely night," he said. "The moon's as bright as day."

"It's cold," I said.

"I don't know why we do it," he said. "Shall I tell you what I wanted to do tonight? I wanted to go for a long drive in the moonlight. It's something I've not done for years."

"Why didn't you?"

"Need you ask? We can't always do what we'd like to do."

"Can't we?"

Suddenly, seeing his expression of wistfulness as he looked out of the window, I was in his mind and the white ribbon of road was running high into the hills.

It was then that I understood what I had to do. And it seemed to me that I had always understood. There was nothing to be frightened of any more.

George looked away from the window.

"We'll have to be off," he said. His face regained its normal expression of cool amusement.

"I think your father-in-law has briefed Arthur," he said. "I don't need to brief *you*, do I, Joe?"

"Don't worry," I said. "I've got it all worked out."

When I returned from the Town Hall, Susan was reading. She didn't look up as I entered the room but made a vague noise from behind the book to indicate that she'd seen me.

The room was lit only by a table lamp; momentarily its soft light seemed to make her not younger, but older. It might almost have been her mother sitting there; for a moment I was tempted to knock the book out of her hands. Her composure was too much to bear; I knew the sense of impregnable superiority it was based upon.

I sat down. It was as if what I'd done in the Council Chamber that night had no significance except to spite my father-in-law. The memory of his face when I'd voted against him would be always something to treasure: but it would alter nothing. And then I remembered how livid his face had been; I'd defied him in the most public way possible, I'd made a fool of him before not only his friends but also his enemies.

He would never forgive me. He would never forgive me, and that was exactly what I wanted. I had blown open the prison door; the sound reliable man, the understanding forgiving cuckold, had set himself free. And soon I was going to wipe that superior expression off Susan's face. But there was no hurry, there was no need to speak until she had spoken. I loosened my collar and sprawled back in my armchair.

She looked up from her book. "You look pleased with yourself," she said. "You wouldn't like to get me a drink, would you? A very weak brandy and soda."

"Certainly, darling," I stood up. "I think I'll have one too."

When she took the glass from me she looked at me suspiciously. "You haven't been drinking, have you?"

"You know where I've been."

"I ought to. It's your second home, isn't it?"

I went back to my chair. "Not any more," I said.

"Don't tell me you're resigning!"

I nodded.

She smiled. "Joe, that's marvelous. I can't believe it."

"It's true," I said.

She came over and kissed me. "So you've come to your senses," she said.

"You can put it that way if you like," I said.

"And this silly business with Norah Hauxley — you've come to your senses about that?" She laughed. "Oh Joe, I don't really blame you, I know how you still must feel about Mark — but she wouldn't be suitable for you, honestly she wouldn't. You wanted to get your own back — you've done it now." She sat on my lap. "Admit it, Joe, she terrifies you really. She's so *bossy*, she'd manage you all the time. There's too much of her, she's so damned overpowering. You'll be far better off with your silly little wife." She took my hand and put it on her knee. "Joe, I want —"

I jerked my hand away. "Get up," I said. "I'm leaving the Council because I'm leaving Warley. And you. I've had my bellyful, I can't stand it one moment longer. Just for once I'm going to do what I want to do. I'm going to marry Norah. I'm going to give her children. I'm going to forget that I ever was married to you or that I ever worked for your father. You said I hadn't the guts. You thought you had me just where you wanted me. Under your thumb. Didn't you? Didn't you?"

She sat down heavily.

"Is that all?" she said.

Her face was scraped dry of color.

"I'll sleep in Harry's room tonight," I said. "Then I'll find somewhere to stay until I go to London. I don't want to stay in this house any longer than I can help." I would have added something about my resentment about it not being my house; but now that my moment of triumph had come I had no enemy: she looked too small, too sick, too hurt.

"What about the children?" she asked.

"I can't do any more for the children. I can't keep up a front for their sake. Not any more. They'd suffer in the end. *You* wouldn't be able to hide what you really felt either."

"I have so far."

"When Barbara grows older, will you be able to? Will I? No. Let's stop deceiving ourselves. It's better to have a clean break."

"I wouldn't have called it clean," she said. "How many lies am I going to have to tell Barbara? And Harry?"

"Harry won't be bothered very much," I said. "How much does he see of me anyway?"

There were two ugly patches of color in her cheeks now. She drew in her breath sharply. "Ah. That's written off Harry, has it? What about your favorite? What about the one you love the best? What about Barbara?"

I looked away from her. There was something about her expression now which frightened me. She was triumphant now, her face was distorted with the effort of it like a runner breasting the tape.

"I'll come to see her," I said. "And Harry."

"You don't think it might unsettle them?"

"Christ, they're my own children. Be reasonable, Susan. Naturally I want to see them."

"Oh. You're quite sure? Quite, quite sure? Wouldn't it be better *really* to make a clean break?"

"Of course I'm going to see them," I said. "You can't deny me that."

"I never would, Joe. I'm just asking you to think very carefully about it."

"I don't need to."

"All right then. I'm asking you for the last time. Do you want a clean break or do you want to visit the children?"

I refilled my glass.

"You can't stop me visiting them."

"You can sleep on it if you like," she said. "You don't have to give your answer now."

"I'm going to visit them. That's final."

She bit her lower lip. "You always do what you want to do," she said. "Don't you?"

"I do now."

"You'll leave me and eventually there'll be a divorce. I expect the number of visits will be settled by the lawyers. In chambers, isn't that it? But you'll write, and I'm sure we can arrange something in the meantime. It won't be difficult during term. The school's quite near London."

"And I'll be able to get up to see Barbara every other week. I can call and take her out. I needn't even see you. I mean, you could have someone in to look after her and you could go out before I come —" I stopped. "Don't look like that. I'm only thinking about your feelings."

"Don't concern yourself with that, Joe. But I can see you've gone into this matter most carefully. I expect you've discussed it with Norah. She's not the sort of person to leave anything to chance. There's just one thing, though: you'll only want to visit Harry."

Her color was more even now and her voice had stopped trembling; she had breasted the tape and was slowing down for the cameras and congratulations.

"What do you mean? What do you mean?"

"You'll only want to see your own child."

"You're mad," I managed to say. "You're mad."

"Oh no. You're not Barbara's father. I'm absolutely certain of it." She began to laugh hysterically, her arms folded as if to keep out the cold.

I took hold of her shoulder. "You whore," I said. "You dirty whore."

She continued to laugh. "If you kill me you won't be able to marry Norah," she said.

I released her. "You're not worth killing," I said. I went towards the door.

"Don't you want to know who it was, Joe?" She had folded her arms again: somehow her face seemed to have fallen in round the mouth.

"I don't need to ask," I said. "You must have had a lot of quiet fun these last four years, mustn't you? Watching her with the Pudding-faced Bawlers. Watching her with her sisters —"

"It wasn't like that at all," she said, wearily. "It only started again this May. It wouldn't have if it hadn't been for you. I tried, really tried to love you." She stopped. "No, I didn't try. I didn't have to try. Because I did love you. I tried to make you love me. But you couldn't because that isn't you." She frowned. "It's like explaining color to a blind man."

"All right," I said. "You tried not to be a whore. For

four years. Nearly five, in fact. That's a long time to stay faithful to your husband, so at the first excuse you went back to Mark. You've done well, haven't you? Nearly five years."

Then I remembered something. For a moment I could not speak.

"You bitch," I said hoarsely. "You're a bigger whore than I thought. It isn't Mark. Can't you ever tell me the truth? Who is it? *Who is it?*"

"I think you're going mad," she said. "Why shouldn't it be Mark?"

"He only came to live in Warley three years ago."

"You wouldn't remember my visiting him and Sybil the year before Barbara was born, would you? When I went to stay with Aunt Cora in Hampstead? You don't remember that row we had before I went? And the pretty things you said to me."

"That's all over and done with," I said.

"Well, so's this. Or it would have been but for you. He doesn't know anything about it."

"I bet it was easy," I said. "I bet he just had to ask the first time he met you. Or did he bother to ask? Did he just sniff at you like a dog at a bitch?" I became more explicit; but her expression was merely of detached amusement.

"It's strange," she said. "You talk of Mark as if I'd met him for the first time five years ago. But I've known him for fifteen years. You don't remember anything at all about me, do you? I'm just an object, a thing, I'm not supposed to have a mind of my own. Shall I tell you what the thing did?" She was breathing hard. "Shall I tell you what the thing did when its feelings were hurt? How often and where?"

I felt a blow on my cheek and then another; I looked at the hand that had hit me and it was mine. I heard myself asking questions; I heard the answers, but it was hardly necessary to listen to the answers. I would have known them a long time ago if only my conceit and stupidity had not smothered my instincts. I hit myself again, but not so hard this time; the violence of the first two blows had made me a little sick.

"That's enough," I said. "I know what to do now."

For the first time she looked genuinely frightened.

"Joe, it wasn't as deliberate as that." She moved over to the telephone. "I told you I was tired. I told you to leave me alone."

"You can leave the telephone alone," I said. "You're not worth hanging for."

"It's your fault," she said. "You've never understood. You've never wanted to understand me."

Suddenly I found myself against my will desiring her; and looking into her eyes, dilated as if by drugs, I knew that she, against her will, desired me. But it was a voyeur's excitement and sent no signals to my loins. I turned away without speaking and went upstairs to pack.

When I came back into the drawing room Brown was there, standing in front of the electric fire. He looked at my suitcase.

"What the hell's this?"

"Joe's leaving me, Daddy," Susan said.

"Who's the woman?"

"Norah Hauxley. He's going to live with her in London."

"I had an idea he was up to his old tricks." He took out the packet of cheroots, hesitated, then brought out his leather cigar case. "We won't be honored with his presence at work tomorrow then." He pierced the Corona and lit it with an air of celebration.

"I'll work my notice out if you like," I said.

"We can do without you. You can't go too soon for me." He blew out a cloud of smoke.

There was an unopened tin of Capstan in the cocktail cabinet; I put it in my case.

"Help yourself to anything you want," he said. "Why don't you take some liquor with you, too?"

"They're my cigarettes and it's my liquor."

"You are getting above yourself, aren't you? Well, don't let me keep you. You can mail your resignation." He clenched his fist. "You've made a right fool of me, haven't you?"

"That was the idea," I said. "Not that you can make me resign. I can vote how I please and there's not a single damned thing you can do about it."

I poured myself a large whisky. There was a drink still untouched beside my chair, but it seemed important, seeing him standing by the fire in that proprietorial attitude, to assert at least the ownership of the contents of the cocktail cabinet, and to make it plain that I wasn't offering him any hospitality.

"We're very clever, aren't we?" His face was darkening. "May I ask how you're proposing to live?"

"Tiffield's offered me a job. You didn't know that, did you?"

"I thought he was up to something," he said. "But he's too clever by half. He doesn't want you because you're such a bright young man, you know. He wants you because he thinks you're my blue-eyed boy and he thinks it'll break my heart to see you go. You're not as good as all that, Joe. You're still the little Town Hall clerk at bottom, you've gone as far as you ever will go —"

"Shut up. I may have to listen to you at the works, but I'm damned if I will in my own house."

"It's not your house. I made sure of that. You're a lodger here, you cheap no-good womanizer, and I'm giving you notice."

I turned to Susan. "Let him rave," I said. "I'm going now. Tell Barbara I'm going away to — earn pennies. Promise?"

"You'll just be in time for the ten-thirty train," Brown said.

"I'm driving down."

"Oh no you're not. That's the firm's car, in case you'd forgotten." He held out his hand. "The keys."

I tossed them on the floor. "There you are," I said. "Root for them like a pig. Susan, will you lend me your car?"

She picked up her handbag.

"No," Brown said. "I gave you that car. It's not his."

Susan handed me the Morris keys. "If it was a present to me, it's mine. I can lend it to whom I like. Joe, you needn't go tonight. Stay here, wait until you've calmed down. It's a long journey."

"I must go," I said. "You know why."

She looked at me appealingly. "Joe, you're tired. You've had something to drink. Wait until morning at least, dear."

Brown snorted. "Dear!" he said. "He's leaving her and she calls him dear! Let the bastard kill himself and good riddance!"

"Keep out of this," Susan said. "I want to talk to my husband. In fact, I think you'd better go."

His mouth sagged open in astonishment. "Go? I'm your father, it's my duty to look after you. By God, you can't look after yourself —"

"Get out."

She was shaking with temper. "You've pushed me around all your life. You've treated me like a puppet, you treat your grandson like one, you try to boss everyone. You're a bully and a tyrant. I won't have you here telling me what to do. And I won't have you talk to Joe like that. He's still my husband."

"Not for much longer if I can help it." He put his arm round her; she shook it off impatiently. "You're all wrought up, love, you don't know who your real friends are. I warned you against him from the start —"

"Yes, you did," she said in a quieter voice. "Perhaps if you hadn't tried so hard to stop it, I would never have married him."

"I'll deal with him. I'll make him suffer. You're too soft-hearted, Susan, that's your trouble."

"You don't know anything about me, Father. Or about Joe."

"Not know my own daughter! I know you inside out. And him, too." He scowled at me.

"Do you know why he's leaving me?"

"You needn't tell him, Susan," I said.

She stamped her foot. The childish gesture was oddly shocking. "I've been having an affair with Mark," she said.

Brown's face seemed to grow smaller; he swayed forward, then checked himself.

"I don't believe it," he said.

"It's true. Ask Joe."

He clenched his fist. "It's your fault," he said to me. "You can't have been a proper husband to her. It's your fault."

"You'd better go now," Susan said quietly.

"Mark," he said. "She always wants the worthless ones . . ." He looked round the room as if he were surrounded by a hostile mob. "You don't see," he said. "I did my best . . ."

He stumbled out, his foot kicking the car keys. They jangled noisily across the parquet floor; he didn't make any movement to pick them up, nor was there any indication that he'd noticed them.

"I'll brew you some coffee for the journey," Susan said.

"I don't want it." Suddenly my knees gave way. I sat down and began to cry.

"Why did you do it, Susan? Why did you have to do it?"

She knelt down beside me and stroked my hair gently. "Poor Joe," she said. "Poor Joe is tired."

"I'm sorry," I said.

She took my handkerchief from my breast pocket and wiped my eyes.

"Poor Joe," she said. "Being sorry won't help us now." She took my hand. "Come with me while I make the coffee." I let her take me into the kitchen.

Watching her set out the cups, warm the milk, fill the percolator, there was no need to talk any more. I had even a feeling of contentment: there was nothing left to happen to me.

I finished my second cup of coffee and looked at my watch. "I'll have to go," I said.

She corked the thermos.

"Joe, this is your home. You can stay the night if you want. Or why don't you rest for a while?"

"I can't rest now." I picked up the thermos flask. "I'll write you."

"Phone me. Phone me as soon as you've reached London. Promise."

"All right."

She started to cry. "Take care, Joe. Oh, do take care!"

I looked at her in surprise; I had not felt so close to her since we were first married. But I made no move to comfort her.

twenty-three

"I'M GOING to collect the car today," Norah said.

I poured myself a second cup of tea, reflecting that the combination of London water and the cheapest brand of Ceylon didn't make a very enlivening brew, even had she been able to bring herself to put more than two teaspoonfuls into the pot.

"That's very exciting," I said. "Have you made your final choice?"

"I told you," she said impatiently.

"I remember," I said. "A Morris Minor."

"You should," she said. "There's one standing outside at this very moment. And has been for a fortnight."

"All right, darling. I'll arrange for it to be returned."

"Just the same, you should take it back yourself. You'll have to see her again sometime, if only to arrange for the divorce."

"The lawyers will arrange that. I don't want to see her again, and that's final."

"You really have written her off, haven't you?"

"She's dead as far as I'm concerned. Dead and buried."

"What will you do if she asks for the car back?"

"Never mind the damned thing," I said harshly. "I've told you to leave it to me —" I swallowed and continued in a calmer tone. "I'm sorry, Norah. Honestly, Susan won't give a damn what happens to the car. Besides, she'll use my car. Or rather the firm's car. She's on the payroll of Brown's, you know."

"Clever as well as pretty. And doesn't care about a trifling little thing like an almost new Morris Minor."

I looked at the black ring on the kitchen table. All the furniture and fittings in the flat seemed to bear similar signs of hard usage and carelessness: the top of the little gas refrigerator was scratched and the door to the ice compartment broken, the chain of the bathtub plug was missing, the W.C. functioned but only at the second attempt, every doorknob had at least four inches of play; none of the many people who had lived there had ever cared enough about the place either to make the necessary minor repairs or not to do the damage in the first instance.

"I don't know whether she's clever or not," I said. "She doesn't actually do any work for the firm."

"The usual tax dodge, I expect." She made the peculiar snorting noise which now I knew to express moral indignation. "It makes me sick. It makes me sick at the stomach."

She was in fact looking extremely healthy that morning, clear-eyed and rosy and exuding a cleanliness which one would have thought impossible to acquire in the chilly little green-distempered bathroom which stood next to the kitchen and from which now I could hear gurglings and rumblings from the geyser as if it were resenting the fact that the two of us each bathed daily.

"No one likes paying any more tax than they can help," I said. "The money might as well be paid to Susan as to the government."

I saw with pleasure that Norah was beginning to be angry. Before I had lived with her I had always avoided argument; but now I went out of my way to provoke it. It was as if, I thought sardonically, we were already married.

"If people like your father-in-law didn't evade so much tax, the rest of us would have less to pay." Her voice was becoming strident.

"We wouldn't have less to pay," I said. "The government would find something else to waste it on, that's all."

"I won't argue," she said. "I've got two interviews about that damned Russian dog this morning."

She kissed me perfunctorily.

"You can do better than that," I said. I pulled her down onto my knee.

"No," she said. "There isn't time." She sighed. "No. Ah God, you are disgusting, you know I've told you . . ." She looked over my shoulder at the divan bed in what the landlord called the living annex. She sighed again, her face so caught up in pleasure that it had an almost icy dignity; she stood up, with her own hand holding mine where it was.

"Love me," she said; and then, as we went into the living annex, used a far different word, smiling as she repeated it.

"It's so lovely to have it whenever one wants it," she said, half an hour later.

"Didn't you when you were married?"

She fastened her stockings.

"Not really. Eric had a set time for everything. I tempted him one Saturday morning when we were having our elevenses, and he never really forgave himself for succumbing. Or me for tempting him. Eric was frightened all the time. Frightened of leaving Leddersford, frightened of having babies before we'd saved up enough for a house, frightened of what the neighbors would think . . ."

She picked up her skirt from the armchair beside the divan, then put it down again and knelt beside me, her head against my thigh.

"It's better in London," she said. "Everything's better in London. I've never been so happy anywhere." She sighed and looked around the room. "I know this is an awful dump, but I love it, even that damned shilling-in-the-slot gas meter. We're in London, that's all that really matters. I'll walk out of here this morning and I'll be in London. Did I tell you I used to have a Tube map on my bedroom wall when I was at college?"

"Never," I said. "I never dreamed you liked London."

"I've told you a thousand times," she said. "It was a rhetorical question." Her voice grew dreamy. "Sloane Square, Victoria, St. James, Westminster, Charing Cross, Temple . . . Joe, if we get that flat in Hampstead, I want to think about having babies quite soon."

"When I fix myself up with a job," I said.

"We'll have two — no, three. One more —" She stopped. "I'm sorry. That's bitchy. And unlucky."

"Don't worry," I said. "You can have four if you like. We'll name them after Tube stations."

She suddenly jerked her head away.

"Darling, no. I can't believe it."

She put on her skirt.

"What can't you believe?"

She flung over my dressing gown. I took hold of her wrist.

"Your appointment's not until eleven," I said.

"I must call at the office first." She helped me into the dressing gown and tied the belt.

"Don't bother. Tell them you had to have another parting kiss."

She giggled; then as I touched her knee the look of pleasure came back to her face. She pushed my hand away and went to the door.

"No," she said, the look still there. "No, I'll see you at Poppin's at lunchtime. You have a rest, darling."

She opened the door.

"Don't worry about sending Susan's car back. I've just had an idea. Tony's going to Leddersford next week. Couldn't he take it back?"

"Tony?"

"He works with me. He's quite sober and reliable for a journalist. His people live in Leddersford. Would that be all right, do you think?"

"I suppose so," I said indifferently. I went towards her.

"Not again," she said. "Stay there, you old goat."

I kissed her; for a moment her body went lax in my arms, then she freed herself.

"I'll scream," she said. "You know I'm late."

I looked at her glowing face.

"Everyone will be able to tell why you're late," I said.

"I don't care," she said. "Joe, will you remember something?"

"I've always something to remember when I've been with you," I said.

"I can run to three babies if you really want them," she said. "That'd be one more than her, wouldn't it?"

She closed the door. I heard her running down the hall.

Her words did not register until I had returned to the kitchen to make myself a pot of tea. I sat down suddenly, the packet of Earl Grey dropping from my hand to the floor.

It still hurt; and the only reason for its not hurting more was not that I was living with Norah, but that I was, for the time being, alone. I tried to think of the three children Norah would have; I could not see their faces but for a moment had a clear picture of us both in a great bustle of happiness with voices floating in from a large garden. A large house, I thought, holding on to the picture, a large house in the country; an old house. Like the one in Pudney Lane, a house in which there'd be room to breathe. Remembering the house in Pudney Lane, I remembered Barbara.

If the definition of an enemy was someone who by mere existence caused one grief and humiliation, then she was my enemy. But I could not think of her otherwise than with love; it was too late to break the habit.

I picked up the packet of tea. Filling the kettle, I gave way to love, I let myself remember her, I let myself be, wearing as I was the fuzzy dressing gown, the warm giant. It was as if the flat were illumined, it was as if, ugly as it was, nothing in it had been chosen by a stranger. And as I drank the tea with its familiar aromatic taste — oranges, lemons, spices, smoke — the sensation of her actual physical presence became more and more real. She was next door, sleeping late with her panda or her poodle; I would finish my cup of tea and set out her breakfast. Cornflakes, cheese, orange juice; and there was a jar of strawberry-flavored yoghurt in the refrigerator. And after breakfast I'd take her to the Zoo. She'd never been to a zoo, though she knew most of the animals.

I took my cup of tea into the living annex. There was no one there; I had known there would be no one there. And now I was alone in a furnished flat in Earl's Court with a yellow mist licking the dirty windows. The divan bed was unmade, the faded green carpet and the cracked gray linoleum were unswept; but even when the bed was made, even when the floor was swept, the room would be no different. And the dust would settle again, and the fawn three-piece suite would grow a little mangier, the floorboards would creak a little louder, the patch of damp over the pelmet would grow larger; and no one would care because no one lived here and no one had ever lived here.

People didn't live in Earl's Court; they stayed here for a while and moved on, as Norah and I would soon move on. And they came here to hide. I was hiding from my wife, I was hiding from my father-in-law, I was hiding, above all, from a four-year-old child.

Reaching in my dressing-gown pocket for cigarettes my hand encountered the letter which, from the Warley postmark and the heavy spiky writing, I knew to be from my father-in-law. It had been there for ten days now; and for ten days the mere act of taking it out, the thought of returning it unopened, had been an unfailingly effectual reminder of the completeness of my severance from Capua. This was Norah's name for Warley; it now came absolutely naturally to our lips. Like the Roman town, Capua was a place where one led a life of luxury and ease, a place where everyone had sold out. One didn't open letters from Capua, especially when they were certain to be full of abuse. Silence and indifference was the only answer to letters from Capua.

I put my finger under the flap of the envelope nevertheless and then, realizing what I was about to do, tore it across and set fire to it with my cigarette lighter. When the letter had burned away it occurred to me that I'd made a mistake; I was the only one to see the letter burnt unopened. It would have annoyed him more if I'd posted it back to him. To burn it was too ceremonious. It attributed too great an importance to him and to Capua.

I went into the kitchen and poured myself a large whisky. As I raised it to my lips I saw the pattern of the whole day unfold itself before me. As I always did, now at this time I would have this one drink, no more; I would dress, I would walk to Earl's Court Tube station, I would have a cup of tea at the ABC or Lyons, I would take the Tube to Leicester Square, I would go down Bedford Street to the Strand, I would walk along the Strand to Fleet Street, looking at the shops on the way. I would go into Poppin's at half past eleven and sit in the corner by the staircase waiting for Norah. I would drink three pints of bitter before she came at half past twelve; we would have lunch and then I would go to a matinee and return to collect her at about half past five.

Today we were lunching at the Cock where we might possibly run across Nick Halberton, a friend of hers who might know of a suitable job for me. I wouldn't have to commit myself, of course, but Nick was a very useful man to know. You mustn't drift, darling . . .

I put the whisky down untasted. Drifting was exactly what I wanted to do. I didn't want to take the job with Tiffield, even presuming that the offer was still open; I didn't want to see a friend of Norah's who was a very useful man to know. I wanted to drift for a while. I wanted to do nothing. I had rejected my old life and was on the verge of a new one; but was I sure that I wanted either? I drank the whisky quickly and then, for the first time, broke my rule and poured myself another.

When I had finished it, I put the bottle away in the cupboard. It was an unpainted whitewood cupboard, the only new article of furniture in the flat: I looked at my flushed face in the mirror on its door and wagged my finger at it.

"Watch your step, Joe," I said. "Watch your step."

twenty-four

THE ROAD was jammed with cars in both directions. I looked for a turning to the left but could see none. The car in front of me went forward for about a hundred yards; I followed it, and then it stopped suddenly; I avoided running into it only by an inch. I looked into my mirror: the car behind me too, had only just stopped short of a crash.

I cranked down the window; the night air smelled cold at first then hot and stuffy and curiously animal. After five minutes I switched off my engine; as if taking their cue I heard all the other engines go silent. Now there were a great many voices; I closed the window and began to tremble. I was on the outskirts of Barnet going into London; but now I wanted to turn back north again.

Then I saw the light in the sky and looked at my watch incredulously. It was three o'clock in the morning; I was driving overnight to avoid the heavy traffic. And there, on a road somewhere on the outskirts of Watford, was the heavy traffic that had no business to be there at that hour and at that season. The light grew stronger; now I could see that I was on top of a hill.

Ahead of me, interminably, stretched the line of cars; people were getting out of them now, looking towards the light that was filling the sky. It was not a light that I'd ever seen before; and it was not a light that I'd see again. This was the end, and even through the closed voices I could hear the voices and now they were screaming, more and more people were dismounting from their cars, they had stopped looking at the light, they were running away from the light, they were running up the hill towards me, their mouths wide open; an old fat woman banged at the window of my car, banged again, banged until the window cracked; the smell came in now, unmistakably what it was, a smell like the lion house at the Zoo — horror, helplessness, rage, despair and the fat hand hammering at the cracked window and the poplars lining the road giving no shelter. I moved over to the other door; the handle came off in my hand and I too started to scream, knowing inside the dream that this wasn't a dream, awakening, now knowing the dream was a dream but feeling that I could never disentangle myself from the rug which was bunched up at my throat and, finally, it was afternoon and my eyes were open. Rain on the window, a nap after lunch. Norah was lunching with a visiting comedian at the Ivy today; I had heated a tin of casserole steak for myself and the flat still reeked of it.

I went into the bathroom and lit the geyser: after ten minutes rumbling a brown-colored water began to trickle into the bath. I lit a cigarette and turned my back; if not watched, then within fifteen minutes the trickle would turn into a steady flow. I inspected my face in the mirror which hung from a nail above the washbowl; it seemed more blotchy and more puffy than ever it had been in Warley.

I took off my pyjamas, shivering as the draft from under the door rippled the linoleum. There were gas fires in the kitchen and the living annex; but the only heating appliance in the bathroom was a rusty oil lamp which stood by the W.C. I put on my dressing gown again, grateful for its warmth.

The geyser began to mutter; I turned on the cold-water tap and the light brown water became a bit darker. As I looked at it and at the brown ring round the tub that no scouring would remove, I knew that it would be only a matter of time before the daily bath would become a bath every two days and then weekly. Norah didn't seem to notice it, just as she didn't seem to notice the streaky green distempered walls and the scabrous wooden W.C. seat; but I had been in Capua too long. I lowered myself into the tepid brown water, trying not to touch the sides of the tub.

But when I had dried myself and was drinking tea by the gas fire in the living annex I began to feel more cheerful; if there had been little pleasure in the bath itself there was pleasure in not being in the bathroom. And there was, now that the tea had removed the thickness of daytime sleep from my mouth, a certain satisfaction in doing nothing at half past three in the afternoon.

It was what I needed: the abdication of responsibility, the retirement from the arena. Looking back, I saw nothing but struggle: struggle to reach Dufton Grammar School, struggle to pass my matriculation, struggle to become a clerk in the Treasurer's at Dufton, struggle to marry Susan and the long struggle, which only since summer I'd known to be so, of marriage itself. The new life would begin soon, the new life that had chosen me: at last I was living in the present. I ran my hand over my chin and took down my electric shaver from the mantelpiece.

A bell rang.

I did not immediately recognize what it was; it had a softer note than the telephone, almost as if it were part of a carillon. For a moment my mind was befogged by vague fears, as if the dream had not ended. This was not a sound I had ever heard in my three weeks in London; no one had ever called at the flat.

I didn't want to see anybody and I was all too conscious of being unshaven and still in my dressing gown at four o'clock; I wondered whether to let the doorbell ring, something which, like leaving the telephone off the hook, I'd always wanted to do. But slowly and reluctantly I went to the door.

It was Mrs. Brown, immaculate in a white belted raincoat. I noticed that her black glacé shoes were dry and her umbrella still furled; there was nothing extraordinary about this, since she presumably had come by taxi, but I reflected that I knew no other person who was so little affected by the weather. She would look exactly the same if she'd walked twenty miles through a cloudburst.

"May I come in?" she asked.

"By all means."

I helped her off with her coat. She was wearing what was for her a closely fitting dress of black nylon jersey; briefly, despite her gray hair, something about the line of her back reminded me of Susan. I was surprised to feel not hatred or pain, but a kind of physical affection.

She sat down on the sofa and folded her hands in her lap.

"I expect you're wondering why I came," she said.

I smiled. "I'm sure you won't have any hesitation about telling me, will you?"

She stared at me. "Is that what you think?"

"You've come to tell me how right you were about me. Haven't you? You've come to give me what your sort calls a tongue-lashing, haven't you? I'm only surprised that you haven't come before. And where's your husband? Can't he do his own dirty work?"

"He wanted to come," she said. "But not for the reason that you suppose."

"For Christ's sake don't give me that." It occurred to me that everything I said was given a strangely disembodied quality by the fact that there was no name that I could bring myself to address her by.

"You needn't blaspheme," she said, coldly.

"All right. But tell me what you came to tell me. You needn't bother about sparing my feelings. Nobody else does."

"It's difficult," she said. "It's difficult. Because you're so wrong about me. And Abe, too. You always were."

"Was I?" I lit a cigarette. I had rehearsed this conversation many times: but now that she was here I seemed to be missing all my cues. "You may as well tell me what you came to tell me. But it won't be a surprise to me."

I took a drink of whisky from the glass beside me. "Your husband's fixed it up with Tiffield so that I won't get a job with him. And he's passed the word around elsewhere so that I won't get a decent job anywhere. And it's entirely my fault that Susan was unfaithful to me, because I'm so low and brutal and rotten. And the house and everything else is in her name. And you're going to hire a good lawyer and she'll get custody of the children, and you'll see to it that they forget they ever had me for a father —"

I stopped. I had spoken of myself as my children's father — and so Barbara's father — to Norah and had felt nothing. But now looking at my mother-in-law's white face I couldn't go on.

"Come here," she said.

I sat down beside her. She took my hand.

"My dear, I'm so sorry. But you're not doing yourself any good by running away from it. And it's futile to abuse me. Or Abe either. I didn't come down here to hurt you any more."

"You can't," I said. "Nobody can. You can't hurt me any more. Barbara —"

As I pronounced the name I found myself beginning to cry. "I can't see Barbara again; I can't see Barbara again. And if I can't see her I can't see my son. There isn't anything left."

"Susan told me everything," she said.

"She didn't have to."

Suddenly I felt scruffy and defeated, a fat unshaven cuckold weeping in his dressing gown. I pulled my hand away.

"I'll shave if you don't mind," I said. "I'm sorry you should see me like this."

"You needn't be," she said. "I've seen men unshaven before."

I plugged in the electric razor.

"She told you everything?"

"She confirmed everything."

I put the razor down.

"Ah God, how you must have gloated! Seeing me with his daughter —"

"Stop it. She isn't his daughter. You might as well say that Harry's his son. There's more to having children than begetting them."

I sat down beside her again. She put out her hand; I grasped it tightly, not out of affection, not out of desire, but out of the need to reassure myself of the presence of another human being.

"I can't think what you mean," I said. "Nothing makes sense any more. Is Barbara or is she not Mark's daughter?"

"You know him, don't you? He isn't bad, I never thought that, but he isn't good either. He's not unlike you in some ways, but he's never had your advantages."

"My advantages? A back street in Dufton? Dufton Grammar School? I've had to sweat for everything I've got. *He's* the one who's had the advantages."

"I mean what I say. You could only go up; but when Mark's father lost all his money Mark could only go down."

I grimaced. "You're really saying that my beginnings were so low that any change was a change for the better."

"You're ridiculously touchy. Mark was spoiled when he was young, everything came too easily. You've learned to depend upon yourself. For that matter, you've had a far happier childhood than Mark ever had. I knew his father. He was a very bad man, and I'm not saying that lightly."

"I don't care about his early sufferings," I said. "You haven't come here to tell me about that, have you?"

"Early sufferings is accurate enough," she said. "But of course I don't expect you to care."

"Something's happened," I said. "Someone's told him, haven't they?"

"No one's told him. If they had, he wouldn't say a word about it. He's that much of a gentleman." She spoke with a certain vicarious pride.

"So our secret's safe. Because whatever happens he's a gentleman and whatever happens I'm not a gentleman. I'm not going to let him know just how big a fool he's made of me. There's not going to be a scandal. Were you frightened that there would be? Is that why you've come?"

She sighed. "You can't possibly have read Abe's letter."

"I didn't. I burned it."

"Oh God!" Her face seemed to elongate itself grotesquely with pain. "You hate us. You really hate us. Why, Joe, why? Why so much? There was nothing in the letter to hurt you. Abe's sorry for you. He feels a certain responsibility for what happened —"

"He ought to," I said.

"Yes, he ought to. We both ought to. But don't ask too much all at once, Joe. There's no question of your being sacked. Abe realizes you need time to think —"

"He knows too, then."

She shook her head. "There's a limit to the shocks he can stand. I don't see any need for him to know."

"Don't be frightened," I said. "He won't learn it from me."

"I never was frightened of that," she said softly.

"I'm not coming back to Warley. I've seen through you all. You didn't think I'd have the guts to, but I've got away. I'm making a fresh start. I don't want anything from you, I'm sick of the whole damned lot of you . . ." I was crying again.

She stroked my hand gently. "Your fresh start doesn't seem to be making you very happy," she said. "Do you know what I thought when you first married Susan? I didn't like you then, I didn't like what you'd done to Alice Aisgill, I didn't like the fact that you were so obviously using Susan to get what you wanted. But there was something about you — whether you were happy or not you believed you could be happy. You don't believe it now, do you?"

"You can't expect me to," I muttered.

"Don't mind my asking this, but are you sure that you really love Norah?"

"Why do you think I left home?"

"Not for her," she said.

"She believes I have. That's enough."

"It won't be enough if she ever finds out about Barbara."

"I'll tell her when the time comes."

"You've changed, my dear."

The night was already setting in and in the half-dark the harsh lines seemed to have left her face and the grayness of her soft and gleaming hair seemed the consequence of choice rather than of age.

"I don't feel any different," I said.

"You've changed. All that decisiveness has gone. You never used to put things off."

The edge of her slip was showing by a fraction of an inch; it looked very white against the black dress. She looked down at it and frowned slightly, but made no attempt to adjust it.

"I'm resting behind the lines," I said. "This place is only temporary. We're moving to Hampstead soon."

"Are you going to take the job with Edgar Tiffield?"

"I don't know."

"Abe won't stand in your way."

"That's generous of him."

"He's a more generous person than you think. I'm the only one who knows how generous he is. Or perhaps not the only one."

It seemed specially important to hold her hand now; but in the moment of silence that followed it was difficult to decide who was reassuring whom. I did not ask her questions and did not need to; but I knew that we had, in different ways, been to the same place.

"Not the one who's in your mind," she said quietly.

I put her hand against my cheek for a moment.

"It's living with oneself that's the trouble," I said. "I can't go back to her. Does she want me to?"

"You'll have to decide that for yourself."

"Has Barbara been asking for me?"

"You have a son, besides a daughter. It's Harry who's been asking for you."

"He's at school."

"He's run away from school. He won't say why."

"Send him back," I said, impatiently.

She released my hand.

"You were very sensitive a moment ago," she said. "You were suffering then, weren't you?"

"Never mind that. Can't anyone make him see reason? Can't you? Can't his mother? Can't his beloved grandfather?"

"It seems not," she said. "He wants his father." She stood up. "I won't waste any more of your time, Joe. Susan didn't send me, by the way. He did."

"I can't go," I said. "It's just not possible."

"He wants you to come and see him," she said. "I've passed on the message."

I helped her on with her coat.

"You'll just have to be firm," I said. "I can't come to Warley now."

"It's entirely up to you," she said, indifferently. "No one can make you see your son if you don't want to."

"I'll phone for a taxi," I said.

"It's stopped raining. I'll enjoy the walk."

"Need you go?"

"I have an engagement. But it's nice of you to want an old woman's company. Goodbye, Joe."

"Goodbye, Margaret," I said, using her Christian name for the first and the last time in my life.

She smiled and unexpectedly kissed me on the cheek.

"You're nice," she said. "Hang on to that, Joe, it's more important than you think." She half ran out of the room.

twenty-five

FROWNING, Nick Halberton added up the bill. His face cleared as he scribbled something on it; the waiter backed away, bowing, appearing as pleased as if his hands had been stuffed with five-pound notes.

"Delightful," he said. "We must do this more often, much more often." He rose. "No, no, you finish your cognac." He kissed Norah. "And don't forget to phone me tomorrow, Joe."

The waiter moved the table back for him. He walked over to the cloakroom, his head moving slowly from side to side; each time it moved he acknowledged the presence of someone he knew with a little wave.

There was a jerky stiffness about his walk, the effect, so he'd told me, of a bellyful of shrapnel at Anzio. But now, as he picked up his briefcase and was helped on with his dark blue overcoat, he made me think of the City Gent in the set of platform figures I'd bought Harry last Christmas; the coat was the same length and the rather flat face the same shade.

And I thought, like Harry's City Gent, he would probably have a transparent plastic base. He was being pushed. We were all being pushed: he had been pushed into this lunch because he'd gone to Leeds University at the same time as Norah, I'd been pushed into this lunch because Norah wanted me to stop drifting, to be tied down to London and to her: nothing had changed.

Except that my son wanted me, wanted me for the first time that I remembered, and I was not with him. The excuse for my not going to Warley yesterday had been that Norah had been given two tickets to the theatre, the excuse today was lunch with Nick Halberton; there would be another good reason why I shouldn't go tomorrow. By the time I actually went to Warley, Harry's need for me would have passed. He would not forget the betrayal; it would be useless to tell him later that I couldn't miss the chance to see *My Fair Lady* or that I was forced to lunch with Nick Halberton. He would only care for one thing: he had needed me and I had not been there.

Norah leaned across the table. "I think he likes you, Joe."

"Who?"

"Nick, you idiot."

"I don't think that he really likes anybody," I said.

"I can tell when he likes someone. Nick's going very far very fast and he wants good men. He's not such a fool that he'll try to do it all himself. He wants good men and he'll pay them top rates. He's fair, he's generous but if you fail him —"

"I know. He's absolutely ruthless. I've heard it all before. You seem to have been thinking about him quite a lot. You wouldn't mind a job with him yourself, would you?"

To my astonishment, she looked embarrassed. It was not an expression that went well with her type of good looks; momentarily her eyes seemed hard and protuberant, her high color artificial, her low-cut dress to belong behind a pub bar.

"He's offered me a job. But it was charity. It wasn't good enough. He wouldn't have respected me for taking it. I couldn't have got any further."

Her voice was becoming shriller. "I've got to think of these things. I've got to look after myself. No one else is going to do it. My husband never did. My own father never did —"

She stopped, then seemed to regain control of herself. "Joe, you can't go on as you are doing, lounging about the flat all day and drinking more and more. I don't care how much money you've got — it won't last forever. It runs out suddenly, and then you're forced to take a job just to eat. And then you get the lousy jobs that no one wants. Do you think Nick would be interested in you if he thought you *needed* a job? He'd smell the hunger on you, he'd discover another engagement and walk out. Why do you think I've been trying so hard to fix this luncheon? Do you think it's been easy? Do you know the amount of intriguing and phoning and hanging about that I've had to do? Do you think I like asking favors? Do you?"

Suddenly I thought, not of the City Gent in Harry's set of platform figures, but of the Seated Woman. The Seated Woman wore a pleated skirt and clutched a handbag to her bosom. She had sharp breasts under a ribbed jumper and her expression, like Norah's, at the moment, was rather fierce. She didn't have a base because she didn't need one. But, like the City Gent, she couldn't move of her own accord. And I was no different. A hand had come down and pushed me into her arms; a hand had come down and pushed me to London; a hand had come down and pushed me away from my son. And whatever name I gave to the hand that pushed Norah, whatever the name I gave to the hand that pushed me, it wasn't love.

"Joe," she said, "you're not listening."

"I was thinking."

"You're going to phone him tomorrow?"

"I will if I can," I said.

"Joe, when Nick asks you to phone him tomorrow, you phone him tomorrow. If you don't, then it's no use phoning him again. He'll write you off completely."

"That would be terrible," I said. "I'd never recover from that."

"Don't you want the job?"

"I haven't been offered it yet."

"You have, you fool. Tomorrow he'll ask you to see him at his office and he'll hand you on to someone else and bits of paper will be shoved backward and forward and you'll be in. That's the way he operates."

"I shan't be able to see him tomorrow. I'm going to Capua."

"You're going to *Capua?*"

"That's what we call Warley, isn't it?"

"There's something wrong," she said. She straightened her back as if waiting for pronouncement of sentence. "I'd rather you told me, whatever it is. I promise not to make a scene, Joe."

"There's nothing to make a scene about," I said. "Harry's

run away from school. He wants to see me. That's all."

"So you have to go now? It won't even wait one day?"

"I should have gone two days ago," I said. "It wouldn't surprise me if he didn't want to see me now. The poor little devil —" I put my hand to my eyes.

She knocked it down. "Don't be ashamed," she said. "I haven't seen you cry before. It's a treat for me, Joe. I've cried for you, Joe. I cried every night for you when I left Capua. But then I used to dream of the life we'd have when you joined me, and then I'd stop crying."

She tapped the pink table. "This was part of it. I've always liked this place. I don't know why. I could have lunched here before, but I never have. I was saving it up for a special occasion." She looked around. "These pink lights, this carpeting, these pink quilted walls — it's like being inside a box of expensive chocolates, it's almost too good for a business lunch. When Nick said we were lunching here, it was an omen. A good omen. Everything was working out —"

"It'll still work out," I said.

"It won't, love. Will you get me another brandy?"

I beckoned the waiter. When I had ordered the drinks I put my hand over hers. "I'll be back," I said. "I thought you wanted me to go to Capua."

"You don't understand," she said sadly. "I wanted you to go at the right time. Today's the wrong time."

"He's only a little boy," I said helplessly. "I'm his father. I have to go to him."

"You're Barbara's father too," she said. "I know what you feel about her. You talk in your sleep, Joe. You cry her name out in your sleep, but you never mention it when you're awake."

"Barbara isn't —" I began, then stopped.

She shook her head. "Isn't important? She is, Joe. More important than Harry even. More important than the job with Nick, more important than me. Or our children." She laughed. "Earl's Court, Gloucester Road, South Kensington — they're not born yet, are they?" She pushed my hand away gently. "You'd better go back to your own children," she said.

"Norah," I said. "I'll tell you the truth. It's not as you think it is —" I stopped. The time to tell her the truth had passed: now it could only damage her pride irretrievably.

"Don't say any more, dear," Norah said. "And don't worry about me. I shan't do anything foolish."

"I love you," I said.

"I love you too," she said. "Much good may it do me."

"Norah," I said. "I don't want it to end like this. I'll phone you tonight —"

"I told you not to worry," she said. "I'm not trying to compete any more. I saw your face when I mentioned Barbara. That was enough, my dear. I can't compete with that."

When the brandy came she clinked her glass against mine.

"Have a nice time in Capua," she said.

"I'll be back," I said.

"No one ever comes back from Capua," she said.

twenty-six

"If you won't tell me what's wrong, what's the use of my being here?"

I looked round for an ashtray and for the fifth time since nine o'clock stubbed out my cigarette on the floor.

"I wish you'd go away," Harry said. He pulled the bedclothes over his face.

"It's your room," I said. I shifted uneasily on the chair which I'd pulled up beside his bed; again it struck me that it was the most comfortless room in the house, not in essentials very much better than the bedroom I'd had myself as a boy. The little pile of cigarette ends on the black linoleum did nothing to improve its appearance.

I pulled the bedclothes back gently. He turned his face away from me. "Why can't you leave me alone?"

"You asked me to come."

"That was three days ago."

"Don't say it again, Harry, please."

He sat up. "I thought you'd be here when I came home,"

he said. "No one ever told me you'd gone away. Nobody ever tells me anything. And then Granny said she was going to London and I asked her to tell you to come. And you never did."

"I'm here now," I said.

I put out my hand to cover his.

"Let me go," he said. "I know why you didn't come." His face seemed to wizen with the weight of his adult knowledge.

"I heard Mummy talking to Granny. She said that Hauxley woman had her claws in you. She said you were living with her . . ."

"You shouldn't listen to what isn't meant for you to hear," I said.

"And you've been sleeping in my room. I asked Mummy if you had but she said you hadn't. I asked her in the holidays and she said you hadn't. But I knew you had because there's a cigarette burn in my Indian blanket."

"I'll buy you another one," I said, feeling as guilty as if it were his sole possession and I had sold it for drink.

"I don't want another one," he said. "You've spoiled it now." He began to bite his nails. "Why did you sleep in my room?"

I took his hand away from his mouth. "There are things you can't understand yet," I said. "But people make mistakes. I made a mistake and your mother made a mistake."

His hand stayed in mine. "Did Uncle Mark make a mistake?"

"He's made a great many."

"You're hurting my hand, Daddy."

"I'm sorry."

Suddenly the look of loneliness on Harry's face was too much to bear. The mention of Mark's name had brought back the old hatred, the urge to destroy; I would never get rid of that hatred, but I had no time for it now. Harry was by himself, Harry was lost, and there was a cigarette burn in his Indian blanket. I put my arm around him.

"Harry, you feel I've let you down. I didn't mean to, love. Things got too much for me, so I ran away. Grownups run away too. I came back because I thought you needed me. You're my son. If you need me, I'll always be there."

"Big deal," he said. "You still didn't come when I asked you. You never bothered to write to me. You never came to the school. You were too busy with that old Mrs. Hauxley. I know what you were doing with her, but I've not to say it. I said it to Mummy and she smacked my face —"

"You say it if you want to. Whatever word you use, I'll have heard it. It won't help matters, will it, though?"

He moved away from me. "You'll lose your temper soon," he said. "Everyone loses their temper with me. You're going to start shouting soon. You always do, anyway. I'm not going to tell you. I'm not going to tell any of you anything because you're all silly and rotten and none of you wants me, not even Barbara —"

"She's only a baby," I said gently.

"She doesn't want me. No one wants me. All of you can go to hell!"

He looked up at me to see if I was shocked. I smiled at him.

"Don't get all worked up, Harry," I said. "I can't force you to tell me anything. But whatever it is, I'm on your side. Remember that." I kissed him. "Try to sleep now."

I rose. As I was at the door, he called me back. I smiled at him. "I'll see you tomorrow," I said.

"Come here, Daddy."

I sat on the bed.

"Do you really mean *whatever* I've done?"

"I don't tell you lies," I said.

He clutched my arm. "You won't be angry with me, will you? You promised."

His large blue eyes and the long dark lashes were wasted on a boy, Susan — and others — had always said; looking at him now for the first time in two months, I thought that I understood what had driven him from school. He was a good-looking boy; his features were, when I came to consider it, more delicate than Barbara's. I began to feel angry again; this time the anger was directed against myself. Into what sort of captivity had I allowed him to go?

"Harry, listen. It doesn't make any difference what you've done, I promise you you won't hear one word of reproach from me. We all make mistakes, Harry. A mistake isn't the end of the world."

"They sent me to Coventry," he said. "I couldn't stand it. I hate the beastly school, anyway."

"You might have told me what you felt about it," I said. "But it doesn't matter now. Why did they send you to Coventry?"

He looked at me suspiciously. "You'll not want to speak to me again," he said. He started to weep noisily; I held him tightly against me and wiped his eyes.

He snuffled and gave me back the handkerchief. "I'm soft," he said. "I shouldn't blub." He shook off my arm.

"Ah, Christ," I said. "Cry if you want to. What's the good of holding it in? What are they training you to be at that bloody school? A Red Indian?"

"They wanted to whitewash me," he said. "I wouldn't let them. It's an initiation ceremony for your second year." He took my handkerchief from me and wiped his eyes.

"It sounds pretty stupid to me," I said. "But I never had your advantages. What do you mean, whitewash you?"

"They whitewash your — thing," he said. "They do it to everybody."

"Did the headmaster know about this?"

"Of course he doesn't," he dropped his handkerchief. "You won't tell him, will you?"

"No. But they didn't send you to Coventry just because you wouldn't let them initiate you. If that's the word for whitewashing your private parts. What did you do?"

"There were ten of them," he said.

"All right, there were ten of them. What did you do to these ten heroes?"

"I knifed one of them."

"Is that all? Is that what all the fuss is about?"

"In his hand. He wasn't hurt, really. I only had that titchy penknife you gave me."

"You should have stuck it in the bastard's guts," I said, smiling with relief.

"You're not angry, Daddy?"

"Angry? What else could you do?"

"They said I was a murderer. They said I wasn't English." The tears were still flowing.

"Who the hell cares, Harry? You did right. If anyone

tries to push you around —" I stopped; I could see that for the time being he'd exhausted his stock of courage.

"You won't send me back there, will you, Daddy?"

"We'll talk about it in the morning," I said. "If you still don't want to go back, then I promise that you won't go back."

"Daddy. Your handkerchief." He gave me it back.

"Sure you won't need it?"

"I've got one of my own." He sniffed. "Yours pongs, Daddy."

Norah had washed and ironed it last night and this morning as she put it in my breast pocket had, in one of her skittish moods, dabbed it with eau de cologne. The handkerchief was initialed, the letter J being so placed that it was on display dead center when it was in the breast pocket. Like the eau de cologne it was a present from Norah: I hadn't wanted to wear it either with or without scent, but she had insisted that I did. I put it in my trouser pocket.

"It'll wash," I said. "Goodnight, Harry."

"Daddy, come here."

"You're as bad as Barbara," I said. "What now?"

"Daddy, I don't have to work for Grandfather, do I?"

"I think we can defer consideration of that for a few years yet," I said. "What's put it into your head?"

"I don't know," he said. "I thought you were keen on it."

"I thought *you* were," I said.

"*You* thought I liked that rotten old school," he said accusingly. "Everybody thinks they know what I like better than I do."

I straightened his pillows.

"We'll talk about it tomorrow," I said. "Your mother and I will work something out." I ruffled his hair. "Go to sleep, son."

When I went into the drawing room Susan was busy with a letter at the writing desk. She turned her head as I came in.

"Have you solved the mystery?" she asked.

I told her, briefly.

"You're very clever, aren't you?"

"I wish I were," I said, sadly.

She lit a cigarette. "You've succeeded where we've all failed, haven't you?" She exhaled noisily. "That letter's to his headmaster. I might as well tear it up now."

"I've promised him he wouldn't go back."

"That's very easy to promise. Not that they'll necessarily want him back."

"I promised him," I said.

She looked over her shoulder at the eighteenth century map of the world on the wall to my left. She went over to straighten it. Her thumb on a dolphin, she said coldly: "Has she got sick of you, then?"

"She was trying to arrange my future only this lunchtime."

She stepped a few inches back from the map, her head on one side.

"Including your new family?"

"There isn't going to be a new family," I said. "I have one already."

"Do you want to stay?"

She seemed to be standing more erect than I remembered; but there was a slight droop about her shoulders as if she were aware of some new burden.

I sat down. "It isn't easy," I said.

"Do you want to stay?"

Suddenly I remembered her handing me the keys of the car. It was something I should not have forgotten. She had been on my side. She had been on my side as I had been on Harry's side tonight.

"I want to stay," I said.

She knelt down and unfastened my shoes. "Do you really want to stay or are you just being noble?"

"I don't know whether I'm noble or not, I only know what I've got to do."

She brought over my slippers. "He's like you," she said.

"Who's like me?"

"Harry." She put on my slippers. "He wants to please everybody and he wants to be his own master, too."

"I don't know much about him. Or you."

She smiled. "We know more now, don't we?"

I heard a voice from upstairs, growing from a whine to a yell.

"That's my daughter," I said. "Does she know I'm here?"

Susan shook her head. "Keep quiet, Joe. Maybe she'll go back."

There was the sound of footsteps. Susan went to the door, frowning. Barbara stood there weeping, her poodle under her arm. She ran to Susan.

"I want a drink juice, Mummy."

I knelt down and put my arms around them both.

"Where've you been, Daddy?"

"Earning pennies."

"A big lot of pennies," she said, drowsily. "A big lot of pennies."

Susan put her down on the sofa. "Stay there with Daddy while I get you a drink, darling."

"No," she said. "Daddy get the juice! With ice in it. And straws."

I went into the kitchen and opened the refrigerator, then remembered that she didn't drink orange juice at night. I mixed a drink of Kia-Ora in her Flopsy Bunny mug and took it into the drawing room.

Barbara was sitting on Susan's knee, her eyes closing. She opened them as I came into the room. I gave her the mug; she emptied it greedily and noisily. My hand under the mug, I watched her face for some sign of recognition. But only the Kia-Ora and Susan were real to her now. She let the mug drop; I caught it before it hit the parquet floor.

"Shall I take you up, darling?" I asked her.

She burrowed deeper into Susan's arms. I kissed her on the forehead.

"Daddy's back," I said. "Sleep tight, pet." But she was already asleep. I could not see her face, only the back of her head that like all young children's was large in proportion to the rest of her body.

She might have been anyone's child, I thought; and then as Susan carried her to the door, I stopped thinking. The decision had been made now; love had caught up with me at last. I had not been prepared for it to take quite this shape, I had not expected its demands to be quite so uncompromising, I had hoped at least for some kind of accolade, even if self-awarded. But I felt no different from before; I hadn't changed, I wasn't a better person, I had been given no new access of strength: I was alone in a big drawing room with cream and gold wallpaper and a parquet floor, a drawing room which despite its immaculate good taste had something of the melancholy of an old battlefield.

Susan came into the room and sat down on the arm of my chair.

"Don't be hurt because she didn't make a great fuss of you, Joe," she said gently. "You've been away over a month. It's like ten years to someone of Barbara's age."

"I'm not hurt," I said. "She'll soon get used to me again."

She put her forefinger inside my waistband. "You've lost weight," she said. "Mother said you weren't looking well . . . Joe, what did she say to you?"

"A great many things," I said.

"I didn't send her, Joe." She sat on my knee. "What did she say?"

"She told me Barbara wasn't Mark's daughter."

She stiffened. "Ah Christ," she said. "Joe, I wish I'd never told you the truth, but it's no use denying it. Not now —"

I held her waist tightly.

"It took me a long time to work it out," I said. "But she's right. Children don't choose their parents, but parents choose their children. I know you told me the truth. But I love Barbara, and I can't stop loving her now. She's my child just as much as Harry is. I've made myself her father. It's easy for you to know who your child is, but I've got to find out by loving the child. Perhaps Harry wasn't my son until tonight."

She stroked my hair. "You won't go back on what you've said, will you, Joe? You won't be bitter?"

"I won't go back on what I've said. I don't know whether I'll be bitter or not. But I'll try."

"Do you want to leave Warley? I will, if it makes you happier."

"No one leaves Capua," I said.

She looked at me inquiringly.

"It's a saying."

"I know whose," she said. "We'll both have to be very careful about sayings, won't we?" She stood up. "You're tired now, darling, we'll talk things over tomorrow." She yawned. "Would you like a cup of tea?"

"I'll make it," I said. "You must be tired, too."

Her eyes moistened. "Joe, you are good. You're the only one, Joe, you're the only one —"

I took her in my arms. "Won't anyone else make you a cup of tea at bedtime?"

"You're the only one," she said. "I've only got you, Joe, I only have you in my mind all the time. Joe, you don't hate me any more, do you? We'll forget all about this, won't we?"

"We'll try," I said.

"Is it really all over with Norah, Joe?" I looked towards the phone and back again at Susan.

"As much as these things can be," I said.

She nodded. "You can't switch it off, can you? But it does stop hurting, Joe."

"It's hurting others that hurts," I said. "There's no end to it . . ."

"Joe, perhaps it doesn't help, but I always loved you. You won't believe it, but I love you."

I kissed her. "I love you, too," I said. But the words were hard to speak; I could only speak them because she had long black hair and large brown eyes, because she was a pretty girl and there was a double bed not far away; it was as if I was seducing someone else's wife.

"I love you," I repeated, this time more firmly.

She moved away from me. "I'm going to believe you," she said. "And you're going to believe me. We'll have to keep on saying it. All of us."

I went into the kitchen and filled the electric kettle; after I had filled it I ran the tap for a moment longer for the pleasure of seeing clear water. I plugged in the kettle and set out the tea things on the tray that Harry had made during the summer holidays. When the kettle had boiled I remembered the Orange Pekoe tea that I had bought at Twining's in the Strand; after I had fetched it in from my case in the hall I stood by the whistling kettle for a moment, wondering whether to blend it with Indian tea, and then decided against it. As I took up the tray to carry it to the drawing room I saw that I had forgotten something.

I took out a lemon from the vegetable rack. I cut a slice from it, then stopped and put down the knife. With no warning, through no conscious effort, I was happy, happier than I had been since childhood. It could not last, it was already evaporating as I began to be grateful for it; but I knew it would come again.